A FATAL BEGINNING
(a prequel to the Fatal Series)

Adda Leah Davis

A Fatal Beginning

copyright © 2018 Adda Leah Davis
ISBN 13: 978-1722827441
ISBN 10: 1722827440

ACKNOWLEDGEMENTS

Thanks are first due to my precious Lord and Savior, Jesus Christ for the gift of writing. I've been writing since I learned to make my letters. I have always had this keen desire to tell stories and thus to write.

As a child I poured out my loneliness, my grief, and my sorrows, but I also wrote about the sunshine in my life. The most important person in my early life was my grandfather, Cicero Wagner . . . he was my sunshine then and still provides me with wonderful memories to draw upon.

My wonderful brothers and sisters whose escapades were like a kaleidoscope of motion, color, and ideas presented to my eager mind are to be praised and thanked. I wouldn't be who I am without them.

My good friend and editor, Rachel Riggsby is owed much more than I could ever give for the innumerable hours we talk and the diligence she gives to the task of editing. Thanks much, Rachel.

Linda Hoagland, a friend and fellow writer who helps me in marketing my books. I truly do not know how I would get to some venues without Linda's assistance. Thanks and many blessings, Linda.

This book would not have seen the "light of day" without the talent and skills of Victoria Fletcher, Hoot Books Publishing. Being introduced to this lady's skills and her love of writing has been the much-needed blessing in my writing life. Thanks, Vicki.

Last, but not least, are my many, many readers who inspire me to keep writing. With your kind words and prayers, I hope to use my gift until my Savior calls me home. Thanks to all of you and may God's love keep you warm and safe.

INTRODUCTION

This book, A Fatal Beginning, is the story of Margie Meadows, the mother of Bill Larkin in the Fatal Series, which contains three books. This book should have been the first book in the series and much of it was written before the other three books. However, when some of my friends said it was too dark, I left Margie's story and started writing about her son's family.

This book then, is a prequel of the Fatal Series because it should have been told first. When my readers read the other three books many of them wanted to know more about Margie Meadows. Almost every day for several weeks, Margie Meadows kept coming into my mind. I imagined how awful it would be to carry around the secret she revealed during the trial of her son's murder.

I love Margie Meadows, but not because she had a terrible childhood, which was heart wrenching, but because she didn't give up. She is living proof that people can overcome adversity if they have the will to keep on trying.

So, dear reader when problems and obstacles crop up in your life, please don't give up. There is always an answer and with patience to wait it will get better. Believe in yourself and trust that the Creator that formed you has put you here for a purpose. We often do not know what that purpose is, but what if it is waiting for you to take that next step. You may have been born for some great purpose and it may be waiting just around the corner. Dare to take that next step and please, please, continue to read.

A Fatal Beginning

Some are born in terrible trauma
Seen as a miracle to survive
Yet unseen strength seemed to hover
Repelling strife to stay alive.
Finding faint joy in every triumph
Gleaning strength from every pain
One resists the path of failure
And a brighter future tries to gain.
Never hoping for approval
Dashed hopes cloud each day
Even from a fatal beginning
With determination, life finds a way

A Fatal Beginning

A FATAL BEGINNING
"You just can't beat the person who never gives up"
-Babe Ruth

CHAPTER 1

"Sh-sh, don't cry," were the first sounds that little Margie Elaine Pierson made. All jumbled together, it sounded like "she un ki." Rebecca, her mother, began noticing that her baby was frequently repeating the same sounds, "she-un-ki," but she had no idea what the sounds meant.

I wonder what in the world she's trying to say, thought Rebecca as she recalled her baby uttering those sounds frequently, especially when Tom was near. When Margie later began putting her hand over her mouth after making that sound Rebecca finally realized that her baby was copying her words and actions.

I've said 'sh-sh, don't cry' and have put my hand over her mouth when she did cry since she was born, she reflected.

She hugged Margie close and whispered, "You are a very smart little baby. I'm going to have to watch what I say." She smiled proudly and silently thanked the Lord for such a smart child.

Every morning from the day her baby was born, Rebecca had walked, winter and summer, barefooted from the window to the door with Margie in her arms.

Please Lord make her a quiet baby, she silently prayed as she walked. Margie always awoke early to be fed and Rebecca lived in fear that her baby would make some noise that would awaken her increasingly volatile husband.

When Margie was first born, Rebecca thought that Tom Pierson, her husband, would love their baby since she looked so much like his mother. Rebecca had never really seen Tom's mother; only her picture. Mrs. Pierson had died before they married.

Although forced into this marriage by her father, after Tom had raped her, Rebecca had come to this isolated farm, in Forks, Washington determined to make the best of it. She set out to make everything orderly and neat. One day when working on the clothes in the dresser drawer used for Tom's underwear, she felt something hard and pulled it out, just as Tom entered the room.

"What a pretty woman! Tom, is this your mother?" asked Rebecca, looking at the shining auburn curls that framed a beautiful face.

Tom had jerked the picture from her hands raking a long scratch down her arm as he did so. He then shoved the picture back into the drawer and covered it up with a jumble of clothing.

"It's my mother, but I don't want to see it or her so leave it alone. Don't you bother that picture again," he ordered in a rough, choking sound and quickly left the room.

Rebecca dabbed the scratch with her apron as she slowly closed the drawer. *So, that's where he gets that beautiful head of hair,* she thought and wondered why he didn't want to see his own mother's picture. She stood deep in thought about all the girls at school being attracted to Tom Pierson. Even she had thought he was a very handsome man, but that had changed. Rebecca sighed as she thought, *Mom always said that looks could be deceiving, and she was right. His looks are just a covering. Tom is not a beautiful person, that's for sure.*

She wrapped her apron around her arm and left the room, hoping that Tom was outside. Most of the time she walked around like a timid, frightened mouse, not knowing what he would do if she made him angry.

Even though Rebecca was afraid of Tom's anger, she often looked at the picture of his mother, but only when she knew he was at work. The woman was so beautiful and had such a kind, pleasant, but worried expression on her face. Rebecca wondered at that look, but she made sure to put the picture back in the drawer just the way she had found it.

Rebecca had learned early in her marriage that Tom Pierson had a vicious cruel streak, especially if he drank alcohol, but until after the baby was born he had only cursed and glared at her.

On the day Margie was born, Tom had gone away and hadn't come back until he thought the midwife would be gone on the following morning. He came through the bedroom door and first looked at Rebecca. He nodded and in a gruff voice asked, "You all right?"

He turned to go when Rebecca said she was, but the midwife stopped him. "Don't you want to see your baby? She's pretty."

Stepping to the bedside, Tom took one look at Margie and gasped aloud, clenched his fists, and with a wild-eyed stare, immediately swung around and dashed from the room.

"Well, I never in my life saw a daddy act like that? What's wrong with him?" The midwife gave Rebecca a curious look.

Rebecca shook her head. "I don't know, Mrs. Croix. Maybe he was hoping she'd be a boy."

"Naw, it ain't that, little mommy. He didn't even ask nor look." She shook her head. "It's quare, but it ain't that . . . It's something, but if you don't know I guess I'll never find out. You've got a pretty baby though, whether he likes her or not."

When Mrs. Croix, the Indian midwife from the Hoh River Indian Reservation, finally left and Rebecca was sitting up in bed she heard Tom come back inside. He stopped in front of the bedroom door and stood looking at her.

He snarled, "Keep that damn ugly brat out of my sight. I don't want to see her nor hear her."

Rebecca started to reply, but he turned so quickly that she didn't get to say a word. So, from that time, Margie Elaine Pierson was kept as far away from her father as possible.

Rebecca, however, loved to look at her chubby, rosy-cheeked baby, whose crown of bright auburn hair lay in curls from the day she was born.

She loved her baby so much that tears often crept down Rebecca's cheeks as she gazed in wonder at this beautiful being that she had helped to bring into the world. She just could not understand Tom not wanting to see her or love her.

It was one month after Margie was born that Tom hit Rebecca for the first time. Everything happened so quickly and unexpectedly that she didn't know how to react. She had gotten used to his curses and threats, but she had never dreamed he would be physically violent.

That evening, Margie was asleep in the next room, and Rebecca was hurrying to get Tom's supper. Everything except the bread was on the table when Rebecca heard Margie's whimper.

Knowing Tom's temper, especially when he'd been drinking, she wanted to get to Margie before she cried aloud. She knew, as soon as he stepped through the door, that he had been drinking, so she put the bread on the table and turned toward the bedroom.

She didn't get far before Tom grabbed her hair and jerked her around.

"Get my supper ready, woman. I'm hungry," he ordered as he shoved her back toward the table.

Startled, Rebecca turned to face him and saw a strange, wild look in his eyes. Still not wanting the baby to upset him, she again started toward the bedroom since Margie was now truly crying. A snarl erupted from Tom as she started to pass him. Like a flash his hand shot out and slapped her across the face so hard that she fell against the table spilling food from every bowl.

"I told you to get my supper ready. Can't you hear?" Tom bellowed and drew back his hand again. With frightened speed Rebecca regained her footing, and quickly darted out of his reach.

"You're wasting all this food and your supper is ready," Rebecca gasped as she put her hand to her face. Tom suddenly stopped and looked at her as if he didn't know what had happened. He stood for just a moment and then took his seat at the head of the table.

"You'd better go on and take care of that bawling young'un. I can't stand much of that."

Rebecca silently left the room, thinking, *he looked like he wanted to kill me.* From that moment on, Rebecca Meadows Pierson lived a life of pure misery.

By the time Margie was two months old, Rebecca realized that her baby's resemblance to Tom's mother was even more remarkable than she had first thought, and her worries increased. *He doesn't want to see his mother's picture and seeing Margie will be a stark reminder,* she thought with a sense of dread.

Tom worked long hours for a lumber company located on the east side of Forks, Washington toward the Pacific coast and he walked home from there unless he hitched a ride. Margie was usually asleep by the time he came home so he seldom saw her since Rebecca kept her out of his sight.

One evening, however, Tom came home early and Rebecca was sitting in the kitchen with Margie in her lap. When he stepped through the door and saw his little daughter his face first turned white and then red with an angry frown and he glared at her for a moment before swinging around and leaving the room. Rebecca shivered at his look of pure anguish or was it hate at the sight of his own child.

After that he never looked at the baby, unless there was no way to avoid it, and Rebecca wondered how he could think anything as beautiful as their baby was ugly. *He must have hated his mother* was her thought since he seemed to dread looking at his own child.

Margie's looking more and more like that picture of his mother was Rebecca's daily dread and she often gazed in amazement at this beautiful child that she had produced and couldn't seem to stop herself from constantly stroking the petal soft cheeks. As the days passed Margie grew and changed from the small curly-headed baby to a "Gerber baby" with shiny ringlets of auburn hair, round, rosy-cheeks, and wide brown eyes that seemed to be checking out her surroundings. She gurgled, blew bubbles, and smiled as her face filled out and a dimple peeped out in each cheek.

As Margie grew, her hair became thick, shiny, and curly and Rebecca thought it was the most beautiful head of hair she had ever seen, but Tom certainly didn't like it.

The first time Tom noticed her hair and the dimples he hissed in wild-eyed anger. "Put a cap on that damn ugly brat. Whose brat is she? Something that ugly don't belong to me that's certain."

Rebecca gasped in surprise. "I don't know how you can say that. She looks just like that picture of your mother."

Rebecca had started to put the baby down and almost dropped her when Tom grabbed her hair and jerked her face around. "You've been lookin' at that picture again, ain't you? I told you to leave that picture alone."

Rebecca looked into his red face and blaring eyes and swallowed the fear that made her mouth dry. She whispered, "No, Tom. I swear I haven't touched or looked at it since you told me not to," feeling ashamed of lying, but fearing to tell the truth.

He dropped his hold on her hair and stepped back, but still snarled. "Put a cap on that damn brat and leave my stuff alone or you'll wish you had." He turned and abruptly left the house.

This put Rebecca on the alert since Tom had such a violent temper and she cautioned herself to be more vigilant in keeping Margie out of his sight.

A Fatal Beginning

CHAPTER 2

From that day forward Margie's hair was always covered when Tom was home, with a knitted bonnet or cap, which Margie was constantly losing or tearing. Rebecca finally told her that her daddy wanted her to wear something over her hair. Margie wanted to know why, but Rebecca didn't really know the answer. "I think your hair must remind him of his mother," said Rebecca since she had no other explanation.

Finally, Rebecca resolved that issue by saying, "Your daddy likes you better when you wear your hair covered," and since Margie wanted her daddy to like her, she gladly donned the despised cap or bonnet. She soon learned that it didn't seem to make much difference, except that her dad didn't yell at her quite so much.

Perhaps sensing her mother's fear, Margie learned not to cry aloud or make any kind of sounds when her father was at home. A visitor wouldn't have known there was a child in the Pierson home.

As Margie aged she constantly heard, "Sh-sh, don't make any noise. You'll wake your daddy and he's not feeling well. We have to be quiet when your daddy's like that. Take this coloring book to the kitchen. If we make noise in there, your daddy can't hear it."

Margie always carried her shoes in her hand every morning as she tiptoed from her room into the kitchen. She learned early that any noise could cause her dad to slap her mother and throw things. One time Margie had a bad cough and couldn't stop. Her daddy had slapped her mother because she couldn't make Margie stop coughing.

When she was three years old she awoke one morning with a sore, aching throat and awoke her mother with her crying. She only did that once, though, because she had also aroused her father. He jumped to his feet in a rage, picked her up, and threw her across the room.

Thankfully she had landed on the bed, which left her only bruised, but with a big knot on her head where it had connected with the bedstead.

Anyone seeing Margie Pierson would have said she was a very pretty child, even with the habitual head-covering, but she was seldom seen. Hearing herself described as ugly and having to hide her hair caused Margie to believe she must be terribly ugly. Also having her father say she'd been slapped in the face with ugly constantly reinforced this belief.

Rebecca tried to dispel this belief, especially when Margie's large brown eyes sparkled and her freckled face came alive with its dimpled impish grin. This often happened while she watched the antics of the many animals on the farm who were her friends, and Rebecca held her close saying, "Oh my beautiful Margie!"

Because of her father's disparaging description of her, Margie didn't grin very often, and never around her father. She became a silent and very shy little girl, who had a habit of putting her hand over her mouth when she talked, but that was only when she was inside the house.

Outside, Margie not only grinned she laughed and played with the various small animals on their farm. Each chicken had a name and the barn cat, Big Ells, was a special friend to Margie. He was a big cat and her name was given to him after hearing her father saying he would get rid of him one way or another.

"I'd give him away, but nobody but big owls would want him." Her father was having one of his 'sick spells' at the time, which caused him to slur his words together and what Margie heard was that nobody would want him but big "ells,"

I hope nobody does want him. Maybe that man called Big Ells won't take him, thought Margie hopefully as she scouted out several hiding places in case Big Ells did appear. So, the cat became "Big Ells," and when nobody came to take him away he became Margie's best friend.

Since she was free to laugh and make noise outside, especially when her father was away, Margie grew into a nature loving tomboy. No tree was too large for her to climb, and no grapevine on the farm lasted long before it became a swing for herself and Big Ells. The cat was constantly in her arms or following her from the time she went outside in the morning until she went to bed at night.

She wanted to take him to her room and allow him to sleep with her at night, but she couldn't do that. Once he came into the house and when her father saw him, Big Ells was kicked completely through the open kitchen door. Margie couldn't defend her friend, but she ran out and scooped him into her arms and ran to the barn with him. Thankfully, he had no broken bones, but Margie soon realized that he could not see out of one eye.

"That's where he kicked you, isn't it Big Ells? One day, we'll scratch his eyes out and then he won't be able to see at all." Margie promised as she tenderly stroked his fur.

Rebecca often worried that Margie would fall from her daily climbs and other escapades. "Margie, honey, please be careful," she admonished as she thought *Tom won't take her to the doctor no matter what she breaks.* Other than scraped knees, arms, and shins, however, she remained unscathed.

When her daddy was home Margie still wore a cap with her hair up in braids, so it couldn't be seen. She always kept her cap in her pocket when she was out playing and if she heard any footsteps she quickly covered her hair with the cap.

If I do what he wants maybe he'll hold my hand and walk me to the school bus like Jennifer Logan's daddy does, she thought and then tried harder to please him.

"You're beautiful now, honey, but you're going to be gorgeous when you grow up," whispered Rebecca as she plaited Margie's silky hair into long burnished auburn braids.

"I know you don't like to wear that cap and your hair in braids, but your daddy don't like for your curls to show. I think they are so pretty though. I wish I had curls."

When Rebecca said she was pretty, Margie didn't believe her. *Mommy wants to make me feel better,* she thought because her daddy's words always made her sad. Hearing herself described as ugly so often, took its toll.

Margie's braided tresses hung to her waist in the back, but she was never allowed to leave them hanging down. She was dressed in clean clothes every morning even though both she and her mother only had three outfits each.

"Try to keep your clothes clean, honey," cautioned Rebecca. She knew that using the washing machine more than once each week would infuriate Tom Pierson.

When Margie started to school and found so many friends to play with she thought school was the best place on earth. She didn't even want to leave in the evenings, but she knew her mother would be waiting at the bus stop to walk home with her.

When she heard her friends asking each other to go home with them and spend the night, she became very excited. As soon as she stepped down from the bus and took her mother's hand, her first words were, "Mommy, can I ask Jennifer to come to our house?"

Rebecca stopped dead in her tracks and looked at Margie fearfully. "Honey, you didn't ask her to come did you?"

"No, Mommy, I didn't ask her, but I don't see why I can't and Jennifer's daddy likes her, and she doesn't have to wear a cap on her head. Why can't I just cut my hair instead of wearing this old cap? Then I wouldn't be so different." Margie said with pleading in her voice. When Rebecca didn't reply, she took courage.

"Mommy, if my hair is short, I won't look like his mother and he may like me," she continued, but Rebecca shook her head.

"No, Margie, I wouldn't dare cut your hair. You'd look more like that picture if I did. Seeing your dimples and your head of shiny curls makes him mad and we don't want to make him mad."

I can't understand it since he sometimes shuts himself in the bedroom and when he comes out he looks real sad. That one time I opened the door he was holding that picture of his mother in his hand, thought Rebecca.

Margie put her arms around Rebecca's waist. "Well what about my friends, then?"

Rebecca stooped and hugged her close. "Honey, we live so far out here that parents don't like to bring their children this far out and we don't have any way to take them back home," explained her mother.

"But, Mommy, Jennifer Logan's mommy said she could come and stay all night sometime," said Margie with pleading eyes.

"Stay all night! Lordy mercy! No, Margie, don't you ever ask any girls to come home with you. Your daddy wouldn't like to have visitors and you know how he sometimes comes in feeling bad and it's hard to tell what he might do."

Rebecca shivered and dropped to her hunkers in order to look directly into Margie's troubled face. "Promise me that you won't ask any of your friends to visit."

Margie promised and she kept her promise, but often cried to and from school because she was so lonely. *If I didn't have Big Ells and my other animal friends I wouldn't have anyone at all*, she thought sadly.

She heard her mother whispering prayers as she worked around the house on a daily basis and now she thought, *I wish she'd beg the Lord to send me some friends.*

I want friends like the other girls have. I'd like to find somebody to like me.

The only consolation she had was her ability to learn. Lessons were easy for her. All of her teachers liked her even though they had difficulty breaking her habit of putting her hand over her mouth and whispering.

"I can't hear you, Margie. Why are you whispering?" her teachers asked almost daily.

Margie had not been aware that she did this so much. Now she tried to break that habit, but only while at school. School was her favorite place to be and she feared being told she couldn't come.

Margie had first started to school at Forks Elementary School. Rebecca walked the three miles down Hoh River Road with her to reach the bus stop on Highway 101, which stretched the entire length of the Pacific coast from Washington to southern California. Rebecca was also there to meet her in the evenings. Her dad, Tom Pierson, was on the day shift for her first two years of school and he never found out. Then he was changed to the second shift and from then on Margie walked to the bus stop alone, but her mother met the bus in the evenings.

CHAPTER 3

When he wasn't working, Tom Pierson controlled every waking moment of the lives of both Margie and her mother, except when Margie was at school. There, she was free until she had to return home in the evening.

I get away when I go to school, but Mommy never gets away, thought Margie and often cried for her mother. *When I get big I'm going to run away and take Mommy with me,* she daily promised herself.

Once each June, Tom Pierson took Margie and her mother into Forks, Washington, which was fifteen miles from their farm. Their small farm of five acres was located on upper Hoh River Road. The lower end of Hoh River was the home of the Hoh Indians.

Margie gazed around in wide-eyed wonder the first time she went to Forks. She'd never seen houses with two stories before, nor had she seen walkways, made of wood or something hard and black, nor stores with all kinds of things displayed in their windows. They passed a beautiful red-brick building and even her mother slowed as they passed.

"Margie, that is the Olympic Pharmacy where people get their medicines when they are sick," said her mother, but Margie was only half-listening. She'd stopped and stood almost drooling as she looked at a large sign describing the ice cream to be had inside.

"Look at that Mommy. I'd like to taste that, wouldn't you?" she asked almost whispering since she didn't know whether to talk aloud or not. Rebecca smiled. She bent down close to Margie's ear and whispered, "Yes," but hurried her on since Tom was several feet ahead

Walking behind her dad she saw a stream of water running along the side of the street "Is that part of the Hoh River that runs by our house?" She was so curious she momentarily forgot her daddy's aversion to even noticing her.

"No, dummy, that's the Bogachiel River. That's why this town is called Forks. It's in the forks of the Hoh and the Bogachiel Rivers," snarled her dad smugly and hastened his steps so that she and her mother were soon trotting to keep up with him.

When they reached Groffman's Dry Goods store, Margie and her mother were allowed to buy shoes and enough cloth to make three dresses each, and each got three pairs of socks and three sets of underwear and two head scarves which Margie now wore instead of a cap. At the same time, Tom bought Margie a coat to wear to school. Until that time Margie had worn a coat made from the only coat her mother owned.

When Margie saw her mother cutting up her coat she was surprised. "Mommy, why are you cutting up your pretty coat? You look pretty when you wear it and you'll get cold without a coat."

"I want you to look pretty and stay warm. Anyway, you're outside more than I am," answered Rebecca, who wore an old coat that Tom Pierson no longer wore when she went outside.

The coat Tom Pierson bought her on that trip was a serviceable brown. It was a couple of sizes too big, since he said it had to last several years. Margie looked at it and wanted to cry, but seeing the scowl on her father's face she smiled and thanked him.

"You'd better be careful with that coat, girl. Money don't grow on trees," was his surly warning.

As much as she disliked the coat Margie had to wear it to school or freeze. Rebecca insisted she wear it since she feared either of them getting sick. There would be no going to a doctor.

Other than the one time that Margie was thrown into the wall, Tom had not beaten her, but she often received slaps across the face and ears that left her with ringing in her ears for hours. He cursed, yelled, and threatened so much, however, that Margie lived in agonizing fear. She often thought that just seeing her made her father turn on her mother. It broke her heart when her daddy knocked her mother about, but she was afraid to try to help her.

I wish it was him with black eyes and purple cheeks, she thought and then shivered since she knew that inside she was glad he hadn't beat her up like he did her mother. Knowing this made her feel ashamed and guilty and furthered the feelings of fear and helplessness that she had grown up with.

She often found herself wishing that her father would die. She even daydreamed of ways it could happen. Sometimes she had him getting sawed to pieces at the saw mill where he worked or sometimes run over by a logging truck. She could hear him screaming and at first, she'd stop her daydream since she didn't really want him to hurt. By the time she was eight or nine years old, however, she let her daydreams play out in horrific, gory details with him screaming the whole time.

Her mother being constantly abused and her own frequent slaps also made her begin to doubt if there really was a God. *Where is he? If he really loved us he'd help us,* was her thoughts each time Tom Pierson was in a foul mood. She wanted to believe her mother, but could not help her doubting thoughts. *If she's right, then we must be doing something that God doesn't like. He never answers and she prays all the time.*

"Mommy, I don't know how to be good enough so God will help me and you. Do you reckon he knows where we live?" She often questioned her mother about that distant God that she told Margie to believe in

"Margie, honey we have to believe that God is real and will take care of us. He will honey, but in his own time, not ours."

Well, if He can't save us when we're being knocked around I don't think we need him no other time, she thought and wondered why her mother kept depending on somebody who was never there.

The pattern of abuse changed when she turned ten years old. She was now in the sixth grade and could no longer go to the elementary school, which was only fifteen miles from the small farm on Hoh River road. The middle school she would now attend was several miles further away. Margie was happy to get away that much longer each day.

Tom Pierson grumbled because she would be later getting home, but other than cursing if everything wasn't done when he got home, he stayed fairly calm.

Margie's three years in the middle school were lonely and full of dread, but she did get to attend. Her dad would have taken her out of school altogether if her mother hadn't convinced him that he could be sent to jail for keeping her out.

"Tom, the law says that Margie has to attend school until she is sixteen and she'll be through school by then," explained Rebecca.

"Where'd you hear about a law like that? Have you been making friends with the sheriff and his deputies? You'd better not or some dark night you'll meet your end and your law friends won't know where I am," threatened Tom Pierson giving her a suspicious look.

"I never leave this farm unless you're with me, so you don't have to worry about me talking to anybody," said Rebecca in as calm a manner as she could before continuing. "When she first started to school she brought papers home that said parents would be fined and even jailed if they did not send their children to school." This seemed to satisfy Tom and he said no more about her attending school.

Often when Tom looked at Margie, he, for some reason, lashed out at Rebecca, and cursed violently with almost every breath. Both Margie and her mother were always glad when he went to bed. The times they dreaded most were when he returned from town drunk. These trips usually ended in Margie being slapped or shoved and Rebecca getting knocked around.

Margie often thought back to the few times she had approached her father, trying to get him to notice her. Once she was helping him dig potatoes. She had her hair completely covered and was working really fast. When he didn't grumble or curse for what Margie thought to be an hour she drew in a long breath and looked at her father. "Daddy, are you going to sell these potatoes?"

Tom Pierson turned a scowling face in her direction, but only answered, "Yep, and I'll get a good price too. They'll not cheat Tom Pierson."

Margie felt so good. She smiled showing her dimples. "They wouldn't dare cheat you would they, Daddy? You're strong enough to beat them to pieces, I bet."

For the first time in her life Margie thought she saw a grin on her dad's face, but if so, it quickly turned to a red angry glare when he saw that smiling dimpled face. "Get back to your job. You're as lazy as that sorry mommy of yours."

Margie remembered being so hurt and puzzled. *I must be really ugly. He seemed fine until he looked at me*, she thought as she bent her head and crouched to pick up more potatoes.

One other time, Margie felt he was proud of her or something. She had gone with her parents to gather mountain tea berries and to catch some salmon. She knew it would be a lot of work to salt down and can the salmon as well as washing and brewing the mountain tea leaves, used for medicine. She didn't think of that, however, since she felt so proud to be doing something with both her parents.

I'll bet Jennifer Logan doesn't get to do this with her parents, she thought in a happy daydream.

Margie had settled herself on the river bank at a spot just below the falls, where the river tumbled down over the rocks. She'd learned in school that salmon swam upstream to lay their eggs or whatever they did to make young salmon. That is why she chose the spot below the falls and it proved to be a good spot.

An hour later she heard the voice of her mother. "Margie, Margie, where are you?"

"I'm here below the falls, Mom, and I've caught a lot of salmon. I don't know if we can carry all of it home," said Margie.

"Are you lyin' again, girl?" The harsh voice of her father made Margie quell. She had thought her dad would be so proud of her with each salmon she hauled to the bank, but he didn't sound proud.

Just as her father came into view footsteps were heard from the other direction. They turned to see a man and a boy of about twelve or thirteen making their way downstream.

"Hello, there, young lady. Looks like you've caught every salmon in the stream," said a nice jovial voice.

Before, anyone else said anything Tom Pierson, who had come to a stop beside of Margie and her pile of salmon, looked upstream at the man and boy and said with a smirk, "That's what being taught by a true fisherman can do."

The stranger laughed. "If your teaching helped her catch that many salmon I want to take some lessons. How much do you charge?"

Margie sat basking in the silent glow that flooded her heart. *He's proud of me,* she thought and wanted to jump up and run to hug her father, but feared to do it.

Other than those two times Margie had no memories of anything passing for goodness or gentleness coming from her father.

A Fatal Beginning

CHAPTER 4

Half way through the seventh grade Margie hit a growth spurt and suddenly changed. Her face and body filled out and her brown eyes sparkled mischievously, especially when she smiled. Now, her hair not only gleamed but stray curls had a tendency to escape the tightly woven braids and creep out around the edges of her head scarf. This drew attention to her beautiful face and boys began to notice her. Margie didn't know this, however, since she was afraid to raise her head around boys.

Rebecca loved to wash and comb Margie's hair, which fell in waves down her back. Margie no longer looked like a little girl. This certainly did not go unnoticed by Tom Pierson, since seeing this almost adult daughter seemed to make him act more belligerent than he had when she still looked like a little girl.

"If I hear tell of you talking or having anything to do with any boys you'll regret it for a long time, girl," he threatened as he shook his fist menacingly in her face. Margie was already petrified around her daddy and now she stood shivering in almost speechless fright.

"Ain't you got no tongue, girl? Are you going to strut around them boys and act flirty?"

Margie had no idea what acting flirty meant, but she whispered, "No, Daddy, I promise I won't."

"You'd better not. That's what got your mommy in trouble. That's why you're so ugly. She couldn't claim something as ugly as you off on me," he stormed as he went out of the house and slammed the door.

Margie looked to the couch where her mother was cringing. "What's he talking about, Mommy? Ain't, he my daddy?"

Rebecca rose wearily from the couch and went to look out the window. When she saw Tom's back as he marched down the road she turned with a sigh. "Yes,

Margie, he is your daddy, but sometimes I wish he wasn't. He was always so jealous that he just wouldn't accept that I hadn't been with other boys. I hadn't though." *I think he wanted me because I didn't want him,* thought Rebecca.

Rebecca grabbed Margie and hugged her close. "You look just like his mother, but it'd probably be better if you didn't. She was a very beautiful woman, poor soul. I wish I'd met her before I married your daddy. If I had I might have learned about Tom. I think I'd have run away even after he ruined me."

"I don't know what you're talking about and I don't know what he means about being flirty with boys. Mommy, I told him I wouldn't, but what is it I'm not supposed to do?" asked Margie.

"Just don't be around any boys by yourself on the playground. If other girls are around you I guess it will be all right," explained Rebecca.

Margie didn't understand how being around boys could hurt anyone, but she was too afraid of her daddy to even think of questioning him. Anyway, she didn't think there was any need to worry about boys noticing her. "What boy would look at me, with my hair braided around my head like an old woman," she mumbled, yet knew she didn't want to make her daddy mad. Her dad hit out and asked questions later, but so far, her mother had been the main recipient of his anger.

Until she started to the new school he had just slapped, cursed, and threatened her, but now when she heard his voice or knew him to be near, she quaked inside.

If there is a God, why doesn't he just let Daddy die? He just loves being mean to me and Mommy. Another man would knock his brains out and I wish somebody would. I'd sneak and hit him with a hammer myself, but I may not kill him and then he'd kill me and Mommy both, she often thought.

It was then that Margie's stomach began hurting every evening as soon as she stepped out of the school bus. Rebecca always said, "It's probably something you ate." Margie, however, felt it was her fear around her father that made it hurt. .

What if I'm flirty, she thought, wondering what flirty meant. One time he had seen the bus pass and a boy was sitting in the seat beside her. Margie hadn't wanted the boy to sit there, but he did anyway, and all the other boys laughed when she asked him to take another seat.

From the time she got off the bus that evening she was afraid she had been seen. She didn't make it inside the door before she was slapped so hard she fell backwards onto the porch. Rebecca ran to help her and took the rest of the beating Margie would have gotten.

Margie made good grades, but had no friends. When a boy approached her, she smiled shyly but backed away. *When I get to high school I'll be older and won't be so afraid of Daddy*, she thought but knew that wasn't true. She had lived with fear so long that it seemed normal, or almost normal.

Margie was slapped frequently during those years, but never was she actually beaten. That didn't ease her fears of when it might happen. She had thought her life was terrible in middle school, but her high school years would prove to be a literal hell on earth. It was as if fear and dread became a heavy fog that permeated the road she traveled and the house in which she lived. The house seemed to take on a persona of evil and she hated the sight of it.

Margie was very eager for school to begin in August the year she was thirteen. *I'll be fourteen in October and I'll be in high school. That means that I will have nine hours of freedom from fear*, she thought.

Getting on the school bus and riding away from the farm each day was like escaping from prison. Quilleyute Valley High School was located in Forks also, but she had more classes and the day was longer. This was wonderful in Margie's mind. This meant she wouldn't be at home nearly as much.

She was a little uneasy, however, when the new term actually started. This school was much bigger and everything was so new and different. She knew she would have no friends; she was 'that different girl' to her classmates since she didn't have the saddle oxfords, nor skirts and sweaters, and a nice coat like the other girls had and she had to wear her hair in those braids.

She was cheered to discover that the high school had a much bigger library and that meant more books to escape into. She was assigned to her classes and each class issued books. Margie knew she couldn't rent a locker, but she was strong. *I can carry my books home,* she thought as she shifted the heavy load into her other arm.

All day long she walked from one class to the other lugging her load of books. She had no friends and didn't sit with anyone at lunch, but she did hear the other girls talk about going skating, or seeing a movie at the Olympic Theater on Division Street, or buying milkshakes at the Olympic Drugstore on Main Street, which her mother had called a Pharmacy. This made her more alone than ever because she knew that she would never do any of those things.

This went on for the first month of school and then she met Rick Mullet. She had noticed him in her English class the first day and thought he was nice and nice looking as well. As she came out of her chemistry class on Monday, he stopped her.

"Here, let me have half of your books. That many books have to be heavy."

Margie looked startled. *A boy was asking to help her. Was that being flirty?* Margie wondered uneasily, but knowing that there were lots of other boys and girls around her she smiled and thanked him.

"My name is Rick Mullet and I ride your bus," he said and reached for the top four of her books.

Margie smiled again. "My name is Margie Pierson. I saw you in my English class, but I didn't know you rode my bus. Where do you live?"

Rick laughed. "You don't know me because you never look around you. We both ride down Highway 101 since it is the only highway in this area, but the bus makes several stops and I get off two stops before yours," Rick answered.

"How did you know which stop was mine?" Margie asked with a penetrating stare.

"Your name is Pierson and your folks are the only Piersons living in this area, so the road leading to your farm is two stops beyond my stop." He laughed. "Why? Don't you want me to know where you live?"

Fearing her father would find out that she was talking to him, she asked, "Do you know my dad?"

Rick looked at her with compassion, but said, "Not personally, but everybody knows about Tom Pierson."

Margie gave him a wary look. "What do they know about my dad?"

Rick hesitated. "Well, they know that he never allows you and your mother to go anywhere. Until you started to school nobody knew Tom Pierson had any children. Do you have any brothers or sisters?"

'No, I'm the only child," said Margie.

"Mom and Dad were surprised that you are getting to attend high school. They didn't think Tom Pierson would allow you to attend."

When Margie didn't answer, Rick blurted. "It must be the truth. I've always seen you in school, but never anywhere else. Does he let you go anywhere else?"

Margie dropped her head. "No."

"Do you mean that you never go anywhere at all? Rick questioned in astonishment.

"Mom and I go into Forks once each year to buy school clothes, but dad is with us."

She looked so forlorn that Rick touched her arm. "You always look beautiful, Margie."

Margie's head jerked as if stunned. She always hid her head scarf as soon as she reached the bus stop, but still no other girls had to wear their hair in braids and Margie was embarrassed.

"You . . . You're just being nice. Dad won't let me cut my hair and Mom has to make all my clothes." She looked down at her skirt. "Mom can't make slacks, but Dad wouldn't let me wear them if she could."

"I like girls with big shiny brown eyes and braided hair and I like girls that wear dresses, Margie. Your mom makes pretty dresses, and I mean that. I'm not just being nice, for you are a very beautiful girl even with your hair in braids." Rick smiled and Margie swallowed the tears trying to break through and returned his smile.

From that day on Margie sat with Rick Mullet on the bus, but she made it a point that they always sat where they couldn't be seen from the road. Margie's dad always walked that road on his way to and from work. She felt free at school since she knew her dad would never come there. So, when she and Rick met in the halls they stopped to talk. When other boys saw her talking to Rick they also began to be friendly with her, but this made her more afraid.

CHAPTER 5

One day during their lunch in the cafeteria, Rick asked, "Margie, would your Dad let me take you to a movie?"

Margie cringed as her eyes widened in fright. "No. Rick, don't ever come down our section of Hoh River. If any boy comes down our road Dad goes into a rage. He accuses me of secretly meeting some boy." She shivered involuntarily.

"Margie, does that man beat you? If he does I'll call the police." Rick's face had taken on an angry red hue.

Margie jumped up from the table. "The police!" came out in a whispered shriek. "No, Rick, please don't do that. I'm all right, just please don't come out our road."

Rick talked to his father. "I'm going out and have a talk with Tom Pierson. I just want to take Margie to a movie or something."

Paul Mullet shook his head. "Son, from what I've heard about that man he'd first beat you up and then those poor women would really get a beating."

Rick stomped angrily to the kitchen door then turned. "Well, if Margie doesn't get to go to the senior prom I'll do something."

Mr. Mullet arose from his seat on the sofa and followed Rick into the kitchen. "Rick, I can see you've got it bad for that girl, but don't do anything rash. I'll ask around. Pierson may have some friends or someone we could use as a go-between. The prom isn't until May and this is only the first of April, so just keep your shirt on and I'll see what I can do."

As it turned out Mr. Mullet didn't have to do anything, circumstances did. Ridgeway Lumber Company, where Tom Pierson worked, cut back the hours of the crewmen. Tom came home in a rage, saying that something would have to be done or he would lose his farm.

Margie worried all night since she knew that having her father home meant more punishment she and her mother would suffer. However, the next day at school, some of the girls told Margie that Jack Fraker, who owned a big orchard near upper Hoh River Road, was hiring pickers.

"How old do they have to be?" asked Margie as an idea formed in her head.

"A man at the post office told Daddy that Mr. Fraker was hiring after school students. They won't be working that many hours and it would save him money," said Beatrice Hayley.

Margie sat deep in thought. *I could get off the bus there in the evenings and then walk home when I finish. If I can make some money to help out, Daddy will be more apt to let me work. It would also keep me away from him that much longer.*

That evening as she and Rick took their seats on the bus she turned to him with a smile. "Rick, I'm going to get a job."

"Where? Your Dad won't let you. You know that, don't you?"

"He might since he has had his hours cut back at the lumber company. If I could work I wouldn't have to be home where he is."

Rick smiled and grasped her hand. "Where is this job you are dreaming about?"

"Jack Fraker wants to hire after school students to pick apples. I could walk home from his orchard," answered Margie.

Rick sat for a moment deep in thought. "Margie, let's both try to get a job in Mr. Fraker's orchard and I could walk back with you. Since I will be with you we can take a path through the woods. It's a short cut that will save us a lot of walking. My place comes before yours and nobody would know I was walking with you."

If Daddy ever heard about me walking through the woods, he'd get angry, but walking with a boy . . . he'd kill me, she thought. She turned to Rick and said, "Well, I'll have to talk to Daddy about it. I dread it, but if he knows that I'll give him most of what I make maybe he'll not get too upset."

When they came to Rick's stop, he squeezed her hand and then impulsively leaned over and kissed her cheek. He quickly went down the aisle and jumped from the bus since the bus driver wasn't the most patient person he'd ever met.

Margie put her hand to her cheek and without knowing it turned red. That was the moment that Margie Pierson fell in love with Rick Mullet.

Leaving the bus, Margie dawdled along in a bemused state. *I feel like singing and dancing. Maybe this is love. What if he loves me too? I know he likes me or he wouldn't have kissed me in front of all his friends*, she thought, smiling to herself. The smile left her face, however, when she turned the last curve before her house came into view.

Margie heard her father's voice raised in loud cursing. "You damn slut. I'll knock some sense into you if I have to kill you. You damn well know we can't buy milk and eggs or nothing else for a while."

"Tom, no, don't. Please, Tom, please," was the pitiful plea Margie heard. Her banked down rage boiled up and overflowed. She broke into a run.

As she jumped up the two steps leading to the porch, she heard a loud crash. She burst through the door. Her mother was lying in a crumpled heap with blood oozing from a cut on her head.

"You've killed her! You've killed my mother," she screamed as she tried to get past her father. She didn't get by him though. Instead she felt a fist strike her jaw and she was sent sprawling back out the front door. Then she didn't know anything else.

She awoke to cold water drenching her face. She sputtered and raised her head, but the world was spinning around and around. She closed her eyes again.

"Quit pretending and get in here to help your mother."

Margie opened her eyes again and finding the world steady she gingerly rose to her feet and stumbled drunkenly up the porch and into the living room.

Tom Pierson had carried Rebecca to the couch, but she still looked dead to Margie. She stood just inside the door looking with dread at her mother.

Her daddy turned toward her. "Well, don't just stand there. Go get some water in a pan and wash her face and hands."

Tom Pierson wiped his fist across his face and winced when his knuckles touched his face. Margie saw blood on his face when he dropped his fist.

"Why do you treat us like this? Do you hate Mom and me so much?" she mumbled through trembling lips.

"Shut your damn mouth," he snarled and turned away.

Margie wanted to jump at his face and claw his eyes. Hate bubbled up again. She looked around the room for something to use as a weapon, but then had to grip her hands together to keep from lashing out. Her jaw, however, was swollen and aching and she knew that saying one word would bring about more of the same.

When he left the room, she hurried to her mother. "Mom, Mom, are you all right?" whispered Margie through her own swollen lips as she lifted her mother's head.

Rebecca opened her eyes, so filled with anguish and pain that Margie wanted to cry. Through swollen lips her mother whispered, "Help me sit up, Margie. I think he broke some ribs."

When Margie tried to lift her mother, Rebecca fainted. Margie thought she was dead and anger filled her with uncaring valor. She turned and walked to the back porch where she knew her father was. She jerked the door open.

"You've killed my mother, you dirty scum. I'm calling the police," she screamed as she turned and ran back into the house and not stopping ran out the front door. She was halfway down the road when her dad caught her.

He grabbed her arm and jerked her to a stop. "She's not dead. You go back to her and I'll go bring the doctor."

At his words and tone Margie looked up in unbelief. Tom Pierson was white as a sheet of paper. "Go on and help her get into bed. She's still on the couch."

Margie stood staring, with hate blazing in her eyes. "You won't get the doctor. You'll get drunk. You know you can't fool the doctor. He'll know what happened to her and he'll report you. I hope to God he does," she stormed and then began to shake.

Tom Pierson turned red in the face and took a step toward her with fist raised, but suddenly dropped his fist and turned toward the road. He muttered dire threats as he went on down the road until he could no longer be heard.

Margie's shaking eased when she realized that her dad wasn't going to hit her anymore. She couldn't believe she had spoken to him the way she had. *I'm surprised he didn't kill me*, she thought as she turned back to the house.

Rebecca was still on the couch and conscious, but was having trouble breathing. She turned her head when Margie came through the door. "He's gone for the doctor," she gasped and then waited as she tried to breathe.

"He'll get drunk and not come back tonight. I'm going to go down to the highway and find a phone. That way, I'll be sure you get a doctor," said Margie as she brushed the hair back and saw the dried blood that clung to her mother's forehead.

She turned to get a wet wash cloth from the bathroom, but Rebecca stopped her. "Margie, stay with me. He'll bring the doctor. He knows he's gone too far this time. He's afraid I'll die and he'll be locked up."

"I'm just going to get a wet wash cloth to get that dried blood off your forehead. I guess that's where that blood on his fist came from," replied Margie who suddenly realized that she had a terrific headache.

Margie brought the cloth and tenderly washed Rebecca's entire face and neck, which was beginning to turn a dark blue. Rebecca put her hand up to Margie's cheek.

"He hit you, didn't he, Margie?" Rebecca put her hand on her chest and struggled to breath and when she seemed calmer she said, "I told him after that last time he hit you that I'd call the law if he ever hit you again."

Her words pleased Margie, but she knew that her mother shouldn't try to talk. "Mommy, don't try to talk. You might make things worse. Don't get upset. I'll not do anything now. *But, if he doesn't have a doctor here in an hour I will go make that call*, thought Margie as she turned to take the cloth back to the bathroom.

Forty minutes later a car pulled to a stop in front of the house and Tom Pierson came in with the doctor beside him. Rebecca had begged Margie to stay in her room while the doctor was there, and Margie promised she would. When they'd heard the car, Rebecca had clasped Margie's hand, "Go on to your room, Margie. I don't want you to witness what the doctor will have to do." Margie, however, knew that her mother didn't want the doctor to see her own swollen cheek. She'd have to lie about that too.

Obediently Margie went to her room and closed the door. She could hear voices, but since her room was at the back of the house she couldn't make out what they said.

She lay on her bed and thought about her life and her mother's life. *What have we done to have to stand so much punishment*, she thought. *God, if you are real, why don't you help us? What kind of a God are you, anyway?* was the questioning thought that popped unbidden into her mind.

When she heard the car leave, she hesitantly cracked her door and not hearing any sounds, walked quietly back to the living room. It was empty, but she heard sounds coming from her mother's bedroom. *I'll go to the door and ask if she wants me to cook supper,* she thought with the hope that her daddy wouldn't lash out at her for coming to their room.

As she neared the door it opened, and her dad stepped through into the hall. Margie gulped and stepped back as if to leave, but her dad said, "Your mother wants to talk to you." Then he went past her and left the house.

She found her mother propped up in bed with a bandage around her head and also around her chest. The usual petticoat worn by Rebecca was missing, but the bandage covered her entire upper body.

"Were your rips broken, Mommy?" Margie asked looking at the bandages.

"Yes, I have three ribs broken, a concussion, and a broken finger, but the doctor thinks they will all heal in time. I told him that the cow butted me into the side of the barn and I couldn't get away."

"Why, Mommy? Why didn't you tell him the truth?" asked Margie. "The doctor would have had to report it and the police would put Daddy in prison. Then we'd never have to be afraid or be beaten up again," explained Margie as if her mother wasn't thinking clearly.

Rebecca raised pain-filled eyes to her daughter's face and whispered, "I can't do that, Margie . . . he knows I can't. I'm caught, but he knows I'll do anything it takes before I'll let him hurt you again." Rebecca was having trouble breathing and Margie bent to kiss her cheek.

"Sh-sh, don't try to talk, just rest," whispered Margie in a soothing voice.

"He won't hit us no more, Margie. He knows he went too far. He could tell the doctor didn't believe my story and I feel sure he'll give Tom a warning. It'll be different, you'll see," said Rebecca as if bestowing a promise.

When Tom Pierson came back he seemed different, at least with Rebecca. "I don't know what we will do without my full-time wages. I don't get hardly enough to live on now. I had to pay that doctor half of what I had saved."

Margie saw this as the best opportunity and she took it. "I can help, Daddy. I can get a job. I'd give you most of the money." Margie was talking very fast and loudly, but she didn't realize it.

Tom Pierson glowered at her, but he didn't act like he was going to hit her. "What did you say?"

"I said I could get a job in the evenings to help out," said Margie more slowly.

"Where could you get a job? Some beer joint may hire you, but you ain't working in no beer joint."

"Jack Fraker, the man with that apple orchard on upper Hoh River Road needs pickers and he wants to hire school kids in the evenings. Some of the girls from school are going to try to get work," Margie anxiously explained.

"How would you get there and back? I'll not have you walking that highway by yourself."

Margie's heart slowed, and she drew a steadying breath. "I wouldn't be by myself. Beatrice Hayley that lives a mile or two out on 101 is going to ask for a job also. In the evening we could get off the school bus there at the end of the road where the orchard is and then Beatrice would be with me on the way home."

Her dad seemed to think about it and finally said, "If that Hayley girl gets a job too, I'll let you try it. You'd better be telling me the truth, girl."

Margie didn't go to school the following day, which was Friday, since she didn't want to explain her black eye and swollen cheek. *They'll be almost better by Monday*, she thought as she studied herself in the mirror.

This was the middle of April and the apples weren't ripe until May. This gave Rebecca time to recover enough to cook, but Margie did the laundry and cleaned the house in the evenings until she started work in the orchard. From May through the end of June, Margie worked two hours every evening. When she received her pay she kept out five dollars and gave her dad the other fifteen.

Rick had also gotten a job and he walked home with Margie and Beatrice. They always took the path through the woods since it was much quicker. Margie really enjoyed being with her friends, especially Rick.

Beatrice soon knew that she and Rick were a "couple" and thought it was wonderful. "Margie, you look happy for the first time in all the years we've been in school together," said Beatrice, watching the color change in Margie's cheeks.

Margie smiled. "I didn't think I could ever like a man. Daddy turned me against men, or I thought he had, but Rick is not like Daddy."

"No, he isn't. Rick is a really nice guy and he's from a nice family also. Everybody likes the Mullets, especially Paul Mullet, his dad," replied Beatrice.

Meanwhile an uneasy truce seemed to be in place in the Pierson home. Her dad didn't speak to her unless he needed her to do something. Then he cursed her if she didn't do it fast enough or the way he wanted it done. This was a blessing as far as Margie was concerned and her stomach didn't hurt as much now.

A Fatal Beginning

CHAPTER 6

Rick asked Margie to go to the senior prom with him and Margie wanted to, but knew she couldn't. It was to be held the first Saturday night in June since school wasn't over until June fifteenth that year.

"Rick, you know that Dad won't let me go. I can't even go alone, so going with a boy is out of the question."

"Talk to your mom. Maybe she can talk to him. You say he's not beating on her now, so she may have some influence," Rick pleaded.

"I'll talk to Mom, but I don't feel like she can make any difference," replied Margie doubtfully.

She was wrong though. She never knew how Rebecca had talked him into it, but Margie did go to the prom. After that Margie talked to her mother about Rick and shared her joy in meeting somebody who really liked her. Rebecca listened to her daughter's first experience of youthful happiness and then prayed that this boy would love her daughter and get her out of the misery she'd had to live in.

"You have to go to Beatrice Hayley's house and tell your dad you went with her to the prom," explained Rebecca. "I hope he never finds out that you went with a boy, though."

The next day Margie bought the material and when Tom Pierson wasn't home Rebecca worked on her dress. When Margie got her first look at the finished dress she gazed in open-mouthed awe. It was the most beautiful dress she had ever seen and she was going to wear it to her first dance. When she tried it on and looked at herself in the mirror, tears came to her eyes.

"Mommy, I look . . . pretty, don't I?"

Rebecca wiped her wet cheeks. "No, Margie, you look beautiful and it isn't the dress. It is you, Margie. You are truly beautiful."

Prom night was the most wonderful night in all of her seventeen years. On the way home Margie listened eagerly when Rick said he'd worked out a scheme, so they could see each other once each week away from school.

"School will be out, Margie, and you know how I feel about you and I can't stand not seeing you," Rick begged when Margie was hesitant about the idea.

"Rick, I don't think I could stand another beating. I believe I'd try to kill him, even if I had to do it while he sleeps. I don't want to go to prison and that's what would happen. I just can't take that kind of chance."

"We'll be careful, Margie. I'll always leave a note somewhere and you can ask to visit Beatrice," insisted Rick.

"What if he asked Beatrice?"

"He won't ask Beatrice. He doesn't speak to people. How's he going to find out if he never speaks to anybody?"

Since she loved him so much and he begged so urgently, Margie agreed. All that summer Margie lived in constant anxiety, but she loved Rick too much not to take a chance. They managed to meet in the woods once each week where they grew close to each other.

Margie was surprised, though, when Rick started begging her to marry him.

"Margie, I've been thinking and I have a plan." He sounded so excited. "There's no work around here right now, so, I'll join the army and after basic training I'll get leave. Then we'll sneak away and marry. I'll take you back to base with me and you'll never have to be afraid again."

Margie threw her arms around his neck and cried. "Oh Rick, do you really want to marry me?"

Hugging her so tight she could hardly breathe, he said, "More than anything on earth, Margie. I'd rather die than lose you. What do you say, honey?" Suddenly Rick dropped to his knees and looked up, "Margie Pierson, will you marry me?"

Margie dropped to her knees and soon they were rolling over and over in their joy. They didn't hear the wind sighs, the leaves crackling beneath them, nor the twittering of the birds startled on their perches.

Later, Margie couldn't really say how or what had started what changed her life forever. At the time her only thought was that she was making Rick happy. When it was over, Margie was too ashamed to look Rick in the face, but he tilted her chin and kissed her.

"Please don't look like that, Margie," Rick begged. "We love each other and now, we'll have to get married. I didn't mean that to happen, Margie, but I have a plan. I'll go tomorrow and enlist in the army. It'll be all right. You'll see," promised Rick as he stroked her hair and held her close and Margie was reassured.

Margie didn't hear from Rick and didn't know what had happened until she received his first letter six weeks later, but what that letter disclosed made her very happy.

Dear Margie,

The day after we promised to marry I went to Port Angeles as I promised and enlisted in the Air Force. I thought I would have several weeks before I would actually have to leave. That wasn't the case.

I got to Port Angeles early and by ten o'clock I had filled in all the forms they gave me and thought I was free to go home. Instead, I was sent to another room for a physical examination and then I was taken back to another room and told to wait to be sworn into the United States Air Force.

I sat there thinking they were really rushing things up and boy was I right. You know how I'd planned to just join the regular army so we could get married sooner. Well, I guess we'll have to wait longer than I thought.

Finally, a sergeant came and motioned me through another door. A man with several stars on his uniform was seated behind a desk, looked up and said, "Have a seat, Mr. Mullet. You have one more paper to sign, and then we'll swear you in."

Margie, I'd already signed so many papers that my fingers were stiff, but I signed the paper pushed toward me and then dropped my hands to my knees.

I was tired, aggravated and certainly didn't expect what happened next. The sergeant barked out, "Stand and raise your right hand."

Of course, I jumped to my feet, not having any idea what was happening and before I realized what was going on I found I had been sworn in and was now officially a member of the United States Air Force.

This officer, who I now know was a Lieutenant, rose from behind his desk and saluted as he said, "Congratulations, Mr. Mullett. You're in the Air Force now. You are to report here tomorrow at 1300 hours (one o'clock to you) and we'll fly you out to Fort Ord."

I know my face must have been red. I was as mad as a hornet as I stormed out, "Tomorrow! But I can't go tomorrow. I have to see my fiancé."

"You signed this paper and agreed to be sworn in and by doing so you said you agreed to serve in the United States Air Force, didn't you?"

"Yes, I... guess, I did, but I need to get some things done before I leave."

The Lieutenant looked at his watch. "You have twenty-eight hours to get everything in order. I'll see you tomorrow at thirteen hundred hours." I stood with my mouth open as he turned and walked out.

Honey, I swear I was so stunned that I just stood there like an idiot. I don't know if I'd have moved for several more minutes if that Sergeant hadn't poked his head around the door and said, "Soldier, you'd best get a move on if you have things to do."

I'll bet he laughed his butt off when I broke into a run saying, "I have to see Margie. She won't know what to expect if she doesn't hear from me."

When I got to dad's truck I was still trying to figure out what to do. I had decided that I would call Beatrice and tell her to get word to you that same evening, thinking we could meet for a few minutes in the woods.

Margie, I still can't believe it, but I swear it seemed that from there on everything that could go wrong did. I didn't get the chance to contact anyone. I drove around a curve on Route 101 and jammed on the brakes. There was some kind of big smash-up just ahead of me. A tangle of cars and trucks were blocking the road on both sides. Flashing blue and red lights seemed to be shining from every direction.

I was shocked and thought, God what a mess! I hope nobody is killed. I jumped out and went to investigate, but a cop stopped me before I even got close.

He said I couldn't go any nearer, that the gas tanks were apt to blow. The police were trying to get as many people out as possible before that happened. He looked so upset that I felt sorry for him as he scurried away.

You know me, old nosey Rick. I didn't get back into the truck. I crossed a rail fence around a hayfield and walked along the edge to get a better view, but before I'd gone five feet a loud blast shook the earth all around me. Flames shot high in the air and then more blasts went off. Bits and pieces of debris were flying through the air and I dropped to the ground and crawled behind a thicket of shrubs to keep from being hit.

When no more blasts erupted I crawled out and made my way through the smoke, dust, and fumes to where I'd left Dad's truck. I thought I'd faint when it wasn't there. Well, yes, the frame and melted metal stood in its place.

A Fatal Beginning

It was like that picture I told you about of a bombing raid in London. Margie, I've never seen such a sight. Dozens of similar frames cluttered the roadway.

I stood there thinking that Dad was going to be real upset. I wasn't even in the pile-up but his truck is gone anyway. That was my first thoughts, but then knowing how they love me, I knew they'd be worried to death. And I needed to let them know I was all right.

I saw a state trooper standing by his patrol car shaking his head as he spoke into his radio. I almost laughed when he said, "We don't even know how many are dead. All these lives are lost because a damn elk decided to cross the highway."

I asked if somebody had really tried to miss an elk and caused all this, but the officer didn't even hear me. He just kept on talking and of course I stood listening as he explained, "A truck was going one way and a car was coming in the other direction. They hit each other head on and over a dozen other cars piled up behind them. The damn elk walked away. I saw him standing over in the field until the first gas tank exploded," explained the officer with tears in his eyes. Finally, he turned around and looked at me.

With all he was trying to deal with I hated to bother him, but I didn't want to worry Mom and Dad, so I asked if there was any way he could get word to them since Dad's truck was gone.

With everything pure chaos around him that officer still helped me, even though I didn't think he would. My heart sank when he turned to go, but he looked back and said, "Wait here! I'll see if anyone is being sent to the Community Hospital." He hurried away toward the waiting ambulances.

Guess what, Margie! Jack Fraker had escaped damage and was on his way home, so he gave me a ride, but Honey, by the time I got home it was so late in the night I couldn't contact you or Beatrice.

Margie, honey, believe me I tried, but there was no time the next morning to make any contacts except that I called Beatrice and asked her to get in touch with you and explain what had happened.

I told her to tell you I'd write as soon as I got there and I'd send the mail to her. She said she'd get it to you and then I had to leave.

Dad hired Jack Fraker to drive me back to the recruiting station in Port Angeles. I was worried sick about not getting to see you, honey, but I didn't have a choice. Margie, leaving without seeing you was the hardest thing I've ever had to do in my whole life. Margie, just remember that I love you more than life.
Rick,

Rick did write, but he had the address wrong and did not realize it for several weeks. After a week had passed Margie was worried and she began having problems with her stomach, but didn't dare mention it to anyone.

A Fatal Beginning

CHAPTER 7

Once he realized his mistake, Rick kept his promise and wrote faithfully to Margie. She always replied as soon as she received his letters. Rick didn't know it, but Margie always made Beatrice wait there in the woods until she answered his letter. She never knew when she could get away, and her Dad had been acting suspicious in the last few days.

Their letters flew back and forth for a little over two months and both of them were anxiously awaiting Rick's leave. Then the letters stopped.

Margie later found that Rick was on a training mission out in the field and couldn't write, but even if she had known, she was living in too much anguish to write. She was sick all the time.

The first morning she awoke and felt sick she thought she had a virus. She ran to the bathroom to vomit and felt a little better until she went in to breakfast. The sight of the food made her stomach roil again and she hurried back to the bathroom.

She heard her dad's roar, "What's wrong with her? Has she lost her mind? Tell her to get back to this table. We don't waste food around here."

Rebecca knocked on the bathroom door. "Margie, are you sick? Your daddy wants you to come back and eat."

"Mom, I can't eat right now. I must have picked up a virus. Tell Daddy I don't want him to catch it. Save my food and I'll eat it at lunch," whispered Margie and started vomiting again.

Rebecca went back to the kitchen. "She's got some kind of virus. She is vomiting and has diarrhea also. She don't want us to catch it." She stood waiting to see Tom's reaction. He stared at her angrily, said, "Humph" and continued to eat.

Margie finally stopped vomiting and cracked the door to see if her daddy was coming. When she didn't see him, she hurried to her room and crawled back into bed.

Later she heard her dad's footsteps coming down the hall and swung her feet off the bed to stand up, but he passed her room and went on to the bathroom.

She waited with bated breath until he went out again and then lay back down. She heard the front door slam and knew that meant her dad had gone to work. She breathed a sigh of relief and dropped off to sleep.

She didn't awake until she heard someone calling her name.

"Margie, Margie, Are you asleep?" She opened her eyes and realized that her mother was calling her. She sat up and looked out the window wondering what time it was. It looked to be almost noon since the sun was warm against the window.

She swung her feet out of bed and got slowly to her feet, fearing that she would be sick again, but she wasn't. Opening the door, she called, "Mom, did you call me?"

Rebecca came hurriedly to her room. "I was afraid you'd sleep til your daddy got home and he would go into one of his rages." She looked at Margie and smiled. "You was awful sick. Do you feel better now?"

Margie walked into the hall smiling. "I don't feel sick at all right now, but I sure was this morning. It may have been something I ate."

"You eat the same things me and your daddy eat and we didn't get sick. I don't believe it was that, but whatever it was, I could tell you was real sick," replied Rebecca as they both walked back to the kitchen.

"I may get a letter from Rick today. What shift is Daddy on? I need to meet Beatrice and if he's here I can't get away," said Margie as she took her breakfast food from the warming closet of the Majestic cook stove.

Rebecca looked at the clock on the shelf above the table. "It's one o'clock right now. You should have time if you hurry. He won't get home 'til three-thirty unless he gets a quicker ride."

Margie hurried to finish eating and left the house, telling her mother she was going to Beatrice's house. "Tell Daddy that Beatrice may know of a job I can get to help out. Maybe, he won't get so mad about me going to her house if he believes that."

Walking along the road Margie puzzled over her sickness. She'd always had trouble with her monthly periods. She never knew when they would occur, but she'd never been really sick. That time of the month was the only time she had ever felt nauseous or hurt in any way. Then her back and pelvic area cramped, but she hadn't had that lately.

At that thought her eyes widened. *No, that couldn't be, could it? That just happened one time and people were married a long time before they got pregnant weren't they? Well, there was Jane Bigelow who had a baby not quite nine months after the day she was married*, thought Margie in a sense of dread.

Rick had been gone nearly three and a half months and after Rick had corrected the address error, Margie had gotten letters twice each week. She always answered the letters while she was visiting Beatrice and gave her money for stamps.

Today, she wasn't as worried about the letter as she was about her morning sickness. She was afraid to talk to anybody, not even her mother and Beatrice. She didn't want to hurt either of them. *I know they'd think I'm pure trash*, thought Margie as she came into sight of Beatrice's house.

Beatrice's first comment was, "Your eyes look too big for your face, Margie. Are you missing Rick that much?"

She handed Margie her letter and Margie grasped it to her chest. "Yes, I do Beatrice. It seems a year since I've seen him."

Beatrice sat waiting until she read the letter and then patted the sofa. "Come here and sit down. I've got some news which may please you."

"Let me answer Rick's letter because I can't stay long. If I'm not back when Daddy gets home, he'll throw a fit."

"Write your letter while I talk. This may be the answer to you being cooped up out there and living in fear," replied Beatrice, looking at Margie with so much compassion.

Margie looked up. "Well, tell me. I'm listening."

"Dr. Leibold, the local doctor, needs a receptionist. He wants somebody who can type, take shorthand, and do some bookkeeping. You can do all those can't you, Margie?"

Margie dropped her pen and looked at Beatrice in unbelief. "You're not kidding me, are you?"

"No, Margie, I would never kid about something that would help you. You're my friend."

Margie jumped up and hugged Beatrice. She wiped the tears from her eyes and stepped back.

"Do you think he would hire me? Everybody knows how Daddy is and I'm pretty sure that doctor is at least suspicious."

Beatrice shook her head. "I don't know how you and your mother have survived, but that won't keep Dr. Leibold from hiring you. In fact, I think it will encourage him to hire you."

Margie was so excited that she forgot about morning sickness or her suspicions. She finished her letter and asked Beatrice how she could get in touch with the doctor.

Beatrice left the room and soon came back with the paper opened to the classified section. "Take this paper with you and say that I had to go to my sister's and I put the paper in your box as I passed. Say that you had asked me to look for work for you."

Margie looked at the clock, jumped to her feet and clutching the paper in her hand as she went out the door. "Thanks so much, Beatrice. I'll pay you back someday." Margie hurried down the road in a trotting gait.

Meanwhile, Rebecca did her work and the work Margie was supposed to be doing and thought about her daughter. *I wish to God something would happen, so she could get away part of the day. She looks so pale and she's about plum quit eating,* she thought worriedly. "I guess she's just missing that boy," she said aloud. Margie had told her that she and Rick were engaged to marry. So, now that Rick was gone Rebecca blamed the miss of him for Margie's malaise.

On the way home, Margie walked along not really seeing anything. She had too much to think about. She knew that if what she suspected was true, her dad, who watched her constantly, would soon notice something and would demand an answer. *If I can get this job with the doctor and help on expenses, he may not pay so much attention to me,* she thought.

She hurried on home hoping she'd get there and have time to talk to her mother. She made it and immediately told Rebecca as she handed her the newspaper.

"Mom, will you help me convince Dad to let me apply for this job? We need the money and I'd feel better if I had something to occupy my time."

Rebecca must have been pretty persuasive for the very next morning her dad said, "Your mother says you want to go to work. Where's this job you're after?"

He looked so scornful that Margie trembled. "It's in the doctor's office in Forks. Beatrice left a newspaper in our mailbox with the job circled. I always did want an office job. That's why I took typing, shorthand, and bookkeeping."

She thrust out the newspaper toward him, "Here is the advertisement. Do you want to read it?"

He shoved the paper back with a snarl. "You know I can't see to read no newspaper." Margie looked puzzled since this was the first she'd heard his vision mentioned.

Her dad jumped to his feet and went stomping out of the room. Margie dropped her head in dejection. *I'll have to run away. I can't stand it here any longer.*

She slowly got up and went into the kitchen. Rebecca saw she was teary-eyed and quickly walked to her side. She whispered, "Just wait until in the morning."

CHAPTER 8

Margie got up earlier than usual the next morning. *If I get sick I can go outside. I'll say I was feeding the chickens since it's my job anyway*, she thought as she breathed in the fresh air. She didn't feel nauseous, but she did feel anxious since she didn't know if she would be allowed to work.

When she stepped back through the kitchen door her dad came into the kitchen.

"I guess you've been out feeding the chickens. It's a good thing you have for you'll still have to do your work around here even if you do go to work. You ain't no better than anybody else in this house," said Tom Pierson, scowling in Margie's direction, but when he looked at Rebecca he shrugged his shoulders and sat down at the table.

Margie had seen the look that passed between him and her mother and was puzzled. She made no comment, however, since whatever eased the situation was a blessing.

She poured herself a glass of water and sat down at the table. "What's the matter you're not drinking milk?" asked her dad.

Milk was what brought on the vomiting the morning before, or so Margie thought, so she said, "I just didn't want it this morning, Dad. I may quit it altogether since milk is so expensive now that we have to buy it."

He gave her a gimlet stare. "That cow won't have her calf until November, so you'll not be drinking no milk for a long time. Suit yourself, though. It'll save more milk for me and your mother."

Rebecca gasped. "Tom, you don't mean that. I'd rather do without as to have my child doin' without."

"Child! She ain't a child no more. She's big enough to be a mother herself," he snarled.

Margie's eyes widened in fear, but her dad was shoveling food into his mouth and didn't look up. *Oh Lord, please don't let him get suspicious*, thought Margie as she took her last bite and pushed back her chair.

She stood hesitantly for a moment, not knowing if her mother had gotten approval for her to apply for the job or not. She looked at her mother and then said, "I guess I'd better hurry or I'll miss the bus. I don't want to be late and give somebody else a chance to get the job."

Her dad pushed back his chair and rose from the table. "I didn't say you could go to work," then he looked at Rebecca.

"Well, I reckon you can go and find out providing your mother goes with you. If you get the job, I'll have to have half of your payday."

Margie relaxed. "Thanks, Dad, I don't mind. I'll give you half," she said turning quickly to leave the room.

As she and her mother walked down the road to the bus she felt light and her breathing became easier and easier. She didn't realize she'd been holding her breath in her anxiety. *I'm almost free, thank you, Jesus, thank you, thank you,* she thought and smiled as she remembered the many times she had doubted that there was a God.

She looked to the east in shame-faced awe as the sun peeped over the mountain east of the farm. The panoramic display was beyond what any earthly artist could ever produce.

"Oh Mommy, didn't God make a beautiful world?"

Rebecca stopped and hugged her. "Yes, he did, Margie. I wish he made people just half as beautiful."

They didn't have to wait long at the highway. The bus came lumbering along at a seeming snail's pace. On its local runs the bus stopped at practically every gate and usually picked up a passenger. Many of the people in the area did not own cars and thus the bus was the standard mode of travel.

She walked through the door of the doctor's office at exactly eight-thirty to find the doctor standing as if waiting for her.

"I am Margie Pierson and I guess you remember my mother," said Margie looking at her mother. The doctor nodded at Rebecca and smiled, but then looked back at Margie as she asked, "Am I too late to apply for the position you advertised in the paper?"

"No, no, Miss Pierson, you're right on time, Beatrice Hayley said you wanted to work. I've been looking for you, but I feared that Mr. Pierson would put a stumbling block in your way. I'll bet he had a lot to say, didn't he?" asked the doctor.

Rebecca dropped her gaze to the floor, but Margie smiled. "I was afraid he would, but he needs the money I'll make if I work, so he didn't say too much."

"Come on back to the office for the interview," said Dr. Leibold and made his stoop-shouldered way down a short hall and opened his door. He then looked back at Rebecca. "You can come in too if you want to." Rebecca shook her head and remained seated.

Once they were inside and seated he asked, "You won't have to give him everything you earn, will you? That wouldn't be fair at all."

Margie had taken a seat in front of his desk and placed her auburn manila envelope in her lap before picking up the notepad and pencil that lay on the desk in front of her. Now she looked up.

"No, not all of it. I have to give him half though."

Dr. Leibold shook his head. "He should be proud that he has a daughter who wants to work and help out. Well, it takes all kinds I suppose. Did you bring your high school transcript?"

Margie pushed the auburn manila envelope across the desk to the doctor. He sat silently going over it for a few minutes. "I see that you can take shorthand, type eighty words a minute, and you can also do beginning bookkeeping, hm-m. Beatrice Hayley said you had taken all business courses."

He looked up and studied her intently. "You're not thinking of marrying any time soon are you?"

Oh no, thought Margie, but then thought, *nobody knows that Rick and I are engaged and I don't know how long he'll have to wait before he gets a leave.*

She looked at the doctor and said, "No sir. I don't plan to marry soon."

Dr. Leibold, gave her an intent look. "You seem to be better qualified than the others who applied so, the job is yours, but you'd better not leave as soon as I get you trained."

Tears welled up in Margie's eyes and she blinked rapidly to keep them from spilling down her cheeks. "Thank you, Dr. Leibold. Thank you so very much. You won't regret it, I promise."

Dr. Leibold smiled. "I don't think I'll regret it, Margie. It is all right to call you Margie, isn't it?"

"Yes sir. I hope you will."

The doctor then proceeded to tell her that she should be there each morning at nine o'clock and would work until five each evening. "You'll have five full days with an hour for lunch each day, but you only work a half-day on Saturdays.

"Is record keeping all you want me to do?" asked Margie in surprise.

"Oh no, young lady, you'll be my receptionist, secretary, and record keeper. You'll take care of the fees paid by the patients. Since you know bookkeeping I may not have to have so many people working here," he said while laughing merrily.

Margie was speechless with relief and even though she had conquered the urge to cry she was still having trouble trying to hide her emotions. She was so happy she felt suddenly dizzy and grasped the back of a chair.

"You really do want this job, don't you, young lady?" asked the doctor with a smile.

"Yes sir, I do and I thank you very much. I'll work hard, I promise," she replied trying again to stop the tears that were easing from the corner of her eyes.

The doctor arose and patted her on the shoulder. "I'm sure you will or I wouldn't have hired you. You be here at nine o'clock in the morning and begin your first week of work. Do you think you can handle that?"

Margie turned to the door and with a big smile replied. "Yes sir. I'll be here and thanks again."

He followed Margie out of the office and saw Rebecca still waiting patiently. The waiting room was empty since he had freed his schedule for the day to interview.

Dr. Leibold shook hands with Rebecca. "How are you doing, Mrs. Pierson? You look well. Has the cow butted you into the barn anymore?"

Rebecca turned red and dropped her head. "No, doctor that was the last time," she whispered softly.

Dr. Leibold looked shrewd. "I thought it might be," then he smiled, but turned to Margie and asked, "Do you have a way to get to and from work?"

"I will walk if I have to, Doctor, but I think I'll be able to catch the bus. Do you know the bus schedule?"

He stepped over to a desk behind a glass window and picked up a card with the schedule on it. "It looks like a bus runs at eight-thirty each morning that will pass your road. Here, take it with you, but that should work out well for you."

Margie took the schedule and thanked him, preparing to leave when he stopped her. "Aren't you interested in your pay? That's usually the first thing someone asks when they apply for a job," he said as he laughed again.

Margie turned red. "I do need the money, sir, but I was so excited to think I had a job that I forgot to ask."

"I pay ten dollars an hour, and you'll earn every penny of it. I wish you had a telephone out there. Sometimes I have to stay over if some patient has to come in late. What would Mr. Pierson say if she is late getting home? I'd drive her out if she missed the bus." This he had directed at Rebecca.

"I don't rightly know, Doctor, but it might be all right as long as he knows where she is and who she's with," replied Rebecca.

CHAPTER 9

When they were outside, Margie looked at her mother smiling widely. She was surprised to see tears running down her mother's face. "What is it, Mom? Why are you crying?"

"You got the job! Oh Margie, I prayed so hard that you would."

Margie put her arm around Rebecca's shoulder and hugged her. "God must have heard your prayer, Mommy, for I now have a job. I'll be away from the house from eight in the morning until six o'clock at night. I'll also be making money to help Daddy. Maybe he won't be so mad all the time."

The smile dropped from Rebecca's face. "He wanted you to work, but wanted it to be for the lumber company so he could see what you were doing. Your daddy don't trust women, Margie."

"He doesn't like women, Mommy. I wonder why? Did he like his mother? It's almost like he hates all women."

"I don't know, Margie. I've often wondered that myself. He has one picture of his mother, but he keeps it hid in his dresser drawer, or it was there the last time I saw it. He may have moved it to someplace else. Sometimes he goes in the bedroom and stays and once I peeped through the window and he was looking at a picture. It must have been that picture because it's the only one we have. I've never tried to straighten his underwear drawer again after that first time, when I saw the picture. I asked him about his mother that time and he got angry and told me to mind my own business and leave his drawer alone. I've seldom mentioned her again, but the few times that I have he gets very upset."

"He was raised near you, wasn't he? I mean surely people told you something about his family," said Margie.

"All I ever heard was that Mrs. Pierson was a good woman, but she had an awful life." Rebecca walked silently along beside Margie for several minutes and then again spoke up.

"I was just starting to high school. I was lucky to get to go. Papa didn't think there was any need for girls to get an education. Anyway, there was a little store near the school and I went there at lunch time with some other girls. Your daddy was always there. I thought he was real good looking, but I was awfully shy and didn't look at him. The other girls tried to flirt with him, but I never even spoke to him for a long time. He had his eye on me though . . . I wish to God I'd never laid eyes on him."

"What do you mean, he had his eye on you?" asked Margie curiously.

Rebecca walked a little slower. "I think I was a challenge since I didn't pay any mind to him. He always had to be the center of attention around girls. I guess he knew he was good-lookin' and expected every girl he saw to notice him. I didn't though, and he started tryin' to talk to me and wanting to buy pop and chewing gum for me. After the girls shamed me for not speakin' to him, I'd speak to him, but I wouldn't take the pop and gum. That didn't stop him, though. He started following me everywhere I went. It made me feel scared or I guess uneasy. I think I was pleased that he thought I was pretty, but I was still afraid of him."

Rebecca stopped and grasped Margie's arm as if to steady herself. Margie stopped as well.

"Mom, what's wrong? You're pale as a sheet."

Rebecca shook her head. "No, Margie I'm not sick, but it nearly makes me sick to realize how dumb I was."

She drew in a long sigh. "Anyway, he must have learned everything about me and my family 'cause when Papa got sick he started coming over and milkin' the cows, feedin' the pigs, and horses. Mama and Papa both really liked him, but I was still uneasy around him."

They had reached the house by then and as soon as they went inside Rebecca looked at the clock.

"Lord, it's almost time for your daddy to get home and I ain't got no supper cooked." She started hurrying around jerking bowls out of the icebox and kindling the fire in the cook stove.

"You're really scared of him, just like I am, aren't you, Mom?" asked Margie.

"I'd rather have supper ready than to hear his cussin' and hollerin'," said Rebecca as she started mixing cornbread.

When Margie saw him coming up the road she decided to try to delay him to give her mother a little more time. She walked out on the porch and then went down the road to meet her father. He looked surprised when he saw her coming to meet him.

"Guess what, Daddy! I now have a job. I'm to start tomorrow and I'll be paid ten dollars an hour," she bragged, trying to smile.

He stopped dead in his tracks. "Ten dollars an hour! He must be expectin' something more than answering the telephone."

"I have to do a lot more than answer the telephone. I have to do the bookkeeping, write all his letters, keep the patients records, and answer all calls. He says I'll have to work hard and will earn every cent he pays me," explained Margie.

When her father made no comment, she continued. "That seems like a lot of money to me, but he said it's for a lot of work. But, ten dollars and hour, do you think that's enough for all he said I had to do, Daddy?"

"It's probably more than you're worth, but it don't matter to me as long as I get five dollars of every hour your work."

A Fatal Beginning

Margie looked at her dad angrily since she hadn't thought of his half on an hourly basis. She started to protest but before she could say anything her dad blurted.

"You'll pay rent if you want to stay here. Your mother ain't going to do all the work and let you play the big shot."

Margie didn't reply although she felt like screaming and cursing. *He must think it's a privilege to be cursed and screamed at or knocked off the porch,*" she thought angrily as she hurried back into the house.

Margie had thought he'd be happy about the money. *I guess me coming out to delay him wasn't a good idea*, she thought. She was right for as soon as he walked into the kitchen and saw that the food wasn't on the table he turned an angry scowl at Rebecca.

"Where's my supper? You must have stayed in town all day. What did you do there all day? Of course, I know what prissy-tailed women do when they're out by theirselves."

"I'm sorry, Tom. It took a long time to get the interview over with. Her appointment wasn't til one o'clock, so we didn't get back here til about fifteen minutes ago," said Rebecca working feverishly. She looked up and saw that he was angry. "It's almost ready. In fact, it'll be on the table by the time you get washed up."

Margie spoke up. "When I get to work I'll bring us something home for supper sometimes. Won't that be nice?"

Tom Pierson whirled around. "You stay out of this. It ain't none of your damn business. You'll not bring nothing home so your mother can lay around like the lazy slut she is." He was getting red in the face and had that wild gleam in his eye that Margie had seen many times before.

She turned to leave the room, but before she had taken two steps she was grabbed by the arm and yanked backwards. She couldn't catch herself as she went stumbling backward, but the corner of the table did. She felt like a poker had jabbed a hole in her right hip as she fell to the floor.

"Tom Pierson, I told you what would happen if you ever hit her again," shouted Rebecca rushing to help Margie to her feet.

"I didn't hit the damn slut. I just grabbed her arm. She's so clumsy she fell by herself," he snarled but didn't hit Rebecca as he always had in the past.

Margie felt like she wouldn't be able to get up, but she gritted her teeth and with Rebecca's help she made it to a chair. The pain was terrible, but she was determined to not give her dad the satisfaction of seeing her cry. She knew he had been drinking because she smelled the sour scent of alcohol when he jerked her backwards. She sat very still as she thought, *what if he decides to beat me up? I can't get out of his way and I can't run.*

"She come plum out the road to meet me just so she could brag about how much money she's goin' to make. She may have a big-shot job, but she's not goin' to live in my house and walk away from me when I'm talkin' to her. Damn her and damn her education. She can go to hell for all I care. I'm still a hell-of-a-lot smarter than she'll ever be," he shouted. He was working himself into a rage and Margie quaked inside.

"Tom come and eat your supper. You'll feel better when you eat. She wasn't braggin' she just thought you'd be happy to get half of the money she'll make."

That seemed to calm him a little and Margie thought it would be better if she was out of his sight. Being so emotionally shattered she forgot about her hip and pushed herself up from the chair. The pain was excruciating and she teetered on her first step, but in a slow dragging gait she left the kitchen. She was afraid to turn lest he attack her again. She could hear her mother talking in a soothing voice. *I'll get a room in town and never come back here, she thought,* but knew that he would make her come back until she was eighteen which was another three months.

She went to the bathroom and waited to see if he was going to yell for her to come back to the kitchen. When she heard nothing she thought *Oh Lord, he'll beat Mommy up and I can't help her.*

In bed, she lay there thinking, *I'll never make it to work tomorrow.* She tried to sit up and finally did even though her pain was terrible.

Mommy always prays when Dad hurts her. Maybe God will help me. I've never asked him before, but I need to go to my job, thought Margie as she eased herself off the bed and slid to her knees.

She knelt there mumbling words. She stopped and still kneeling she thought, *I've said the words but I don't really know how to pray.* With effort she pulled herself up and fell onto the bed.

After a long time, Rebecca quietly opened the door. "Margie, I've brought some liniment. Let me rub it on your hip. It helps most of the time."

Margie struggled to her feet and lifted the tail of her night gown. A large lump had formed on her hip and Rebecca poured the liniment on the square of cloth she'd brought with her and pressed it against the lump. "Here, Margie, hold this in place and I'll go bring you something to eat." Rebecca was whispering and Margie whispered also.

"Where did he go?"

"He's asleep. He's been drinking. I don't know where he got the money, but at least he didn't bring any home with him," replied Rebecca worriedly.

"I hope I can walk in the morning. I have to go to work. Mom, I'm so tired of being afraid all the time. I think I'd rather be dead than to have to live like this much longer. I wish Rick could come home. I'd get away then."

Rebecca patted her on the arm. "I wish he'd come home too, Margie. I'd rather see you marry and move plum away from me as to have to live like we both have ever since you were born." Rebecca left the room and soon came back with a plate of food.

"Try to eat as much as you can. I can't stay any longer. He might wake up," she whispered and turned to the door. "Put fresh liniment on that swellin' every half-hour until you go to sleep. I'll ask God to help you. Maybe you'll feel better in the morning."

Margie stayed awake until eleven o'clock bathing her hip every half-hour and silently praying that she would be able to walk the next day. Finally, she eased herself down and under the cover. Then her thoughts turned to Rick. With all the excitement of the last two days Margie hadn't had a chance to contact Beatrice. Before she went to sleep she made plans to call Beatrice. *Maybe she will meet me in town and bring my letters,* she thought as she finally drifted off to sleep.

Rebecca eased her door open at seven-thirty. "Margie, are you awake?" she asked softly.

Margie opened her eyes and then sat straight up in the bed. "What time is it, Mom? I didn't hear the alarm."

"It didn't go off. I snuck in here and turned it off early this morning. You had it set for six-thirty and I knew you didn't need to get up that early. How do you feel this morning?"

Margie raised her arms to stretch and winced as pain shot through her left arm. "Well, my arm is really sore. I didn't feel my arm last night. I was too worried about my hip."

She looked up at her mother's worried face and smiled. "Don't look so worried, Mom. I don't have to walk on my arm." Still smiling grimly, she twisted around to get her feet and legs over the side of the bed. When that didn't hurt as much as she feared she dropped her feet to the floor and stood only to sit down again.

Rebecca came quickly into the room. "You can't bear no weight on that leg, can you?"

Margie clamped her jaws together and taking Rebecca's hand pulled herself to her feet once again. She stood there shivering in pain.

"Do you think it's broken, Mommy?" asked Margie, looking at Rebecca for reassurance.

Rebecca pulled up her night gown and looked. "It's all black and blue but the knot has gone down. Just try walking a few steps. It may just be bruised real bad."

Margie gritted her teeth and took a step, holding to Rebecca. The pain made her feel nauseous but she took another step and another until she reached the bathroom. She looked up at her mother. "It must not be broken since I can walk."

"Let me help you get your bath. Maybe soaking in warm water will take some of the pain away," said Rebecca and helped her to the commode.

"You set there 'til I run you some warm water."

"Margie sat and watched her mother testing the water and then she giggled. "I'd rather not be scalded just to forget about my hip."

Rebecca looked at her strangely for a moment and then smiled. "I hadn't thought of that in years, but that's what Papa told me. One time I had an awful, awful toothache and Papa told me that setting on a hot stove would cure it. I remember sayin', "Why you'd set your tail on fire," and he said, "Yeah, but you'd forget all about your toothache.""

Margie looked at her mother and thought, *I've not seen Mommy smile like that in a long time.*

"Was grandpa a kidder?"

Rebecca smiled. "He was plum full of fun. He had us all laughin' especially at supper time when we was all gathered around the table."

The water must have been to her satisfaction for she turned and said, "Come on let's get you in this tub." She grinned. "Maybe you'll forget about your hip."

The water was warmer than Margie usually had it but with the help of her mother she was soon comfortable and even allowed her mother to wash her back. "I can do the rest Mommy. I'll yell when I'm ready to get out."

Forty minutes later Margie came hobbling through the hall into the kitchen. "I didn't yell since I needed to make it by myself. I had a time of it, but here I am. I don't know if I can make it to the bus though."

"Come and eat. I'll help you to the bus. I think you ort to ask Dr. Leibold to check you when you get there, though," said Rebecca, pulling out a chair.

A Fatal Beginning

CHAPTER 10

Margie reached the door of the doctor's office at eight-forty-five just as the doctor opened the door. "I saw you getting off the bus. What's happened to you? You walk like somebody crippled."

Margie was white from the pain and mumbled. "May I sit down, please?"

Dr. Leibold grasped her arm and she winced. "Ouch! My arm is sore."

"Well, you're not sitting down in here. You're going into my office. I want to see what that idiot has done to you," said Dr. Leibold with a deep frown on his face.

After examining her arm and her hip he allowed her to sit up. "Tell me what happened, Margie. I know Tom Pierson did this, but how and why?"

Margie recounted her effort to delay him so that her mother would have a little more time to get supper on the table. "I thought he would be pleased, but I was wrong. He talked like I was trying to put him down or something."

Dr. Leibold had put some ointment on her hip and now on her arm and turned to wash his hands. "You don't have any broken bones, but from the looks of that hip I don't see what saved you."

"He didn't hit me, Dr. Leibold. He grabbed my arm and yanked me backwards and I lost my balance and fell. Part of me hit him and the rest hit the corner of the table. His grip was so tight that it bruised my arm, I guess," said Margie as she slid off the doctor's examination table.

"You can't work today, Margie, but I don't want you to go back home either. He may do more damage."

"I can work, Dr. Leibold. I walked to the bus and made my way here. I'm sore and I hurt some, but I've lived with worse," replied Margie.

I'll bet you have, thought the doctor as he opened the door for her to go out.

A Fatal Beginning

"If you want to try it, you can get out the patient's cards that already have appointments. If you find you can't handle it just let me know," said Dr. Leibold turning to his desk. Margie limped out and took her place behind the glass window in the next room.

She was slow and ached all over, but by lunch time she felt more knowledgeable about her work. This eased fears she had kept at bay since she was hired. She hadn't realized how tense she was, but as she relaxed it seemed also to ease the pain in her hip. She was so engrossed in her work that she didn't realize it was lunch time until a boy came through the door carrying a cardboard box. "Where do you want me to put this?"

Margie looked up. "What is it?"

"It's your lunch. Well, yours and the doctor's. Mrs. Leibold sent it over. She said to tell you both that she made that soup this mornin' and every bite had better be eat."

Just then Dr. Leibold opened his door and seeing the boy his eyes lit up.

"Josh, you brought our lunch. What did Lorraine send today? Here, put it here on this table." Dr. Leibold tossed the magazines from the table onto a chair and took the box.

Relieved of his load the boy swung his arms and said, "Whew, that was heavy and it smelt so good I wanted to stop and take a few bites on the way over." He looked at Margie whose eyes had opened wide and laughed merrily.

"Don't look so scared, Miss. I didn't touch it."

Margie was surprised and touched by the generosity of the doctor and his wife. "I was going to buy a sandwich, doctor. I didn't expect this."

"I know you didn't and you won't get it every day. I told Lorraine, my wife, about you coming on to work in your condition and she wanted to do this for you. That Missus of mine is a good woman," he said with a twinkle in his eye.

After the good lunch and the friendliness of the patients Margie felt like her life was finally making a turn for the better. *If only this hadn't happened*, she thought smoothing her hand over her belly as if she could feel something. *I was scared to death that I'd have to turn and Dr. Leibold would see how my belly is growing*, thought Margie breathing a sigh of relief. *If I'm really going to have a baby, I'll have to keep it hid someway. If Daddy finds out he'll kill me*, she thought as she cleared her desk for the day.

She limped to the bus stop and found a seat up front. It was harder to step down than it was to step up, however, which she discovered when the bus stopped at her road. She stumbled as she tried to step down but caught the handle near the door and finally made it off the bus.

The driver had jumped up to help her, but she had already gotten steady on her feet. "I didn't know you had a bad leg, Miss, or I would have helped you down."

Margie smiled. "Thanks, but I'm all right. I fell into the corner of a table. I'm just bruised."

She was slow, but finally made it home. Rebecca came out on the porch when she looked out the window and saw Margie limping up the road.

"Well, you made it. How do you feel this evening?"

Margie smiled tiredly. "Better than I did this morning. Dr. Leibold said I was just badly bruised. He gave me some ointment to put on it and said the hot bath was good for it."

"Let me help you up the steps. I've got your supper in the warming closet of the stove. Your daddy got home early and wanted to eat."

Margie looked surprised. "What time is it? We always eat at five-thirty even if he does come in early." Her eyes grew round in fear. "Is he drinking, Mommy?"

Rebecca shook her head. "I can't tell. I didn't smell anything, but he wanted to eat so I put it on the table. He said he had a headache and went to bed right after he finished."

"He must really be sick then. He certainly didn't have any alcohol in him or he'd have found someone to knock around," said Margie in relief.

Her dad was sick and stayed sick for that entire week. *This is the best week I've ever had in this house*, thought Margie as the week drew to an end. She and her mother had talked and even quietly laughed a few times. Margie had gotten letters from Rick saying that he had two or three more months before he would get a thirty-day leave.

"He's training to fly airplanes, Mommy. He says it's the most wonderful feeling to soar high up in the sky above the clouds. I can't describe it the way he does, but he really loves it."

"I'd be scared out of my wits, Margie. Ain't he afraid?"

Margie sat dreamily thinking of what he had said. "No, Mommy. He said, that's the way he wants to die, flying high above the clouds."

"What a strange thing for somebody young to say. Don't you think it's strange, Margie?"

"You just don't know Rick, Mommy. He's like that. If he enjoys something he gets carried away with it. He just wanted to let me know how happy it made him to fly. I don't think he meant that he wanted to die," replied Margie in a thoughtful voice.

"Well, we'd better get ourselves to bed. Tomorrow is Saturday and I guess that next week will be a payday for you, won't it?" Rebecca rose from her chair and suddenly bent down and hugged Margie. "I'm so proud of you."

Margie looked up into her mother's face and saw the pride in her eyes. Guilt washed over her. *Oh God, please don't let me be pregnant. She will be so hurt*, she thought as she also rose and turned toward her room.

On Saturday of the next week, Margie got her payday and gave her father his half of the two hundred and seventy she earned. *I hope he doesn't go buy whiskey with that money*, she thought as she passed it to him. He didn't thank her, but put it in his billfold and turned to the door.

"I'm goin' into town. I got some bills that need to be paid," he said and strode hurriedly down the road toward the bus stop.

She and her mother were both surprised when he came back from town sober. He had brought some pork chops. "Here, woman, fix me something decent to eat now that money is comin' in this house."

Although it meant building another fire in the cook stove, Rebecca was happy to have him in a good mood for a change. Margie thought, *if giving him that money makes that much difference I'm glad to do it.*

This held true for another two and a half months and both Margie and her mother were beginning to think their lives had taken a change for the better. Well, better for Rebecca, but now it was evident that she was pregnant, and Margie lived in constant dread that her dad would discover it. She bought clothes which were a size too large and therefore loose on her.

"That job must be good for you, girl. You're getting' fat. You're almost as broad as you are long," said her Dad one evening as she rose from the dinner table.

Margie turned red. "I know, Dad. It must be all this good food Mommy cooks. I'm going to have to start dieting."

"Don't you do that, Margie. You look better than I've ever seen you look since you were a baby," said Rebecca with a smile.

Margie had been saving every penny she could because she planned to run away before the baby was born. *I'll go to Port Angeles and get a room near the hospital. I'll have my baby in the hospital and when it's born I'll get another job and hire a babysitter to watch my baby,* were the plans that constantly ran through her head.

Of course, if Rick got home before the baby came she wouldn't have to do all that. His last letter said that he would be home in three more weeks. Margie cried when she got that letter. *Three more weeks and then I'll be Mrs. Rick Mullet and Daddy can't touch me*, she thought happily.

The next day Dr. Leibold asked her to come into his office at lunch time. *I wonder what he wants* she thought since he had never done this before. When she shut the door behind her Dr. Leibold offered her a chair. She sat down and looked across the desk at him.

"Margie, I've thought you were pregnant for a long time and didn't want to say anything, but it's time you told me about it. Don't you think that would be best?"

Margie gasped and turned red. "How did you find out?"

Dr. Leibold smiled. "I'm a doctor and I can see. You look like you are around six months pregnant. Has Tom Pierson done this to you?"

Margie dropped her head and tears streamed down her face. "No, Dr. Leibold, Daddy didn't make me pregnant. I can't tell you who it is, but it isn't Daddy."

"You were raped then, weren't you? If you were it must have been a good while back. Does your mother know?"

"No. Nobody knows. I didn't know. I kept hoping that I wasn't. When Daddy finds out he will kill me. He told me this week that I was getting too fat. I'm scared to death, but I don't know what to do."

"Margie, I'll talk to Mr. Pierson. A woman can't help it if she's raped. He can't blame you for that. You're not the kind of girl that struts around on the streets. He has to know that."

"Dr. Leibold, please don't talk to Daddy. He'll never believe that I didn't mean this to happen. I worked in Jack Fraker's orchard after school this year and I always took the shortcut through the woods. It cuts off three or four miles. It happened then, but Daddy will not understand that I was and I am in love with the father. In Daddy's eyes I'll be a 'slut.' That's what he calls Mommy and I know she is a good, decent person. By taking the shortcut I did disobey him, but I didn't go that way to meet a boy. Other kids walked that way except for that one evening."

By this time Margie was so over wrought that she began shaking like a leaf. Dr. Leibold reached into a small refrigerator in his office and brought out a coco-cola and handed it to her. "Here drink this. I won't talk to Mr. Pierson if you tell me not to, but I think it would be best."

Margie looked up at Dr. Leibold. She looked like a picture of a tormented soul without any hope.

"Margie you aren't the only girl that this has happened to and you won't be the last. Why don't you tell me what happened? It sometimes helps to have someone to talk to."

When she sat without speaking, Dr. Leibold asked, "Was the man who raped you a stranger?"

"Dr. Leibold, I wasn't raped. I do love him and he loves me. We're going to get married, but we have to wait until he can get here. I've been planning to go to Port Angeles and get a room near the hospital and have my baby there. But, yesterday I got a letter saying he would be here in three weeks. If I can keep it a secret three more weeks then, we can marry and Daddy can't do anything. We were going to some other town and not come back until I was eighteen. Daddy won't have control over me when I become eighteen."

Dr. Leibold sat thinking and suddenly he looked up. "You were friends with Rick Mullett in school, weren't you? Is Rick Mullett the father of your child?"

A Fatal Beginning

Margie lifted her head and looked at Dr. Leibold for a few minutes and then with a weary sigh she said, "Yes, but please don't tell anyone. Mom knows that Rick and I are engaged to be married, but she doesn't know that I'm pregnant."

"Rick Mullett is a fine young man and from a fine family. Why don't you go to them? Paul Mullett would put the skids under Tom Pierson if he came around him."

Margie shook her head. "I can't go to them. They don't know me and I've never told Rick that I'm pregnant. They would think I was just trying to trick him into marrying me. They'd also think I'm a loose woman, but I'm not, Dr. Leibold. I swear before God, that it was just that one time before Rick had to go into service and never since."

She had started shaking again and Dr. Leibold said, "Take another drink and calm down. We'll think of something. Now, I need to examine you to see if everything is all right. Will you allow me to do that? You do want your baby to be healthy, don't you?"

Margie nodded and shyly climbed onto the examination table. Dr. Leibold was gentle, but thorough and when he finished and washed his hands he turned to help her up. "When did you have your last menstrual cycle?"

"I don't remember," said Margie with a woebegone look.

"You're at least five months. Does that sound right to you?"

"Rick and I worked in Jack Fraker's orchard in May and it's now October so I guess that's right. I never knew when I'd have my periods. Sometimes I did and sometimes I didn't, so that's why I had to wait so long to realize I was pregnant," replied Margie with head still bowed.

"Well, so far you seem to be in good health and the baby's heartbeat is strong. From what you tell me your dad has been calm, so let's hope he stays that way."

Margie finished the week out in a fairly happy mood, but on Saturday morning as she sat behind her reception window the door was thrust open and Margie's world fell apart.

A Fatal Beginning

CHAPTER 11

Paul Mullett walked through the door carrying his wife. "Is the doctor in? My wife needs some help."

"Yes sir, just a moment please." She went to the door and opened it.

"Dr. Leibold, Mr. Mullett has his wife . . . she's .." Before she could finish Dr. Leibold brushed past her.

Paul, what's . . . Bring her in here. Did she fall or what happened?" Mr. Mullett closed the door and Margie couldn't hear the rest of what was being said, but she felt uneasy for some reason.

When the door opened again, Mrs. Mullett walked out, but her husband and Dr. Leibold were both supporting her.

"Gradually wean her off the medicine, Paul. Give it to her twice a day for the first two weeks and then cut it down to a half dose at night, then cut it to a half dose in the morning, and so on. If she doesn't begin feeling better after the initial shock wears off call me and we'll take it from there."

Dr. Leibold paused as he released Mrs. Mullett's arm to open the door. When Mr. Mullett was through the door which was left open Dr. Leibold followed him onto the entrance stoop.

"I'm terribly sorry, Paul. I have a son and I can empathize with you. Rick was such a fine young man. It's no wonder she is in this state. She thought he would be home in a few days and now he'll never . . . .. I'm so, so sorry," said Dr. Leibold as he helped Mrs. Mullett down the steps and into the waiting car.

Margie had been listening, but not really interested until she heard, 'I have a son and I can empathize with you' and then she jumped from her seat and walked to the door and onto the stoop. She opened her mouth to ask what they were talking about, but no sound came out.

Dr. Leibold turned back toward his office, but stopped when he saw Margie's face. She was still standing on the stoop with her mouth open and her eyes staring from a bloodless face.

"Margie, . . . Oh! My God. I forgot. You heard, didn't you?" He walked up the steps and grasped her shoulder. He turned her back into the office, but she moved like a robot. Once inside he shook her gently.

"Margie, snap out of it," he said roughly and pulled her toward his office. "Come on into my office and I'll explain."

Still in robot fashion, Margie moved her feet and sat down in a chair when Dr. Leibold pulled it out for her. She sat staring and hadn't made a sound. Dr. Leibold again resorted to a Coco-Cola. "Here, drink some of this."

When she didn't reach for the drink, he waved his hand in front of her face, but got no reaction. Then he wet a cloth and washed her face. Margie jerked her head back and looked wildly up at him.

"What happened to Rick? He's hurt, isn't he? He's not coming home, is he?"

Dr. Leibold sat down in front of her and grasped her hands. Speaking softly, he said, "No, Margie, Rick isn't coming home. His plane crashed this morning. There were no survivors."

Margie put her hand over her mouth and said, "Sh-sh." She looked up at Dr. Leibold from eyes that looked dead. "I'll just go home and if Daddy kills me I won't mind."

"Now, we won't let that happen, Margie. I'm going to take you home. I'll tell Tom Pierson that I'll come to pick you up each morning so he'll be afraid to harm you," said Dr. Leibold, helping her to her feet.

Margie quietly gathered her possessions and walked with him to his car. She didn't speak or make any sound, but sat looking straight ahead as he drove down Highway

101. She trembled when he turned the car onto the road leading to her home, but still did not speak.

Rebecca had seen the car pull into the driveway and came onto the porch. When Dr. Leibold rushed around the hood to help Margie from the car Rebecca hurried down the steps to meet them.

"What's happened? Did you get sick again, Margie?"

"Let's wait until we are inside, please. Margie needs to sit down," said Dr. Leibold. Rebecca ran back up the steps and held the door open for Margie to pass through. She motioned for the doctor to take Margie into the living room. When Dr. Leibold had her seated on the sofa he sat down beside her.

"Where's your husband, Mrs. Pierson? I wanted him to hear what I have to say."

"He's workin' late, I reckon. He's usually home by now since his hours has been cut back," replied Rebecca, looking around worriedly.

Dr. Leibold hesitated for a moment. "I wanted him to be here, but I have to get back. I forgot to call my wife and she'll be worried."

Rebecca had sat down on the sofa beside Margie, but was turned at an angle so she could see Margie's face. She looked at the Dr. Leibold.

"I can tell something has happened. She looks plum bad."

Dr. Leibold arose and walked to the window and looked down the road. Not seeing anyone he turned and took the chair across from the two women. He dropped his hands between his knees and looked down. Then he took a deep breath and raised his head. "Mrs. Pierson, I think you know that Margie was engaged and had plans to marry, but you didn't know that she was pregnant, did you?"

"Pregnant! When? How?" she sputtered. "Margie was never out of my sight unless she was in school. It must

A Fatal Beginning

have happened while you were in school. Did it, Margie?" She jerked Margie around to face her. "Did it happen at school?"

Margie shook her head without looking up. Rebecca grabbed her shoulders. "Do you know what you've done, Margie? Your daddy will. ." She suddenly remembered that the doctor was there and said, "Well, he'll really be mad. You know how upset he gets."

"Mommy, I'm not bad. I didn't mean for this to happen, but Rick said he loved me. He's the only person who ever spoke to me, was nice to me, or ever said they loved me. I know Daddy will kill me, but I don't care. Do you hear me, Mommy, I don't care." For the first time in her adult life, Margie Pierson broke down and began crying aloud and spasmodically jerking as she rocked to and fro.

Dr. Leibold went to Margie's side. "Now, Margie, this kind of reaction won't solve anything. I told you I'd help you, so you're not alone. I know you had planned to be married by this time next month, but that won't happen now."

He turned back to Rebecca and quickly explained that Rick Mullett had been killed in an airplane crash. "About an hour ago Paul Mullett, his father, came into the office carrying his wife, who was in shock. I helped get her back to the car and stood talking to them about what had happened and Margie heard us talking."

Dr. Leibold patted Margie's shoulder. "Margie is in shock herself. I've given her some medicine to take for just tonight. I don't want to give her too much since it may hurt the baby."

He looked steadily at Rebecca for a moment. "The last time I came out here to treat someone that had been beaten up I warned your husband that it must never happen again. I'm repeating that warning. If he beats on Margie or you he will be sent to prison and I mean what I say."

"He's been better since then, doctor. I know Margie fell into the table when she first started working for you, but he didn't actually push her," said Rebecca with bowed head.

"No, he didn't push her, he jerked her backwards and it's a miracle she didn't break her hip. I hate to leave her, but I do have to go home. You be sure to tell him what I said. I'll check on you tomorrow, Margie."

Dr. Leibold turned toward the door and stopped. "If I can't get here early in the morning and she isn't better go to the phone box down the road and call me. Will you do that?"

"Yes, Doctor. I will and I won't let Margie get hurt," replied Rebecca firmly as she arose from her chair and walked to the door with the doctor.

Dr. Leibold looked through his rear-view mirror as he drove away and saw the lonely figure of Rebecca standing on the porch. *I'm surprised that she's still alive having to live with a brute like Tom Pierson*, he thought.

When Dr. Leibold arrived home, Lorraine met him at the door. "Where have you been? Paul Mullett has been calling for the last hour."

Dr. Leibold sank tiredly into a chair. "Is Mrs. Mullett worse? She's probably in better shape than Margie Pierson is about this time."

Lorraine Leibold tilted her head in a questioning pose. "Margie Pierson! What's wrong with her?"

Dr. Leibold laid his head against the back of his chair.

"It won't matter if I tell it now, I don't think." He told his wife about Margie's life and her engagement to Rick Mullett and her pregnancy.

"They were planning to get married when he came in on leave which would have started Monday. That was Margie's way of escaping the cruelty of her father, but she also says she loves Rick Mullett. Nobody knows she's pregnant."

"Why Tom Pierson will kill her. You know he will. Everybody knows he killed his mother."

Dr. Leibold raised startled eyes to his wife. "He killed his mother! Are you sure?"

"You weren't raised around here, but I was and I know that Tom Pierson has always been an overbearing brute. We all knew he raped Rebecca Meadows, Margie's mother when she was only fifteen and we all thought that his mother threatened to call the law and he killed her."

"Did he spend time in prison?"

"Oh no. There were no witnesses and he claimed she fell out of the barn loft and hit an iron anvil. He never served a day. From what I've heard he has beat on poor little Rebecca from the day he married her," said Lorraine scornfully.

"I told Margie, I'd be out to check on her tomorrow, but I've been uneasy ever since I left her there," said Dr. Leibold.

Lorraine patted his shoulder. "Well stop worrying long enough to eat and then get a good hot shower. You're as tense as a fiddle string."

Dr. Leibold had his shower and ate his supper, but Margie Pierson was still on his mind. When he rose from the table he said, "I forgot about Paul Mullett's call. I'd better call him."

When he reached the Mullett home one of the daughters answered. "Daddy went to town and Mom's asleep. Daddy wanted to ask you if it would hurt Mom if he took her to Fort Ord to gather Rick's possessions."

"If I were him I'd wait a week or so. Your mother was in a pretty bad condition."

The doctor stood listening for a moment, then said, "She did! That's good, really good. Usually when someone takes an interest in someone else it means they are turning away from their grief, at least a little."

When the call was over Dr. Leibold paced back and forth from the kitchen to the front door with a troubled look on his face.

On the fourth trip his wife stopped him. "I'll go with you out to the Pierson place. I can tell you are worried."

Dr. Leibold smiled down at his wife. "You don't have to go, but I would feel better if I knew Margie was all right."

"They're probably all in the bed by now, but we'll go out there since I know you won't sleep a wink if we don't," she said as she patted his shoulder.

They left the house at seven forty-five and Dr. Leibold kept the speedometer at a steady fifty-five all the way. *He kept thinking, If he beats them up he's already done it and if they're asleep it won't matter what time I get there,* but he still didn't slow down.

When they turned up the Hoh River Road he did slow down and dimmed his lights as he turned the curve to the house. "If they're asleep I don't want my lights to wake them."

There were lights on in the house and the door was standing open.

"That's strange. Why would someone leave their door standing wide open? It's so cold tonight." Mrs. Leibold said as they came to a stop before the gate, which too was hanging open.

They both got out but eased the doors shut for some reason. With a flashlight in his hand, Dr. Leibold took his wife's arm and started to walk with her to the porch, but suddenly stopped. "Look! Fresh tire tracks." He followed the tracks with his flashlights. "It looks like someone has backed up to the porch."

A Fatal Beginning

They silently walked up the steps. Suddenly his wife gasped and pointed to the porch floor. Dark bloody looking spots marked a path from the door to the steps.

Dr. Leibold clinched his flashlight like a weapon and stepped inside the open door with his wife right behind him. The house was in a shambles with a lamp turned over, the sofa tilted backwards, pictures and glass lay in shattered patches on the floor.

"Oh my! This is awful. Where are Margie and her mother?" asked his wife as Dr. Leibold stepped over the clutter and went to the kitchen. That room had bloody footprints marking a path to the back door. They followed those steps, but they ended on the last step and were buried in the grass of the backyard.

"I'll bet he's hauled them off and buried them or has thrown their bodies in the river," said his wife in a shivery voice.

"They may be in the house. Let's check the other rooms," said Dr. Leibold turning back to the house.

"Nothing was found in the other rooms except a bloody door knob leading to one of the rooms. The door was standing open and they flashed the light around inside, but found nothing. The other rooms and the bathroom revealed that whatever had been done had mostly taken place in the living room.

"We'd best go down the road to that phone box and call the police. I don't know what has happened, but I suspect he's killed them both," said Dr. Leibold grimly.

They made their call and waited there at the box until the police arrived. Dr. Leibold told the police why he was there and what he'd found at the house.

"I hope you didn't touch anything. It would mess up the evidence," said the officer.

Dr. Leibold still gripped his flashlight and now looked at it. "I had a grip on this flashlight to use it as a weapon if I needed it. I never put it down. I didn't touch anything." He turned to his wife. "Did you touch anything?"

"No, uh, yes I did. I pushed that bedroom door a little wider with these first two fingers. "I'm sorry." Mrs. Leibold held up her first two fingers on her right hand.

The officer patted her shoulder. "That's all right, Ma'am. We won't arrest you for that. I'm going to call the ambulance service and see if they have been out here."

"Somebody has been out here. There are fresh tire tracks leading through the gate and up to the porch," said Dr. Leibold.

"I'll bet that Tom Pierson hauled their bodies off to dispose of them," said Mrs. Leibold shivering from shock.

The officer gave her a shrewd look and went to his car radio and soon came back saying, "They said a Mr. Patrick Archer called about two hours ago and said someone had broken into his house and beat up his wife and daughter. They transported two female bodies to the hospital in Port Angeles."

"Were they dead?" asked Mrs. Leibold, shaking so badly that her voice wobbled.

"Doctor, I think you'd better take your wife home. We'll call you if we need to ask any questions," said the officer.

Mrs. Leibold grabbed the officer's arm. "Was Margie and her mother dead," she again asked in a near shriek.

Dr. Leibold took her arm. "Come on, dear. I'm sure they're all right. He probably beat them up and then got scared. The police will find him."

The officer stopped him. "Do you know who did this? Your wife keeps saying he's killed them. Why is she saying that?"

Mrs. Leibold screeched. "Tom Pierson killed his own mother, that's why."

A Fatal Beginning

The officer looked at Dr. Leibold. "Who is Tom Pierson? That wasn't the name of the man who called the ambulance service."

"Tom Pierson is the man who lives here with his wife and his daughter," replied Dr. Leibold.

"Why does your wife believe this Pierson is the perpetrator of this crime?"

The doctor shook his head wearily. "Tom Pierson's mother died under suspicious circumstances about eighteen years ago. My wife has always believed that Pierson killed his mother. It wasn't proven in the trial, however. My wife is over-wrought. I'll take her home."

The officer nodded and started back to his car. "I'll probably be contacting you both again. You seem to know a lot about this family."

"No, we don't and nobody else around here does. We only know that the wife was beaten up once and I was called. She claimed the cow butted her into the barn wall. I warned her husband at that time about abusing his wife, even though they both told the same tale. The daughter is my receptionist and I've been concerned about her also." Dr. Leibold wanted the officer to know that other than those incidents nobody in the area knew the family.

The officer didn't say anything else and Dr. Leibold helped his wife into the car and drove slowly out Hoh River Road and onto Highway 101deep in thought.

CHAPTER 12

Mrs. Leibold had been silent also, but now asked, "Why would they take the bodies to Port Angeles? Forks hospital is closer."

Dr. Leibold shook his head. "This is terrible. I told Margie I would take care of her. I sure did, didn't I?"

Mrs. Leibold patted his shoulder. "Try to stay calm dear. We can't do anything tonight, but tomorrow you can call the hospital in Port Angeles. You can probably get information since you are their doctor, or at least the doctor for whom Margie works."

Early the next morning Dr. Leibold called Olympia Memorial Hospital, introducing himself as a doctor and was told that two females had been brought to that hospital, but that one had died shortly after arrival.

"The one that is still living, is she Margie Pierson? Margie is my receptionist," said Dr. Leibold.

"I'm sorry, doctor, we can't give out that information except to members of the family. The father came to the hospital with the ambulance. You'll have to get his permission."

Dr. Leibold turned to his wife. "I can't believe the audacity of that man. That woman said that the father had come to the hospital in the ambulance."

Mrs. Leibold gasped. "He sure has his nerve or felt that they both would die and he wanted to make sure. He is a psychopath. I can't imagine what those two women have had to deal with, probably on a daily basis."

"We could be mistaken, dear. That may be two other women. If Tom Pierson had killed them I don't think he would have hung around. He was probably drunk anyway. If the police were smart they'd look around and I'll bet they'd find him somewhere passed out drunk."

The evening newspaper reported that the police had been called to a house on Hoh River Road by Dr. Edwin

Leibold. According to the paper the case was under investigation since Tom Pierson, his wife, Rebecca, and their daughter were all missing. The paper further reported that two females had been taken to the Olympia Memorial Hospital in Port Angeles. One of the females died shortly after being admitted and the other one was in a coma. Although the father had ridden in the ambulance to the hospital he had not left an address or phone number for contact.

When Dr. Leibold put down the paper his wife spluttered. "Now that he's seen that one of them is dead and the other one is near death, I guess he felt he should make himself scarce."

Dr. Leibold called the hospital several more times but wasn't given any information. He finally decided that he would go to Port Angleles and see if he could gain admittance in order to see which female was still alive. Two days later on Saturday afternoon he and his wife drove to Olympia Memorial Hospital in Port Angeles.

They stopped at admittance and asked if they could see the female that was still alive who was brought in by her father.

"The father left instructions that nobody but himself was to have access to either of the patients. I'm sorry sir, but when a family member leaves that kind of instructions we have to abide by them," replied the admittance clerk.

"Can you tell us the name of the patient who is alive?" asked Dr. Leibold.

"I'm not supposed to, but since you seem to be so troubled, I will. Her name is Elaine Archer."

Dr. Leibold and his wife looked shocked. "There's something not right. If that person was brought here from a farm on Hoh River Road her name is not Archer. I know that for a fact."

"I don't know where she came from, but that is the name I have and I'll get in trouble if you say that I told you."

"Don't worry. We won't implicate you, but we are going to the police," replied Dr. Leibold, taking his wife's arm and leaving the hospital.

When they reached Forks again they went straight to the police station. An officer behind a desk looked up and asked, "May I help you?"

"I'm Dr. Edwin Leibold and this is Lorraine, my wife. We reported the murder or the event at the farm on Hoh River Road last week. We know that Tom Pierson, his wife and his daughter lived on that farm. We really liked Margie Pierson. She was my receptionist. We drove to Port Angeles where two females were transported there from this area. We weren't allowed to see anyone or speak to anyone, but we did learn that one of the females was called Elaine Archer. Now, I know you've lived here as long as I have and know full well that there has never been an Archer family living in this area?"

The officer pushed back his chair and gave Dr. Leibold a penetrating look. "You're right. I can't think of ever hearing that name around here. Like you say, I've lived here all my life and I'm not a young man anymore, but I know I've never heard that name anywhere. Hm-m-m, that's something to think about. I'll tell the chief when he comes in." He rose from his chair and walked to the door and then looked back at the Leibolds.

"Thank you, folks, for stopping by, we'll let you know if we discover anything. We need to do a little more searching."

"Seems to me a lot more searching should be done. Surely the ambulance men got a good look at Tom Pierson's... oh, I forgot... the father's...face if he rode that far with them," said Lorraine Leibold angrily.

A Fatal Beginning

Fearing that Lorraine would get upset and anger the officer Dr. Leibold hurried her out to the car and drove away.

"I'm so mad, I can't see straight," fumed Lorraine. "I just know that Margie Pierson or her mother is there in that hospital without a soul in this world caring if they live or die. Tom Pierson certainly don't. Oh, I hope to God they find him. He needs to be hung."

Dr. Leibold patted her hand. "Try not to worry, dear. We want something done quickly, but the police have their methods of investigation. Tom Pierson will get his own reward in time."

"I know God will punish him, but that's not going to help whichever one he didn't kill," mumbled Lorraine Leibold with a determined look. "I'm going to find out more about this for I know in my heart that Tom Pierson tried to kill Margie and her mother."

It was three months or more before the Liebolds were able to learn anything, but then they learned that in a small corner room at Olympia Memorial Hospital in Port Angeles, Washington, Elaine Archer, as the nurses called her, was slowly improving. She had been brought in with three broken ribs, a broken nose, a broken arm, and a concussion. Worse than that though, she had gone into labor at her arrival and been delivered of a premature, five-pound, baby boy. The baby was immediately placed in an incubator and was not expected to live.

When Mr. Archer, the man who called himself her father, was told that she had a baby that was premature and not expected to live he insisted that Elaine was under age and wasn't able to care for a child.

"If it lives put it out for adoption. She was raped and she said she didn't want the baby, but, me and her mother don't believe in abortions. Since it is still alive, I want it put out for adoption. A baby should have a good home."

The doctor looked at Mr. Archer. "Are you sure she wouldn't want to keep the baby, if it lives?"

"She wanted to go to some old granny woman and get rid of it, but like I said, she's underage and we wouldn't let her. So, if it lives and you know of some good family who would be good to it, let them have it," said the father. "She may not get better anyway and I can't take care of myself, much less a newborn baby."

The doctor and nurse exchanged glances, but made no further comments.

Mr. Archer asked if he could see his daughter. "I'll probably have to stay in the YMCA for awhile and I may not be able to get back to see her for several days."

The doctor shook his head. "I'm sorry, Mr. Archer, but we can't allow anyone to see her right now. Come back tomorrow."

He did come back the next day and asked about her condition. When he was told that she wasn't any better he turned to leave, but the nurse stopped him. "Mr. Archer, the doctor wants to talk to you." She had risen from her desk. "Come this way, please."

When he was ushered into the doctor office he was trembling and had turned white as a sheet. "What's wrong, Doc? She ain't dead, is she?"

"No, no. She isn't any better, though. I wanted to see if you still wish to give the baby up for adoption. Do you?" The doctor gave him a very serious look.

"You'll have to sign the papers since you are Elaine's guardian and she can't answer for herself."

"I don't care about no papers I just want that baby to have a home," said Mr. Archer seeming to get whiter and looking anxiously behind him where the door stood open.

"Here are the adoption papers and we have a nice young couple who want him very much. They'll be very good to him and he'll be well provided for," said the doctor laying the papers on the desk in front of Mr. Archer. "Sign

A Fatal Beginning

right here on this line, Mr. Archer," said the doctor pointing with his finger.

Mr. Archers face turned from white to red as he looked at the doctor. "I'll have to put my X. I never got no schoolin'." He shakily scrawled an X on the paper.

"That's fine, Mr. Archer. Now let us see your social security card for verification."

"I ain't got one of them either. I think I did have one, once. It may be back at the house, but I can't go back there. I'm her daddy though." Suddenly he jumped up. "You'uns tryin' to trick me or somethin', ain't you? I'm leavin' here and you'uns do whatever you want with the bas. . . uh baby," he said as he headed for the door.

"Don't you want this money the couple wanted you to have? It's three hundred dollars."

Mr. Archer turned and seeing the money in the doctor's hand eagerly grabbed it. He went trotting down the corridor, stuffing the money in his pocket, as he went. The doctor and his nurse looked at each other in amazement.

"That man is scared to death about something. I'll bet we've seen the last of him," said the nurse, smiling grimly.

"He may not even be her father, but until she comes out of the coma, if she ever does, we'll never know. Anyway, a five-month baby only has a fighting chance. If he does live, however, the Larkins' will love him and be good parents. This way, we'll be giving him the only chance he has right now," said the doctor seriously.

"Whoever broke into that house must have been a maniac. The girl was bad enough, but the older woman was beat to a pulp, wasn't she?" said the nurse as she clipped the adoption papers together and put them in a letter-sized manila envelope.

They thought Mr. Archer had left the hospital, but he hadn't. He acted as if he was going outside, but when he saw nobody in the hallway he quickly, with anxious looks, crept up the stairs and at the ICU unit asked permission to look at his daughter. The nurses knew him as the girl's father and allowed him in.

He walked to the bedside and stood looking down on the daughter who had always reminded him of his mother. He had never admitted that though and both Margie and Rebecca thought he didn't like her because he thought she was ugly.

If anyone had been watching they would have seen the anguish written on his face before he suddenly reached out toward the life-sustaining tubes. Before he grasped them, a nurse pulled back the curtain that separated the cubicles from each other and he dropped his hand to his side and leaned back. He waited a few seconds and then gave a furtive look around and seeing there were too many nurses and doctors, he feared getting caught. Suddenly, with a malicious gleam in his eyes he leaned close to his daughter's head.

"That bastard you was carryin' is dead. If I didn't kill you I at least I got rid of that shame to my name. Women ain't nothin' but sluts no way. "

He almost spat in his daughter's face as he hissed, "Did you hear me, girl? I killed your bastard and I killed your mother so you're like me now. You ain't got nobody either and you may as well go ahead and die."

When this got no response or movement from the girl he felt sure she would not live so he turned and left the room and the hospital as quickly as he could.

Meanwhile the doctor and nurse were still discussing the Archer girl and her father. "That girl certainly doesn't look like her father, but he rode in the ambulance with her to the hospital," said the doctor grimly. "She doesn't seem to be responding to treatment so she may never come out of the coma."

He shook his head sadly and then in a more cheerful voice said, "We are assured that the baby will be cared for, if it lives. I don't know of anything else to do."

"The Larkins are a wonderful young couple, so we can be sure the little fellow will have a good home," said the nurse as she picked up the phone and dialed a number.

"Mrs. Larkin, the little baby I spoke to you about is yours if you still want him. Now, as I told you on the phone, the baby is premature and may not live, but the papers have been signed and the money was accepted. So, if you still want him, you and Mr. Larkin only need to come in tomorrow about ten o'clock and sign your papers. The baby will have to stay here for a while, but you will have your own newborn baby."

She put the phone back in its cradle and looked at the doctor with a big smile. "Well, we've made two people happy. I'm glad somebody found some happiness from this terrible incident."

Sometimes, the Lord uses bad things to create a lot of good, but it is hard for us to understand God's reasons," said the doctor going out the door.

He went upstairs to the nursery. He waited while a young nurse changed the baby's diaper and settled him back into his cot. "How's he doing, Nurse?"

Jennifer Jacobs, smoothed the thin blanket covering the small bundle and turned. "He has trouble with his feed, but he seems to be doing better today. I worried about him all night. He's now five days old. I didn't think he'd last as long as he has."

"That girl's father came in and signed the adoption papers and took the money, they offered. The parents will be here tomorrow at ten o'clock. They've wanted a newborn baby for over a year now. If he lives I think the little fellow will have a good home," said the doctor as he stood looking down at the small scrap of humanity.

Jennifer Jacobs made no comment, but her thoughts were with that poor girl who was the mother of the baby. *She's unconscious and what if she wakes up and wants her baby. I think they should wait. She might wake up, but what's she got to wake-up to. Her mother, or I guess it was her mother, is dead, her baby's gone, and if that brute is her daddy he don't care for her at all.*

Jennifer had been raised by loving parents and she suddenly decided that she was going to visit Elaine Archer. *I've heard that if someone will talk to unconscious people it sometimes helps them to come out of a coma*, she thought and thus made it her resolution.

A Fatal Beginning

CHAPTER 13

That evening Jennifer made her way to the ICU unit and asked to see Elaine Archer. At first the nurse wouldn't let her in, but when she told them where she worked and that she only wanted to sit beside Elaine and talk to her to see if it would help. The nurse paged the doctor and asked permission explaining Jennifer's motive.

"Let her, but she can only stay ten minutes. Also tell her she is not to mention anything about the mother or the baby. Talking to her might help since she appears physically healthy except for her broken bones," said the doctor.

After that, Jennifer Jacobs went about once each week to sit beside the bed and talk. She didn't know how to begin, but thought that telling Elaine who she was would be a good beginning.

"Hello Elaine. I'm Jennifer Jacobs. I work here in the hospital. I'm twenty-two years old and I'm a nurse. Why don't you try to get better since I want to have you for my friend?" said Jennifer and patted the hand that lay so lifeless on the blanket. *Her hand is warm and I'm going to get her to move it,* thought Jennifer as she rose to leave.

Mr. Archer never returned to the hospital and the lady he had said was his wife was after a week finally laid to rest in the local cemetery. The husband wasn't there and the daughter was in a coma so the authorities had no other choice.

Jennifer heard about the mother being buried and that made her feel more compassion for Elaine. Her visits in the evenings became more frequent and longer. As she talked she often clasped the limp hand on the coverlet.

For two months Jennifer repeated her visits without any indication that she was being any help. In the third month, on a Sunday, Jennifer came after church where she had asked for prayer for Elaine Archer. The entire congregation had prayed for her new friend and Jennifer left the church feeling excited. *Something is going to happen today. I just know it is. Thank you Jesus*, she thought as she hurried to the hospital.

She reached the ICU unit and quietly seated herself beside the bed. She clasped Elaine's hand and said, "You're feeling better, today, aren't you? I asked the church to pray for you and I think everybody in the congregation prayed. I hurried over here because I knew you would feel better. You do, don't you? Squeeze my hand. Please, please squeeze my hand," she pleaded with tears in her eyes.

Her head was bowed as tears dripped down on her lap. Then she felt something . . . a slight pressure and jerked her head up to look at their clasped hands. She pressed Elaine's and waited. Once again, she felt the pressure only stronger this time.

"Glory to God. Thank you, sweet Jesus," praised Jennifer and jumped to her feet to lean closer to her new friend. "Elaine, you squeezed my hand, didn't you?" Again, she felt the pressure of the fingers clasped in her hand. She unclasped her hand gently and went to the nurse's station.

"She squeezed my hand! Elaine squeezed my hand. She did it three times." Tears were streaming down her face as well as the face of the nurse on duty.

The nurse's eyes opened wide and she smiled. "Let's check this out, shall we?" She turned to the other nurse. "I'm going to check, but you call the doctor. He wants to know of any movement."

Fifteen minutes later the doctor was at the bedside. "Elaine, your friend is so happy she is crying. She would be happier still if you would open your eyes. Can you do that?"

Jennifer, the nurse, and the doctor waited with bated breath as Elaine's eyelids quivered for several seconds and finally stopped. There was no other movement and they all left feeling so disappointed.

After two more days Jennifer visited again at the same time and always squeezed Elaine's hand and always felt the slight pressure in return. On the evening of the second day Jennifer sat holding her hand and praying. When she lifted her head she said, "Elaine, please open your eyes. Please," she begged and sat waiting and the eyelids started twitching again. Then the lids parted, but barely a sliver, but it was enough. Jennifer grasped the hand she was so familiar with and kissed it.

"My friend, oh my friend. Now you can see the ugly girl who has been pestering you to be her friend." Jennifer would have loved to hug this girl who the Lord had blessed her to help, but instead stood watching Elaine's face..

Elaine's eyes moved to find where the voice was coming from and Jennifer said, "Here, I'm here beside you."

When Elaine's eyes finally focused on Jennifer she squeezed her hand and tried to smile. Crying again, Jennifer ran to the nurse's station just as the doctor arrived.

Soon the room was crowded. The doctor tested Elaine's reflexes and said, "Well, Miss Archer, we're glad you're back with us. We'll not tire you anymore today, but we expect great things from you. Your friend, Jennifer, is on cloud nine and you can't let her down, can you?"

Again, they all saw a brief twitching of the lips which appeared to be a smile. The doctor patted the cover. "You rest now and Jennifer will be back to see you tomorrow."

Elaine was tired and soon dropped off to sleep, but had fitful dreams of her daddy telling her he had killed her baby, which made her restless. After checking with the doctor, the nurse gave her a mild sedative and she slept soundly the rest of the night.

A Fatal Beginning

Elaine had been battered so badly that she was kept in Intensive Care and the Critical Care for the first month and then moved to a room near the nurse's station which made it easy for Jennifer to let the nurses know of any slight improvement. Two days after her eyes were opened she was moved to a small room near a window and her bed was raised so she could look out but she didn't seem to notice.

Jennifer still came every day and steadily got more and more responses as to movement. On Thursday evening she sat down and clasped the waiting hand. "Elaine, it is so pretty outside. It is cold, but the snow is so white. It looks like a fairy land."

That seemed to make no impression on Elaine, but she did frown as if concentrating for a moment and then whispered, "Name."

"What? What did you say? Did you say, name?" asked Jennifer jumping to her feet and looking into Elaine's face.

"Name," said Elaine more clearly.

Jennifer smiled. "My name is Jennifer and I'm your friend." She watched as Elaine moved her head slightly from side to side. Then she frowned and tried to speak again.

"Your name is Elaine. Did you think I didn't know it?" asked Jennifer with a smile.

"Not . . . name," said Elaine more loudly.

"Elaine is not your name. Is that what you are saying?

"Yes," grunted Elaine.

Jennifer's eyes widened, in shocked surprise. "We've been calling you Elaine. What is your name?"

"Mar-g-gie," Elaine finally got out.

Jennifer looked stunned. "I'll need to tell the nurse. I'll be back," she said and hurried away.

This information led to a flurry of activity. Now members of the police force wanted to talk to this girl who had been brought in as Elaine Archer, but now she was awake and saying that Elaine wasn't her name.

"My name is Margie Pierson," she finally got out when the police came to talk to her.

"Now, the pieces are falling into place," said the police chief after he had talked to the officer in charge in Forks. He looked at his partner.

"Dr. Leibold kept telling us that the girl taken from the house had to have been Margie Pierson, so I think we need to talk to him again, don't you?"

Everything they learned pointed the police to Tom Pierson who had seemingly disappeared into thin air. "

"Now, that we know who we're looking for I think we should go back out there, don't you?" asked the sheriff, looking over at his deputy who had seated himself in the passenger seat.

"The house is locked up and has been for several months. It is designated as a crime scene, but I want to look around inside again. Who knows we might find a picture or something we've missed," mumbled the sheriff and headed the patrol car toward Hoh River Road.

Even though they went over the house with a fine-toothed comb they found nothing of interest except the picture hidden at the bottom of one of the dresser drawers in the bedroom.

The sheriff stood looking at the young woman in the picture. "This must be her mother or grandmother 'cause that girl in the hospital is the image of this woman. We'll wrap it up and take it to the girl. It may make her remember something she's forgot."

The deputy soon had the picture stowed in the backseat of the car "Mrs. Liebold has lived here all her life. She may know some member of the family that's still living. That Archer or Pierson or whoever he is may be hiding out if he's got any kin in the area."

Mrs. Liebold was a wealth of information. When she saw the picture she said, "That's Elaine Pierson. I don't know what her maiden name was, but I always heard that her folks lived some place up river from here. It may have been across the mountain, but she was Tom Pierson's mother. I never heard of either of them until the family moved to that little old run-down farm way back at the end of Hoh River Road, right close to the reservation."

The sheriff stood thinking. "You said Tom Pierson killed his mother. What made you say that?"

"Well, I was in high school and some of my classmates used to go out that way to hunt and they said they'd hear him cursing and knocking things around about every time they got near the house. One time they said this woman had come stumbling backwards through the door and Tom Pierson had come right behind her with his fists drawn and cursing something awful. When they found her dead with her head bashed in we all thought that Tom killed her. He got off scot free, but we never did believe he was innocent." Mrs. Leibold wiped tears from her eyes as she finished.

"We thought maybe the girl would remember something so we're going to take this picture to her," said the sheriff and got into the patrol car, and raising his hand in farewell as he drove away.

Margie broke down when she saw the picture. "I guess that must be my grandmother, but I don't know anything about her. Daddy wouldn't let us mention her and I was never allowed to see this picture. Mom said the picture was hid in a dresser drawer, so we didn't dare look at it. Mom always said that my grandmother was a good woman. She died just before Mom and Dad married, or that's what Mom told me."

"What was her maiden name?"

Margie laid thinking. "Meadows. Yes, that's what I heard Mom say once and Daddy got really upset."

The sheriff and his deputy left with at least a name and a place to begin. "I hope we find the murderin' son-of-a-bitch.' I'd like to string him up myself," said the deputy vehemently.

A Fatal Beginning

CHAPTER 14

Elaine Archer, now Margie Pierson, was getting better physically, but had a long way to go, according to the doctors. She was very depressed, however, and seemed to not even want to live.

The doctors discussed, among themselves, as to why she never mentioned the baby she had carried for nearly six months. They feared to directly bring it up since she was still so weak and unstable.

"Miss Pierson, do you remember anything from your past?" asked Dr. Jonas, the doctor who had followed her case closer than anyone else.

Margie turned her head quickly as if to avoid either the question or having to answer. Suddenly she broke down and cried, but made no sound.

"Don't get upset, dear. We can talk about this when you are ready," said Dr. Jonas soothingly. He stayed to chat a few more minutes and then left.

During this time the police were busy trying to find Tom Pierson, and the medical profession was trying to heal Margie Pierson in body, mind, and emotionally. She was very depressed, her memory seemed poor, and she couldn't put her thoughts together easily. However, on one visit she did tell them that her father had beaten her and her mother up. Then she suddenly began looking fearfully around the room.

"My mother! Where's my mother? She hit him when he slapped me, but he hit me again and I . . . don't know after that," she mumbled.

The doctors looked at each other as if doubting what to do. Finally, Dr. Jonas said, "Margie, your mother didn't make it. She died shortly after arriving at the hospital. The ambulance men said your mother was holding your hand when they got to the house. She probably died holding your hand."

A Fatal Beginning

Margie seemed to know it was her left hand since that is the hand she put lovingly against her cheek. She didn't act shocked, however. She seemed to be resigned or relieved, but silent tears coursed down her cheeks unchecked.

The doctor waited to see if this would exacerbate the trauma. Margie drew in a long breath and sighed slowly. "Now, he can't beat on her any more. She used to say, 'Margie I've often wished he'd just kill me, but I'd think of you and didn't want to leave you to his fists and feet.'"

Margie twitched at the blanket covering her for a moment. "He did kill her, but she died defending me. She didn't want him to hurt me." Margie wiped her tears away with the back of her hand until the nurse handed her a tissue.

When she had gained control of herself she asked. "Where's my mother now? I'd like to see her and touch her just once more."

"I'm sorry dear, but she had to be buried. You've been here in the hospital for almost two months."

"Oh. I didn't know," said Margie and her forlorn look caused the attending nurse to turn away to wipe her eyes.

Dr. Jonas held her hand as he told her everything that had happened from the time she and her mother had arrived at the hospital. They didn't mention the baby fearing a relapse. "We haven't seen your father after the fourth day you were here. Nobody knows where he is."

The doctor arose and stood waiting for her reaction. Margie shivered convulsively and said, "I hope he's dead too. I hope somebody beats him like he beat us," she said grimly.

"He'll get his own, dear. We'll find him and he won't be alive much longer," said the policeman who was there with the doctor.

Back in Forks, they searched the grounds around the Pierson house, and asked about Tom Pierson at the lumber company where he had worked, but he hadn't been seen.

"I'm surprised he hasn't shown up since I owe him for two days work. He always wanted his payday as soon as he could get it," said the owner before suddenly stopping. "I'll send his money to the daughter if you can't find him.".

Not finding any traces of Tom Pierson in Forks they broadened their search and in Port Angeles they had luck. The owner of a run-down rooming house in a poorer section of town said that a man that looked like their description had rented a room two nights before.

"He looked all done in and said he would pay me the next morning since he needed some change. He left before I got up the next morning and I didn't get a cent from him. I'm glad though for from what the roomer next door to him said he must have been going off the deep end. He cussed two women who he called Rebecca and Margie all night long and there wouldn't no women in that room. I don't run that kind of house. I guess he was just crazy drunk."

The police left there thinking he was holed-up somewhere in Port Angeles. They began asking from one end of the town to the other after getting a descriptive drawing of how he possibly looked.

It was six o'clock in the evening and still they'd had no luck. The two officers who had worked on this all during their shift stopped at a diner for coffee before heading for the station. They had ordered and were waiting when they got a call to check out a possible homicide.

On the other side of the river they found a male body beaten into a pulp. His head and face were so bloody that it was hard to tell what he was. They put in a quick call for an ambulance and checked for any signs of life. There was a faint pulse in the neck, but the odor and the gore made them both nauseous.

When he was loaded into the ambulance the officer stood shaking their heads. "I wonder what that man did to deserve that kind of beating?" said the youngest officer.

The next morning's newspaper revealed that a body had been found that fitted the description of the drawing of Tom Pierson.

When nurse Jennifer Jacobs came on duty she glanced at the newspaper and then picked it up. She read the entire story and stood thinking, *if you live by the sword, you die by the sword, according to the Bible, or so her mother always said. This man had been evil and he died in an evil fashion as well.*

She put the paper down and wondered if the doctors would tell Margie. She was surprised at how natural the name Margie sounded since they had all called her Elaine for over two months.

The doctors didn't get a chance to tell Margie, she read the paper herself. A nurse's aide, with a newspaper under her arm, had brought in fresh water. Margie asked if she could read her paper and the girl left it with her.

When the doctor made his early morning visit Margie was sitting with the paper across her lap. She had her hand over her mouth and tears were streaming down her cheeks.

Seeing the paper lying open to the story of Tom Pierson the doctor stepped to her side. "Margie, I'm sorry. That was a terrible way to die."

Margie looked up with a hard look. "Mom died a terrible death also, but he is the one who beat her to death. I have no tears to shed for him. I was crying because this didn't happen before he killed my mother and my . . ." This last part was almost whispered and since the doctor didn't understand what she said, he didn't delve into it.

There was no easy answer to that and the doctor said, "I understand your feelings, but you must realize that he had to have some kind of problem. A man couldn't be that brutal unless he was deranged in some way."

"You wouldn't feel like that if you had been on the receiving end of his rage. I'm glad he's dead." Margie gave him such a stony glare that he dropped any attempt at empathy for the deceased.

The doctor picked up her wrist and checked her pulse. "How are you feeling otherwise? Are you still having nightmares?"

Margie sighed. "Yes, but not every night. I think I'll feel better now, knowing that I don't have to be afraid of him anymore."

Jennifer Jacobs still visited every day and Margie grew to like and trust her.

"Margie, when you are released, why don't you come out to the farm with me? Mom and Dad will welcome you and you need a place to stay until you get settled," begged Jennifer.

Margie smiled. "I'll have to do something. The police said that Dr. Leibold was selling the farm for me. I'm hoping that will bring enough for me to find some place to live until I can get work. If you're sure your parents won't mind, I may take you up on that."

Jennifer replied happily. "Good! I know they won't care because I've already asked them."

Three days later Margie Pierson was released from the hospital even though she still had to use crutches to walk. James Jacobs, Jennifer's father, was there with his wife to take her to their home. Margie left her contact information with the nurse so that Dr. Leibold could contact her when the farm was sold.

The huge log farmhouse on the Jacob's farm seemed to welcome her as she hobbled along the flower bordered walkway leading to the wide porch. Banisters with flat shelves interspersed with spaces along the top, ran the length of one side of the porch. The other side held a swing and several cane-bottomed rocking chairs.

Inside, the rooms were large, airy, and very clean. Smells of herbs and flowers permeated the air. She was shown upstairs to a spacious bedroom with one large window that looked out over a vast expanse of pasture where a mare and young foal grazed peacefully. The furniture was sparse and simple, consisting only of a wooden bed with solid oak head and foot boards and covered with a hand-tacked quilt of blue knots. Blue and white gingham curtains framed the window and beneath its sill was a wooden table with a blue gingham skirt draped over it. Resting on the scarf was a dark blue bowl with the trailing vines of a sweet potato plant creeping toward the window sill.

Margie sat down on the bed and dropped her crutches against the bed. *This is so . . . peaceful or something. I feel safe, I guess. I can't be a burden to these people though* she thought and suddenly felt overwhelmed with the thought that she had nobody in the world that cared whether she lived or died, and knew that she didn't care either.

"Oh, Mommy and Rick, what am I going to do?" she whispered softly and rubbed her hand across her belly where her baby had rested for nearly seven months. *Why did he have to kill you?* she thought as she gently caressed her belly. Then she thought about how her mother always prayed for help when things got really rough. She shivered as she thought, *Mommy didn't have time to pray when he came out of the kitchen and hit her the day he killed her. We thought he was still at work, but he was hiding and listening to what Dr. Leibold said.*

After all her doubts that there was a God, Margie still buried her head in her hands and silently begged the Lord to give her strength and show her what to do. She stayed like that until Mrs. Jacobs came to the door and stood for a moment looking at the forlorn picture before her.

"Margie, do you feel like coming back downstairs? I thought you could peel some potatoes for me."

Margie jerked her head up, startled. "Oh! I didn't hear you come up the stairs. Sure, I'll be glad to help."

As she made her slow way back down the stairs she realized that this kind woman didn't really need her help. She was trying to keep Margie's mind off her worries.

She sat at the table to peel the potatoes, and make a salad while Mrs. Jacobs finished the rest of the meal. It was ready to put on the table as Jennifer's car pulled into the drive.

The Jacobs farm was a haven of warmth, love, and rest for three weeks, but every day Margie searched the newspaper for some kind of job she could do. Mr. and Mrs. Jacobs told her that she wasn't strong enough yet. "Give yourself another month, Margie, then you can think about work," they both advised.

Since Margie never once mentioned her baby, Jennifer was afraid to mention it. She had kept track of it though. With the risk of losing her job, Jennifer still had looked at the file on Elaine Archer.

She found that William and Mary Larkin, a young couple, unable to have children, had been searching for a newborn baby to adopt. The record revealed that they had adopted a premature boy baby whose mother was listed as Elaine Archer. She saw the paper with the X signature of Patrick Archer which gave the baby up for adoption.

The Larkins lived in a nice house about thirty miles north of Port Angeles in Sequim, a small town just off of highway 101. Jennifer wrote all the information down so that Margie could have it when she was better. *She'll want to know that her baby was alive*, thought Jennifer, wondering how she could discover whether the baby was still living.

I'll tell her that it was alive, when it was adopted. I'd want to know if I'd had a baby, Jennifer thought as she hurriedly put everything back in the folder and closed the file drawer. She quietly closed the door to the file room and started up the stairs when Dr. Jonas loomed on the landing above her.

Dr. Jonas smiled. "Have you been down to chat with Ginger?"

Thinking quickly, Jennifer said, "I couldn't find her. She must have left early."

Dr. Jonas looked at his watch. "It's four. I guess she has already left. That's all right. We can both catch her tomorrow. It's time we went home also, isn't it?"

Jennifer smiled and nodded as she went on up the steps toward him. When he turned and took the remaining steps two at a time she breathed a sigh of relief.

When she stopped by the mailbox at the end of their road, there was a letter for Margie Pierson from Dr. Edwin Leibold. *This will make Margie happy, she thought, but I don't want her to leave. She's like the sister I never had.*

Dr. Leibold had written that the farm had sold for $25,000.00 which caused Margie to gasp in surprise.

"What's wrong dear?" asked Mrs. Jacobs.

"Nothing's wrong. Dr. Leibold sold the farm and look how much he received for it," said Margie, holding up the letter.

"Here's another letter," said Margie, trembling as she pulled out another envelope, opened it, and gasped again as she looked at the short note and the check inside. "It's a check from the company where my father worked. It seems they owed him for two days work. This is . . . Why that dirty skunk! He lied to us. Mom and I never had one cent. I had no idea he earned this much. This is for $200.00 and it's only for two days. This makes me so mad."

"Oh my! That is good pay, isn't it?" Mrs. Jacobs said in wide-eyed amazement.

Mr. Jacobs grunted and shook his head in caution to his wife. "He probably was a good worker, but I like the sound of what you got for the farm better. Margie, how much land did your dad own? That is a good price if he didn't have much land."

"We only owned the house, the hen house and the pasture. I never dreamed it would sell for $25,000.00," replied Margie.

"That's wonderful, dear. You said you wanted to go to school and now you can," said Mrs. Jacobs as she smiled with pleasure.

Margie sat studying the letter. "Dr. Leibold says I'll have to come to Forks to sign the deed and receive my money. He wants me to call him as to what day I can come to Forks. Is there a bus that goes there and back in one day?"

Margie shivered as she thought of the day she learned that Rick had died. "I can't stand the thoughts of going to Forks."

Unconsciously her hand dropped to her belly as if to shelter something, but jerked it back when her hand made contact.

Jennifer noticed this action, but her parents didn't. They both looked at Jennifer. "Don't you have two days off next week, Jenns?" asked her father.

Jennifer nodded as she grinned expectantly. "Why don't we make a day of it and all of us go with Margie?" She looked at her mother and father for agreement.

"I've not been to Forks but once in my life," said Mrs. Jacobs. "We could take some sandwiches and drinks and stop at one of those roadside areas and have ourselves a picnic."

This met with approval since Jennifer had Monday and Tuesday off from work. They decided on Tuesday. Mr.

Jacobs only had a farm truck so they had to go in Jennifer's car.

The evening was spent in discussing the best options for use of the money.

"I want to get a degree in secretarial skills and office management. I can do bookkeeping, but I don't like it as well," said Margie as she thought of how much she had enjoyed working for Dr. Leibold. Thinking about working there, however, brought up all her trauma and she shivered violently.

Suddenly she sat up very straight and looked at Mr. Jacobs. "Can someone change their name? I mean, if someone never wanted to be called by a certain name again is there a way to get it changed?"

Mr. Jacobs didn't even ask why. "I don't know of anybody that's done that, but since you're eighteen and don't have any kinfolk, you might go to the court house and change it."

"I'll check with Mary Castle. She works in the County Clerk's office. If she doesn't know, I'll bet she can find out," said Jennifer excitedly. "Do you want me to check for you?"

"Yes, I want to be Margie Elaine Meadows. It was my grandmother's maiden name, and I look so much like her picture," said Margie with a tender smile. "You check on that tomorrow, but tonight I want to decide what college to attend."

Seeing excitement shining in her friend's eyes, Jennifer quickly asked, "Do you want to go to the university?" Then with brow furrowed she added, "I guess you'll have to since we don't have a state college, or if there is I know nothing about it."

CHAPTER 15

"Why, that university is miles from here in Seattle and it may cost so much that you won't have enough to live on," said Mr. Jacobs, who had come in on the mention of the university.

"Maybe you could get a scholarship. That's the way Jennifer was able to go straight through her nurse's training. She got enough to pay for a room and meals which saved her a lot of money," said Mrs. Jacobs and then smiled, "You could come here on holidays and long weekends and it would be like coming home."

Tears came to Margie's eyes. *These people are treating me as if I were their daughter, too*, she thought.

She swallowed her tears and looked at these wonderful people. "I couldn't impose on you people like that. It wouldn't be fair."

"I don't see why not. The room you're in now has been empty for years and it will be empty until Carl decides he's had enough of the military life," said Mr. Jacobs.

Jennifer jumped up and hugged Margie. "I've always wanted a sister. Say you'll make this your home, Margie, please."

"If you don't come home once in a while James is really going to miss those wonderful biscuits you make in the mornings," said Mrs. Jacobs with a twinkle in her eyes.

"And I'll never learn to knit if you don't come home to finish teaching me," Jennifer added.

Margie grinned. "I'll think about it. It is just hard for me to understand all of you being so good to me. I'm not even related to you."

"Yes, you are. You're my sister, so just accept it and quit acting silly," said Jennifer and hugged her again. She released her and grinned. "Since you are going to be kinfolk I think you'd better drop this Mr. and Mrs. stuff. Don't you both think so?" Jennifer looked at her parents.

A Fatal Beginning

"She can call me anything she wants to as long as she makes biscuits, but James would sound nice," said Uncle James smiling at Margie's red face.

Aunt Amy smiled and said, "Amy is a lot easier to say than Mrs. Jacobs so why not just call us James and Amy."

Tears came to Margie's eyes as she hugged Aunt Amy and put out her hand to Uncle James, but had it pushed aside as he engulfed her in a bear hug. He quickly stepped back. "Well, that makes it official. You are now a part of the family. Welcome home, Margie . . . uh, Meadows."

With tears in her eyes Margie looked around. "I'm not officially Margie Meadows until I get it changed, but I think it sounds a lot better than Elaine Archer and I sure don't want to hear my dad's name again."

"I don't blame you, Sis, but now you have a really super dad, Mr. James Jacobs," said Jennifer turning to her father with a bow.

Jumping to her feet Margie said, "Thank you . . . Uncle James and Aunt Amy. Thank you so much. She then quickly left the room since she was so choked on held-back tears and they allowed her to go.

Tuesday was a day that Margie would always remember. She had called Dr. Leibold and told him they would be in Forks by one-thirty on Tuesday. This gave them time to stop at one of the many roadside picnic areas and eat lunch. Jennifer produced a camera and took lots of pictures.

"We'll start a new family album since we have a new member in our family. Mommy and Daddy have another daughter and I have a sister."

"Yes, and I didn't have to suffer to have her," said Aunt Amy. This caused surprised laughter since that was unusual for Aunt Amy.

In the attorney's office Margie met Dr. Leibold and his wife, as well as Mr. and Mrs. Henderson, who purchased the farm. After the deed was signed and the Hendersons had left, Dr. Leibold said, "Margie, do you want to go back and take a last look at your old home place?"

Margie shivered. "No. Oh no, I never want to even think of that place again."

She looked at Mrs. Liebold. "I don't mean that there's anything wrong with the place, but I don't have pleasant memories about it."

Knowing Margie story and reading the more recent account in the paper, Mrs. Liebold smiled. "I understand, dear, but it'll look like a totally different place when the Hendersons get finished with it."

Margie left Forks without looking back, although she wished she could have searched for her cat, Big Ells. As they got into the car Jennifer saw such a sad look on Margie's face.

"I know it is sad to leave everything you ever knew, Margie, but it will be better from here on out."

"It isn't that, Jenns. I wish I still had my Mom, but this area only reminds me of the miserable life I had here. I just wish I knew that Big Ells has found a good home. I loved that cat. He was the only friend I had for many years."

"Cats are right resourceful, Margie. I'll bet he's friends with some other little boy or girl that needs a friend, by now." Uncle James reached up from the back seat and patted her shoulder.

As she rode along her thoughts were troubled. *Why was I spared to be all alone? Both my mother and baby are gone and Rick is gone so, if there is a God, why doesn't he let me know why He left me here. I don't have anything to live for, so why didn't he kill me too?*

A Fatal Beginning

Jennifer glanced sideways and saw that Margie was fighting tears. "Margie, I think you and I should go into Port Angeles one evening and buy you some clothes and . . . maybe get a new hairdo."

This got Margie's attention. "I could, couldn't I? Mom used to slip and clip the ends off my braids when my hair would get so heavy I'd get headaches from it. I've never had a real haircut though.

"Well, we're going to fix you right up, little Sis. Of course, if we do that all the boys in Sequim will be hanging around our farm," said Jennifer and laughed at the startled look on Margie's face.

Then she smiled. "I guess I could spend maybe a hundred on clothes and things. Do you think I'd have enough to do that, Uncle James?"

Well, I don't know. The clothes maybe, but you've got a lot of hair to cut. It may cost a heap to cut hair like that," kidded Uncle James.

They all laughed and then Margie sobered. "Mom always said she'd love to see me with my hair cut. She said I'd be pretty, but I always knew she just said that to make me feel better. I always knew I had no looks."

"No looks! Why Margie Meadows, how can you say that. Even with your hair up in braids you're the prettiest girl I've ever seen," said Jennifer.

Aunt Amy leaned in from the back seat. "Why do you think you're not pretty, Margie, didn't you have mirrors in your house?"

Margie sighed. "Dad made me wear a cap over my head from the time I was born. He said I was so ugly he couldn't stand to look at me."

"That man must have been blind as well as crazy. Anybody with eyes can see that you are a beautiful young woman. Ain't she, Amy?" James asked, looking at his wife.

"Yes James, Margie is beautiful, but I guess if one was told every day that they were ugly it would make them think they were. Is that what happened to you, honey?" Amy asked.

Margie didn't reply for a moment. "I guess so, Aunt Amy, but then nobody in school, I mean none of the boys in school talked to me," she stopped abruptly and turned pale as she thought, *They did after, Rick, my baby's daddy, started talking to me.*"

Jennifer heard Margie's pause and glancing to the side saw how pale she had become. Switching her eyes back to the road, Jennifer reached across the seat and patted Margie's arm. "Do you ever wonder about the boy you were engaged to, Margie?"

Margie didn't answer and when Jennifer glanced over at her, tears were streaming down her face. *I'm going to tell her about her baby*, thought Jennifer as she turned onto the dirt road that led to the Jacob's farm.

They were so busy that evening getting all the chores done and planning their trip to Port Angeles the next day that they were in their beds before Jennifer thought of it again.

Jennifer didn't tell her the next day, either. They left early for Port Angeles to shop and both girls were so excited that nothing but clothes and the 'long awaited' haircut occupied their minds.

Jennifer pulled to a stop in front of the Sassy Scissors Beauty Parlor. Turning to Margie, she said with a big smile. "Let's get the big thing done first. Several of the nurses I work with come here to get their hair done and they always look nice. Do you want to try it?"

Margie was so excited she'd already opened her door. "Yes ma'am, I do, but I'll come out feeling completely naked. I'll be so light-headed you'll probably have to hold onto me so I won't fly away."

Having seen Margie's hair down, she agreed with that statement. "I know, but I'll hold onto you," said Jennifer as she got out also and slammed the car door.

Linking her arm with Margie's she said, "Come on Sister, let's go look for a new hairdo for you."

Once inside Jennifer introduced them to the owner and then said, "My sister wants a hair style that will make her look different."

The owner's eyes widened. "You're very pretty as you are, but I try to provide what my clients want. There's a pile of magazines showing hair styles. Go through them and find the one you want." She pointed to a table with glossy magazines stacked several inches high.

Margie and Jennifer took the chairs offered and began their search. Suddenly Jennifer plopped her magazine on top of the one Margie held. "Here it is, Sis. This girl has your eyes, your hairline, and your face shape."

Margie looked and gasped in surprise. "I can't look like that. She's a red head."

"No, you'll look even prettier. This is you, Margie," said Jennifer tapping the picture with the end of her finger.

The salon owner stepped over and asked to see the book. She stood first looking at the picture and then looking back to Margie before her face lit up with a broad smile. "Your sister is right. This is the hair cut for you."

Since the stylist's chair was empty she invited Margie to take a seat, so she could get started. When Margie's hair was loosed from its braids and tumbled down her back both Jennifer and the stylist stood looking in awe. The stylist spoke first. "Geez! I've never seen such beautiful hair. It's almost a shame to cut it. Do you want to give it to "Locks of Love?"

"What's that?" asked Margie.

Jennifer spoke up. "Yes, that's what you should do, Margie. It's an organization that makes wigs from human hair for cancer patients. I don't know why I didn't think of it." She turned to the stylist. "I'm a nurse and should have thought of that myself, but I 'm glad you did."

Margie agreed and soon the stylist was snipping away. As wave after wave fell onto the plastic skirted around her chair, Jennifer stood looking on in amazement and said, "I hope you don't charge more for long hair."

Before the stylist had started Margie felt sad, but then she began to feel a tingling awareness of a heaviness being slowly removed. "Gosh, my hair must have been really heavy. I feel . . . well, strange, I guess."

Jennifer smiled in understanding." You're like that song Mom likes about putting off the old coat to put on the new."

When the stylist had finished and combed Margie's hair, it fell in loose, short curls around her head and Jennifer's face lit up with a wide smile. "Like I said, the boys out our way will be making a bee line for the Jacobs farm."

The stylist turned Margie to face the mirror; she gasped and then gazed in astonishment. "I don't even look like me. I wouldn't know me if I saw myself coming down the street."

Jennifer winked at the hair stylist. "I guess we'd best not buy any new clothes, lest I won't recognize you either."

The stylist gathered all the shorn hair into a clean trash bag and turned to Margie. "Do you want to take this to the hospital or do you want me to take it?"

Jennifer took the bag from the stylist hand. "The collection station is on the first floor of the hospital where I work, so I'll take it in tomorrow."

After paying the stylist and thanking her, the two girls left the shop and walked down Main Street. "Where's the best place to buy dresses, Jennifer?" asked Margie.

"Penny's and Sears are places I go. They have good clothes that aren't too pricey. Of course, you have money now and may want to go to more upscale stores."

Margie shook her head. "No, I'm not interested in being fancy. I just want some decent clothes to wear in college. Let's try Sears first."

An hour later they emerged from Sears so loaded with packages and bags that they had difficulty getting to the car. When they finally made it, Jennifer dropped one of her bags and fished her keys from her handbag and opened the back door first. "Try to get all of this in here. My trunk is filled with flat fixing tools, so there's no room back there."

Once all the packages were stowed, Margie looked at Jennifer and smiled. "I'm so glad you brought me, Jennifer. I really don't know anything about shopping. I've read about it, but I've never shopped before."

Jennifer frowned in puzzlement. "How did you get the clothes you wore to school?

"Mom made them. Dad took us into Forks once each year and allowed Mom to buy cloth, thread, and patterns so she could make our clothes."

"Then you've never had a store-bought dress before, have you?" asked Jennifer.

Margie turned red. "No. I've never had anything store bought except socks and shoes. Mom made our underwear and dresses and she also knitted our winter socks."

Jennifer was silent as she drove down the highway. Finally, she looked over at Margie and smiled. "You've really had an adventure today, haven't you?"

"It is like I'm suddenly living in another world, Jennifer. I don't really know how to explain it. I feel uneasy or something, like I'm in a dream and when I awaken it will disappear."

"That's just because you're doing all these new things. You'll get used to it though since you don't have to be afraid anymore," said Jennifer, reaching over to pat Margie's arm.

When they walked into the house, Aunt Amy was working on a flower arrangement in the hallway with her back to the door. She turned and looked at Jennifer and then at Margie, but didn't immediately recognize her. "Where's M . . . Margie! Why Honey, I declare! I can't believe my own eyes." She turned toward the living room and yelled, "James, James, come here."

When James stepped to the door, his wife said, "We've got company. Jennifer has brought a new friend home with her."

Amy took Margie's packages and then ordered her to turn around. When she did, James Jacobs let out an admiring whistle. "I kind of dreaded you getting your hair cut, but I do declare it becomes you. Margie, you are a handsome young woman. Ain't she, Amy?"

Amy put her hand out and touched Margie's soft curls. "Ooh, they feel so soft. That ain't a permanent is it?"

Jennifer laughed. "No, that is not a permanent. It curled up as that woman cut it. I wish you'd been there. The stylist was just as amazed as I was and wait til you see all the hair Margie had on her head."

"You didn't bring it home with you, did you?" asked her father.

"She is giving it to The Locks of Love Project. You know that group that makes wigs for cancer patients or anyone who has lost their hair," said Jennifer.

Margie stood looking, but not saying anything. *It seems like they're talking about someone else,* she thought. She clasped her hands together and stiffened her back and turned a smiling face towards all these wonderful people.

"Well now, since we've all seen my mortal sin, I need instructions about how to go to a strange city, get myself a room, and enroll in college".

The words mortal sin had everyone's attention and all eyes turned to look at Margie.

"Mortal sin? What are you talking about Margie?" asked James.

Margie's eyes widened. "My father would not allow me or mom to cut our hair. According to him, the Bible says a woman should not cut her hair, so I always thought it was a mortal sin."

"When I was little I thought all my classmates were headed for that bad place Dad always threatened me with. Of course, when I was eight or nine he started acting instead of threatening and from then on I lived in that bad place he talked so much about." Margie shivered at the memory.

"The Bible doesn't say that, Margie. Your Dad was wrong. The Bible says a woman's hair is her glory and she should wear it long, but it says nothing about it being a mortal sin to cut it," said Amy.

Margie sighed. "I know, Aunt Amy. Dad was wrong about so many things. I think he was mentally unbalanced and was the devil incarnate."

"He must have been, little Margie. He shore must have been," said Uncle James with a sad sigh.

Wanting to change the mood, Jennifer said, "I'm hungry. Let's go eat and talk about what Margie should do next."

Before they left the table, a decision was made that they would all go with Margie to Port Angeles the next morning to set up a bank account.

.

CHAPTER 16

Margie was wary about traveling from Forks to Port Angeles with a check for twenty-five thousand dollars, but she tucked it and the two hundred dollar check securely inside her billfold and held her purse in her lap the entire trip. Once they reached Port Angeles she was anxious to put it in the bank.

Never having been in a bank nor had a bank account, Margie asked Uncle James for help and together they entered the bank. Margie came out feeling much smarter than she had going in. *I'm a woman of means*, she thought giddily as she climbed back into Jennifer's car.

She rode home with her adopted family feeling the best she had since that dreadful night that her mother and her baby died.

With people surrounding her Margie had no place to hide and release the grief and horror that often wanted to overwhelm her, but every evening when the sun went down, the horror of that night crept upon her. At these times, her foremost thought was, w*hy did my baby have to die?* These thoughts led to fitful dreams and nightmares which she hoped did not disturb her adopted family.

Jennifer, whose room was just across the hall did hear, however. After waking several times hearing Margie's moans, Jennifer knew that Margie was having nightmares. *I just know she's grieving over her baby*, thought Jennifer and prayed for some way to help her adopted sister. *Whether she's ready or not I'm going to tell her about her baby*, thought Jennifer.

The right time to talk to Margie just seemed to elude Jennifer. Something seemed to always occur right when she had started to tell her which hindered the telling.

Even with all these other things to worry about, Jennifer didn't forget Margie's desire to change her name. Mary Castle, Jennifer's friend, who worked at the

A Fatal Beginning

courthouse, had gotten the information Margie needed for a name change. The Jacobs family went with her to fill in the forms and bear witness. Margie was told that she could begin using her new name as soon as it was approved by the state office of vital statistics at the capital in Olympia.

"You will also have to apply for a name change on your social security card," said the office clerk, but the post office should be able to help you with that, I think.

Also, since the Jacobs family did not want Margie to be alone in Seattle, Jennifer checked to see if there was a state business college in the area but didn't find one.

Seeing no alternative, Jennifer said, "You're just going to have to go to the University of Washington in Seattle. That's where most of my friends went, but I got my nursing degree at the Port Angeles Hospital. I hate for you to have to go to the university though. I know you won't like living in the dormitory."

"No, I don't like to share bathrooms and having all those strangers around me. Do you suppose I could find a room close to the university?"

"We'll go with you to Seattle to register and help you find a room, can't we James?" asked Aunt Amy,

James grinned. "You'd better ask Jennifer that. She's the one with the car."

"We can go Wednesday. I'm off Wednesday and Thursday, but I have to work this weekend," said Jennifer as she looked at the calendar.

Margie felt so much love as her "adopted family" climbed into the car with her. *This is what I've always missed*, she thought, but knew that her mother had given her everything she could. *She gave her life for me*, thought Margie as her eyes filled with tears. She quickly brushed them away. More than anything Margie feared that if she allowed herself one tear that she may never stop crying and would be sent to a mental hospital.

She enrolled at the university and applied for work-study. She was surprised when she was told she would work in the President's office as a student helper.

Amy Jacobs had a broad grin on her face when told the news. "Just think, you get to attend college and work part-time as well so you get to keep more of the money from the sale of the farm."

The only drawback, at least from the Jacobs' perspective, was that Margie had to live close to the college. As they were walking back to the car, Jennifer suddenly stopped.

"Margie, let's go back and ask President Rice's secretary if she knows of anyone who has rooms to rent. We may as well get as much information as we can."

"Today's my lucky day," said Margie as they came out of the president's office with a name and address along with written directions.

They found the house, which was on Rayburn Street. It was only one block over on the left of the university. Mrs. Duke, the homeowner, was a widow lady who welcomed them politely and showed them what she had to rent. The room was large and airy, had its own bathroom, and was very clean.

"This is a nice quiet and peaceful area," said Mrs. Duke, which sold the Jacobs' and Margie.

"I have really good neighbors and I want it to stay that way, so don't you start bringing no young men in here," said Mrs. Duke, casting a suspicious look at this beautiful young girl named Margie.

"I won't do that. I don't know any young men and I don't want to know any either," said Margie adamantly.

Mrs. Duke looked at her intently. "You may change your mind when all these college boys start asking you out. You're a really pretty girl, and I don't know when I've seen a young girl with a prettier head of hair."

A Fatal Beginning

Instinctively Margie's hand went to her hair and she turned red. "I just got it cut."

"Well I don't know what it looked like before, but it certainly looks nice now. I think it's the color, or perhaps the curls that make it so becoming. I fear you'll get a lot of attention, whether you want it or not," said Mrs. Duke.

"How much is the rent?" asked Mr. Jacobs in an effort to allay Margie's embarrassment.

"It's forty dollars per month and if she wants breakfast in the morning and dinner at night it will be fifty dollars. I may even let her wash her clothes once every two weeks if she's clean."

"That isn't enough, is it?" asked Margie.

"Child, I have to cook anyway and unless you are a terribly big eater, ten dollars is quite enough," said Mrs. Duke with a gentle smile.

So, Margie drove back to Port Angles with the Jacobs family, chattering all the way.

"Do you think I'll be satisfied, Jennifer? The university is a big place. I'm afraid I'll get lost and what if I'm not smart enough to pass my classes?" said Margie fearfully.

She was in the front with Jennifer and now Jennifer slapped her lightly on the arm. "Don't you act afraid, girl. Remember, we know what you've already lived through, or at least some of it. So, if you've survived thus far, nothing will ever get you down. You're tougher than nails."

Margie drew a long breath. "Mommy always said, the worst thing we have to fear is fear itself. So, I guess I need to look fear in the face and walk right on, don't I?"

"Amen!" said two voices from the backseat and Margie looked around and smiled

"My mom was one in a million. I know that nobody could love a child more than she loved me," said Margie and dropped her head into her hands.

Amy Jacobs leaned up and put her hand on Margie's head. "What a beautiful memory you have. Lots of people can't remember their parents as caring. I know I can't. I can't remember anything about mine. I was an orphan."

Margie gasped. "I . . . I'm ashamed, moaning and going on when you've had it worse. Please forgive me."

"You don't need forgiveness. You had a good mother, but a terrible father. I had really good adoptive parents, but I just never felt like I belonged to anybody."

This brought a chuckle from her husband." Well, whether you like it or not Amy Jacobs, you belong to me now."

Amy lay her head on her husband's shoulder. "I didn't mean now, James. I meant as I grew up."

Margie was moved and settled in her room in the city of Seattle, Washington before the month was out. The first week, a student mentor was assigned to her for orientation for which Margie was very grateful. She felt proud of her accomplishments. She was now working, going to school, and getting acquainted with new people in a totally new environment.

She found her classes interesting, but somewhat difficult, especially accounting. She liked her work in the president's office and she also liked his secretary, Jane Lewis.

Margie missed the Jacobs family, especially Jennifer, since she truly felt Jennifer was the best friend she'd ever had. She wanted to call Jennifer but had no access to a phone. She didn't know how to use a pay phone and had very little spare time to learn how, but Jennifer had Mrs. Duke's number and Margie wondered why she didn't call.

Several weeks later she learned that Jennifer had been assigned to a new department and was trying to get adjusted to all new co-workers.

Margie still had not been told about her baby, but that didn't stop her from grieving. When she finally heard from Jennifer she said, "Margie, I have something to tell you, but it has to be sometime when we can really talk."

Margie thought, *I'll bet she has met a man and wants to tell me before she tells anyone else.* Margie smiled at the thought and put it out of her mind since she too was really busy.

Margie later learned that Jennifer had planned to tell her at Christmas, but Margie didn't go to the farm at Christmas. Jane Lewis, the President's secretary, who Margie had gotten to know and like, asked Margie to spend Christmas with her family and she accepted.

Jennifer called her the week before Christmas to invite her to have lunch with her since she had a workshop at the university that week. When they met Jennifer asked her to spend Christmas with them.

"Oh Jenns, I'm so sorry, but when someone's boss extends an invitation and their family insists it is very difficult to refuse," explained Margie.

"Well, I sure wish I'd gotten to you first. You need some of Mom's cooking. Margie, you are as thin as a rail. Aren't you eating?" asked Jennifer.

Margie assured her that she always ate and could prove it by Mrs. Duke. "I'm just having a hard time adjusting to this new and so different life style."

Jennifer had to leave it at that, but told Margie she had to come to the farm at Easter if not before and Margie agreed.

Margie didn't want to tell Jennifer about her dreams of Rick and their baby and also the almost nightly dreams of her mother. Some nights she awoke in a cold sweat, with her body jerking spasmodically. This usually ended with her being violently ill until she vomited. Then she would fall into an exhausted sleep and awaken in the morning so tired that it was hard to move.

Mrs. Duke noticed this tiredness and the dark circles under Margie's eyes as well as how thin she was. "Margie, I think you need to see a doctor, dear. You are getting thinner every day. Let me get you an appointment with Dr. Samuels. He's my doctor and he's very good. You may just need a tonic."

"I don't have any way to pay a doctor, Mrs. Duke. I'll ask the druggist to give me a tonic," promised Margie. The next evening after class she stopped by Walgreens Drug Store.

"What kind of problems are you having, young lady?"

Startled Margie turned in surprise to face a tall young man in a white coat.

"Who are you?" asked Margie turning very red.

"I'm Henry Jenkins, the pharmacist. Mary Taylor, my assistant told me that you wanted a tonic. If you do, I'll need to know what kind of problems you're having." .

"Well, I . . . I haven't been sleeping well and I don't seem to have much appetite. My landlady wanted me to go to the doctor, but I told her I was just tired and would get a tonic of some kind."

Mr. Jenkins smiled. "Why not see a doctor? Tonics are just kind of "pick-me-ups" that are used mostly by elderly people. You don't look elderly to me."

Margie tried to smile but found she was ready to cry instead. She quickly turned away and started to walk toward the door.

"Wait, Miss. Please don't go. I was only trying to make you feel better," said Mr. Jenkins, grasping her shoulder.

Margie whirled around jerking from his grasp. "I can't afford a doctor and besides I'm not really ill."

The pharmacist's hand fell to his side, but he still wanted to help this very attractive young lady. He felt that she really did need to see a doctor. "Are you a student here at the college?"

"Yes, I am. Why?"

"Dr. Samuels treats students for half price, did you know that?"

Margie shook her head. "Are you sure?"

Mr. Jenkins proceeded to explain that some couple had left an endowment for the program and Dr. Samuels had been working with it for several years.

"All you have to do is take your student ID and your class schedule to insure you really are a student. I wish you would do that."

Margie looked up at him and smiled. "Thanks! I'll go see him tomorrow or as soon as I can get an appointment."

"Let me give him a call and he may see you this evening. I know that he has an evening clinic one day each week."

Margie agreed. Mr. Jenkins smiled and turned back toward the pharmacy. "Sit down here and wait. You may be in luck. I really think you need to see the doctor."

So, that day Margie Meadows made her first male friend since Rick Mullett, who had truly been her first boyfriend and her first love. She was then Margie Pierson and she wanted to put that Margie behind her. Her validation had come through and she was now known as Margie Elaine Meadows.

The pharmacist returned. "You're in luck. Dr. Samuels agreed to see you at five-thirty this evening. Do you want to wait here or go to his office? His rooms are two blocks over at 2012 Dunbar Street."

Margie knew it would be dark before five-thirty and she was afraid to be out alone in the city. She hesitated. "I'll need to go to my room before I go. I thank you very much." She turned to the door to stop when Mr. Jenkins said, "Wait!"

"I always leave at five and if you'll tell me where you live I'll come by and take you to see Dr. Samuels. I wouldn't like for you to roam around by yourself in this town."

Mary Taylor coming from the back said, "Sure, let Hank drive you. He's got nothing else to do since he's not married and can just go home and put his feet up."

She laughed, but seeing Margie's wary look, she continued. "He really is a nice man. You'll be safe with him and truly you shouldn't be out after dark by yourself."

Margie had been feeling strange from the time she walked in the door and now she began shaking. She felt really ill and feared she couldn't make it back to her room, but she was also afraid of men. She looked first to Mary and then at Mr. Jenkins.

"Well, if you're sure it wouldn't be too much trouble. I can pay you, but not much" She stood trembling and then grasped the door handle. "I don't feel very well. May I sit down, please?"

Mr. Jenkins made it to her as she slowly sank toward the floor. He lifted her into his arms and carried her across the store to a row of chairs. Mary came back with a wet paper towel and began to wash her face. Margie opened her eyes. She looked around wildly for a moment and then looked at Mary.

"I must have fainted. I'm sorry. I'm all right now. I guess I'd better go to my room."

"I'll take you in my car. You're too ill to walk." He turned to Mary. "Will you stay with her until I pull the car around and then lock up for me?"

Mary agreed and soon Margie was seated in the passenger seat of a new looking black Chevrolet sedan. Mr. Jenkins got into the driver's seat and looked across at Margie. "Where is your room?"

"I'm on Rayburn Street at 1234 with Mrs. Calvin Duke."

"Oh! I know Mrs. Duke. She comes in all the time and she goes to church with Mom and plays bridge with her also. She's a really nice lady. I'm glad you are with her."

Henry Jenkins, known as Hank, got out when they reached the Duke house and helped her up the steps. Margie got out her key, but Hank rang the bell. When Mrs. Duke opened the door and saw Hank, she smiled. "Oh! So, you brought her home. Did you give her a tonic?"

"No. She needs to go to the doctor and I'm taking her at five-thirty. She fainted there in the store, but I'd already called Dr. Samuels."

CHAPTER 17

Mrs. Duke stepped back to allow them to enter and followed them to the living room. "I told her she should go to the doctor, but she says she can't afford it so I sent her to you to get a tonic."

Margie said, "Excuse me, please. I need to go to my room."

When she was out of the room, Hank Jenkins asked, "How long has she lived with you? She is thin as a rail? I hope there's nothing serious wrong with her."

"She's been living here since this semester started. She is a freshman at the university and she works in the President's office as a student aide. I don't know if she eats lunch or not, but she certainly eats very little breakfast or dinner. She has those meals with me."

"She's beautiful, isn't she? I don't even know her name," said Hank, looking at Mrs. Duty expectantly.

"She is Margie Meadows. I don't think she has any parents, but she was living with the Jacobs family from the Port Angeles area when she came here."

"Do you know how old she is? She looks about sixteen, don't you think?"

"I've not asked her, but she must be eighteen to be out of high school," replied Mrs. Duke just as Margie came back into the room.

She was paler than she had been before she left, but she made it to the sofa and sank into it.

"I'm glad you're going to the doctor, Margie. Were you sick again? I mean vomiting. I know you have been because I heard you last night. I'm a light sleeper," said Mrs. Duke.

"I'm sorry I woke you. I tried to be quiet."

Mrs. Duke smiled. "I know you tried, dear, but like I said, I'm a light sleeper. I guess one gets that way when they live alone."

"Miss Meadows, have you eaten anything today? If you haven't perhaps you should eat before we leave for the doctor," said Hank.

Before Margie could answer, Mrs. Duke jumped briskly to her feet. "I don't know what I'm about. Our dinner is ready. In fact, I was getting worried about you and was just ready to call the college when you came."

"Mrs. Duke, please don't be upset with me, but I really can't eat now. I'm too sick. I'll eat when I get back if you can leave me something," said Margie.

Mrs. Duke looked at Hank and shook her head anxiously. "I'll put your supper in the refrigerator and I hope Dr. Samuels can help you. You need some help or you're going to end up seriously ill, Margie."

Hank helped her out to the car and then drove slowly to the doctor's office. He was hungry himself, but he had forgotten about it until he sat waiting for Margie to come out of the doctor's examination room. He sat thinking, *I hope Mrs. Duke has enough food for two.*

When his wife died, Hank Jenkins had told himself that he'd never put himself into a position to be hurt again, but he now found himself drawn to this beautiful, young girl. He knew that Dr. Samuels had a wonderful bedside manner and hoped that he could help her.

Under this elderly man's gentle questions Margie soon relaxed and found herself telling about what led to her being in Seattle. She was crying and like a dam bursting, she told about her life of abuse, including the savage beating that almost killed her, and about losing her mother, and her father's death. She even told him about changing her name, but she didn't tell him about her baby.

When she had finished and washed her face with the cloth Dr. Samuels gave her, she looked up with a timid smile. "I'm sorry, doctor. I guess I've held all that in too long."

Dr. Samuels smiled and patted her shoulder. "Yes, I believe you have. I saw an account of the entire affair in the paper. I don't blame you for wanting to change your name. None of this was your fault, Margie, but I'm sure you'd like to forget that your father ever existed."

Dr. Samuels pressed on her stomach, listened to her heart, lungs, checked her pulse and blood pressure, and checked her ears and eyes. When he finished he pulled out a stool and sat down.

"Margie, I think you may have the beginnings of an ulcer, but I also think you need a nerve tonic so I'm going to give you some medicine to take for your stomach and also this medicine for your nerves. You won't have to stay on it long, I don't think, but I want to see you again in three weeks."

Margie rose from her chair and put out her hand. "Thank you so much, Dr. Samuels. I feel better just by talking to you. How much do I owe you?"

"You were about to explode, young lady. Everybody needs a release valve and I just happened to be it. Since this is your first visit I have to charge ten dollars, but if you don't have that much I can charge it until your next visit." Dr. Samuels turned to put her record in a file drawer and when he turned back Margie held out a ten-dollar bill.

"Thanks so much, Dr. Samuels, I'll tell Mrs. Duke and Mr. Jenkins that their trust is not misplaced," said Margie with a smile.

Dr. Samuels opened the door to the waiting room and found Hank Jenkins leafing through a magazine. "Hank, I thought you had just given her a lift. You must have brought her. Well, I knew you'd hold out for the prettiest girl around."

Hank grinned. "I'd like that, of course, but to be honest Mrs. Duke sent her to me to get a 'tonic.' You know Mrs. Duke thinks that one only needs to see a pharmacist to be cured of all ailments. Anyway, she fainted while in the drug store, so I took her home and then brought her here. She rooms with Mrs. Duke."

Dr. Samuels nodded. "You did right. She needs a tonic for sure, but not one of your concoctions. She's stressed to her limit and probably has an ulcer or will have soon if she doesn't relax."

The two men turned to look at Margie, who had just opened her mouth to complain about the doctor telling her problems to someone else. Dr. Samuels realized what caused the look on her face. "I had to tell him, some things, Miss Meadows, since he is the pharmacist and has to fill your prescriptions."

Margie's shoulders slumped in resignation. Too many people were getting involved in her life and she wasn't used to that, but didn't know what to do about it. "I'm not used to having people know about my business, but I suppose he would have to know."

Hank gave her a quizzical look. "Have you never visited a doctor before?"

Margie didn't answer for a minute thinking, *I won't tell him about the hospital.* Suddenly she blurted out. "I used to work for a doctor and he didn't tell anyone about a patient's problems."

"If given a prescription, the pharmacist would know what was wrong with the patient being treated because he knows medicines," replied Dr. Samuels.

Margie realized that all or most all of Dr. Liebold's patients left his office with a prescription. She turned red and mumbled, "I'm sorry. I know you're right. I had forgotten."

Dr. Samuels patted her shoulder. "That's all right, Miss Meadows. We understand. Now Hank is going to stop by the pharmacy and fill your prescriptions before he takes you on home. Don't go in to work or to classes tomorrow, and, since it is Friday you'll have three days to regain some strength and also give the medicine time to take effect."

"I can't miss tomorrow, Doctor. I'll lose my job and get behind on my classes and I can't afford to do that," said Margie as tears welled up in her eyes.

Hank, who had been watching her, shook his head. "I'll call Jane Lewis. She is your boss, isn't she?"

Margie nodded. "I'll miss my accounting class and I'm having trouble in that class already. I have to go."

"No, you won't. Jane Lewis is a friend of mine and I'll get her to get the assignment and notes and you can have the entire weekend to work on it. In fact, I'm pretty good with accounting, and if you'll let me, I'll help you straighten it out on Friday or Saturday evening. How does that sound?" asked Hank.

"Why would you do that? You don't know me," said Margie.

Hank grinned. "Mrs. Duke assured me that you were a good person and I like to help good people."

Dr. Samuels nodded in satisfaction. "Why don't you accept his offer of help? I can vouch for him. He is also a good person and sometimes 'one-on-one' help gives more insight into how to approach a subject."

Margie nodded. "Well, all right, if it won't be too much bother, I'll accept your offer."

"Good. Now let's go get your medicine and get you back to Mrs. Duke before she calls the police to see if you're all right," said Hank with a laugh. "You don't know it yet, but when Mrs. Duke likes somebody her heart adopts them and she is like an old mother hen."

Soon Margie was back in Hank's car and on her way to her room and to bed. Mrs. Duke heard the car and had the food on the table when they came in with two places set. Hank gladly accepted Mrs. Duke's invitation and took his seat at the table.

A Fatal Beginning

With Hank and Mrs. Duke looking on, Margie swallowed the tablespoon of tonic prescribed by Dr. Samuels after she had eaten a few bites of the food waiting for her. She looked at Mrs. Duke and smiled.

"See, I'm being good. I ate and took my medicine."

"Now, you go on up to bed and don't set your clock. If Hank said he'll take care of things at the college and get your assignment you can go to sleep without a worry in the world," said Mrs. Duke, pointing toward the stairs.

Margie whispered, "Thanks, Mr. Jenkins", and then turned to Mrs. Duke. "Thank you so much and good night."

"You're welcome, dear. You can thank me more by getting better and gaining a little weight. You've had me worried sick."

Hank grinned. "See, didn't I tell you Mrs. Duke liked you."

Margie nodded and smiled. "Thanks and good night, sir." She hurriedly went up the stairs.

Hank and Mrs. Duke stood watching her go and when they heard her door close, turned back to the dining room.

"She must think I'm an old man, Mrs. Duke. She called me sir," said Hank in a disgruntled voice.

Mrs. Duke laughed. "You may seem old to her. Even though she must be eighteen or nineteen since she graduated from high school, she doesn't look more than fourteen."

Hank snorted. "I'm twenty-eight and that's not old."

"Not to me, it isn't, but she may see it different," said Mrs. Duke with a chuckle, but seeing Hank's look of chagrin she sobered. "Aw, she just uses a formal address with people she doesn't know. You don't look old."

Hank raised his eyebrows. "Well, I sure hope not for I want to get to know her. She's beautiful, isn't she?

"Yes, she is and she is also very shy. I think you'd better take it very slowly. She seems surprised or something when anyone even comments about her being even pretty. She must surely have looked in the mirror and if so, she had to see that she was above the average in looks." Mrs. Duke sounded puzzled.

"You can say that again. She has beautiful eyes, flawless skin, and her hair is her crowning glory. She is certainly a lot more than pretty," said Hank.

"Do you want some coffee or something else to eat," asked Mrs. Duke.

"No thanks, dear lady. I have to get back and put in a call to Jane Lewis. If I don't keep my promise I'll have more than old age against me." Hank left with Mrs. Duke laughing.

He didn't wait to fulfill his promise to Margie and before he did anything else he had Jane's approval for Margie to take a day off and also Jane's assurance that she would have all assignments for Margie in her office by one o'clock the next day for Hank to pick up.

Hank Jenkins, the confirmed bachelor, who had avoided entanglements with women for the past eight years, was planning the approach of getting better acquainted with Margie Elaine Meadows.

He picked up the assignments and couldn't wait for five o'clock to roll around. He called Mrs. Duke asking how Margie was and if she would like for him to bring something with him for their dinner.

"No, young man, that girl needs good home-cooked food to get her back on her feet. She has slept a lot, but I hear her moving around, so I'm thinking she is getting ready for your visit," replied Mrs. Duke.

Margie had been in her dressing gown all day, since she had spent the biggest portion asleep either in a chair or on her bed. She looked at the clock on her bedside table. "Three o'clock," she mumbled and realized that she only had two hours before Mr. Jenkins would be there with her assignments.

Thinking it would rouse her from the stupor she had been in all day, she ran a bath. She did feel better and more alert when she stepped from the tub. She toweled herself vigorously and after getting dressed she left her room and slowly made her way down the stairs.

Mrs. Duke met her at the foot of the stairs. "Well, you look better. Do you feel better?"

Margie smiled. "I feel better, but everything seems such an effort. I know I've been a lot of trouble to you, Mrs. Duke, and I'm so sorry."

"No, child, you haven't been any trouble. You have just been too sleepy to eat all day. I had to force you to pick up your spoon and I feared you'd miss your mouth, but you didn't. After you'd eaten about a cup full I just let you quit. I was afraid you'd go to sleep and choke before you swallowed." Mrs. Duke laughed at Margie's startled expression.

"I don't guess that would have happened, but you kept nodding off. I didn't want you sliding to the floor and drag all the food off with the table linen."

Margie grinned. "I do remember you begging me to eat. I think this medicine is too strong for me. Do you reckon it is?"

"You may just need to get it into your system, but we'll ask Hank when he brings your school work," said Mrs. Duke, turning toward the living room.

Margie followed her and took a seat beside the window. She turned toward Mrs. Duke to only see her back retreating through the door. Soon she came back with a coffee pot and two cups on a tray. Placing the tray on the coffee table she poured coffee in one of the cups and turned to Margie. "How much milk do you take in your coffee? I thought this would help to make you more alert."

"I like my coffee creamy, so make it tan instead of black. You may be right about it making me more alert. When I was still at home, I could never drink coffee late in the evening or I'd be awake all night," said Margie.

They were just finishing their coffee when a car pulled into the driveway. Margie started to get up, but Mrs. Duke said, "Just sit still, it's probably Hank and I'll let him in."

A Fatal Beginning

CHAPTER 18

Soon, Mrs. Duke returned. "Come on into the kitchen, Margie. Hank has brought supper. I made some chicken soup that would be better for you, but since he brought fish from Long John's anyway, we may as well eat it. You do like fish, don't you?"

Margie loved fish, and for the first time in a week she felt she wanted to eat. "Yes, I do like fish, so I'll be glad to eat. I've never had food from Long John Silver's before."

Hank was placing the last plate on the table, but turned. "You must not be as old as I thought or you would have eaten at Long John's by now."

Margie dropped her head. "We didn't eat out much when I was at home."

Hank saw the red creep into her face and winced. "I'm sorry. I didn't mean anything by my foolishness. I need to keep my silly thoughts to myself."

Mrs. Duke was busy putting out silverware, but finished and said, "Well, come and taste this. This will be a real treat. I love their fish, their slaw, and their hush puppies."

Soon they were all busy eating and Margie thought she was eating the best food she'd had since her mother was . . . died. She hated thinking about how her mother died. *Mom was trying to take care of me, but she couldn't and I couldn't take care of my baby either*, she thought and then jumped up from the table and ran toward the bathroom.

Her actions startled both Hank and Mrs. Duke. They also jumped to their feet. Hank looked at Mrs. Duke. "Did I say something that made her cry? I'm trying to be so careful."

Mrs. Duke touched his arm and shook her head. "No, no, you didn't say anything that could have hurt anybody." Then in a low murmur, she continued, "I think some thought from her past brought that on. The family that came with her said she'd lost her mother and had been in the hospital before she came here."

"Oh! I guess the medicine is making her relax and begin to remember whatever she has been shutting out," said Hank.

Margie came back into the room, but with her eyes downcast. "I'm sorry, seeing the fish reminded me of how much my mother loved fresh caught fish and I . . . I still miss her so much." Margie blinked her eyes, striving to hold in the threatening tears.

"Don't worry about that, dear. Anyone who has lost a loved one would act the same way. Grief needs to be let out and talked about, but only when one is ready to do so. Don't feel embarrassed if that should happen again. We both understand."

Mrs. Duke looked at Hank and said, "I lost my husband four years ago and Hank lost his wife and his baby several years ago, didn't you, Hank?"

Hank acted embarrassed, but answered, "Yes, and sometimes, after this length of time, I still want to strike out at something. A drunken sot ran a red light and killed them both. He went to prison, but I still don't have my wife and son."

Margie raised her head and looked at Hank. Seeing the sadness in his eyes made her blink back the tears. "I'm so sorry, Mr. Jenkins . . . so sorry."

Hank smiled. "Thanks! We don't understand why these things happen, but the world is full of people suffering from grief. We have to live with it, because we can't change what has happened; it's done and there's no going back. I'm trying to live for today. I really think today is all we really have since we have no control over the future either."

"Yes, we do," blurted Margie. "I'm never going to allow things to happen to me that happened to my mother."

Mrs. Duke had been sitting silently watching the two young people and now spoke up. "Perhaps you can stop the same thing from happening to you, but we really don't know what is around the corner. It's like going to the drugstore and somebody sneaks up behind you and knocks you out. You had no idea that was going to happen and you can't guard against it."

"But, we . . . my mother lived in fear. I'm not going to do that," argued Margie.

"Nobody should have to do that, Margie, uh, is it all right to call you, Margie?" Hank asked.

Margie grinned and her dimples transformed her sad face. "Well, since I'm enjoying the fish so much, I think it will be all right."

They all laughed and the sad mood was broken up. The talk became general until the meal was finished. Mrs. Duke rose to clear the table, but Hank said, "No, you sit down and I'll sack all this up and take it to the dumpster on the way home."

Mrs. Duke raised her eyebrows. "We can't beat that, can we, Margie? Having our supper brought to us and then not having to do the dishes is a double treat."

Margie, who had remained seated, looked up at Hank. "That's the first food I've really enjoyed for over a week. Mrs. Duke has cooked delicious meals, but I just had no desire to eat."

"Dr. Samuels must have helped you, so you keep taking your medicine and by Monday you may be able to get back to school," said Mrs. Duke.

Margie was suddenly alert. "Lessons, where did you put the lessons you brought for me, Mr. Jenkins?"

"Just hold on one minute. If I'm going to help you, you'll have to call me Hank. I'm not a teacher and therefore you have no need to address me as Mister," said Hank.

Margie smiled. "Okay, Hank, where are my lessons?"

"Wait just a second until I get this all gathered up. I'll get your assignments from the car and we can begin," replied Hank.

Mrs. Duke turned toward the living room. "I'll go watch television, but don't let her work too much tonight. I'm afraid she'll get bad again."

Hank stood a moment in thought. "Let's tackle the Accounting first, but we'll only work an hour tonight. Tomorrow, I'll come a little earlier and we can probably work an hour and a half or perhaps two hours, depending on how you are feeling. How does that sound?"

Margie sighed. "That's fine, but I feel so bad causing you so much trouble."

"No trouble, young lady. If I don't use what I've learned I'll get rusty myself. So, you're doing me a favor," said Hank.

Mrs. Duke rolled her eyes and left the kitchen as she said, "I'm going to time you for one hour and then I'm closing you down, finished or not."

Hank laughed. "Hard as nails, aren't you? We'll stop though for I don't wish Margie to feel worse either."

Soon Margie and Hank were engrossed in the intricacies of debits, credits, and balances not once looking at the time. Just as Mrs. Duke put her head around the door, Margie suddenly lifted her eyes from the sheet she was working on.

"Hank, I understand this. I had no idea what I was doing before. I've always added, subtracted, multiplied, or divided and never once thought of a system of income received and money spent in such a way as to record all transactions in a formula, which will insure an accurate balance."

Margie sat back in her chair relaxed. "Isn't that something? It's almost like I was fumbling around in the dark and somebody turned on the light."

Hank sat back also and grinned. "Gee! I'm sure a good teacher, aren't I?"

Margie chuckled. "I guess you must be or perhaps I was so intimidated by all those smart people in my class that I couldn't think straight."

"Does this mean I can't be teacher anymore?" asked Hank.

"Oh no, you don't get off that easy. This was only the beginning of all I'll have to learn, but I promise I won't take up all your time," said Margie smiling happily.

"What about the other subjects? I have the assignments from four classes. I didn't ask what they were," said Hank.

I have business English, typing, short hand, and accounting, but two of those are just practice and I have no typewriter to practice on so I can't do that," explained Margie.

"Yes, you can. I have a typewriter that I can lend you until you finish your classes if you like," offered Hank.

"Don't you use it at the drugstore?" Margie asked.

"No, it's my own that I have at home and don't use much, so it's yours to use. I can bring it over tomorrow if you want me to," said Hank.

Margie arose from the table and yawned. "I would love to borrow it if you really don't use it that much. I'll take good care of it."

"It's done then. I'll be here around four tomorrow evening with a typewriter under my arm, but right now you need to go to bed. You're so sleepy you can't keep your eyes open," said Hank as he too, arose.

Margie smiled sleepily. "It must be the medicine. I'm sure sleepy. Good night Mr. no, I forgot . . ., I'm supposed to say Hank. So, Hank, I'll see you tomorrow."

Hank smiled and watched her leave the room, marveling at the beauty of her shiny, auburn curls, but thought she was still far too thin.

CHAPTER 19

From that evening on for most of the entire semester, Hank came each Friday evening to help Margie with her accounting homework. This resulted in a strong bond of friendship on Margie's part, but much more for Hank.

The first time he asked her to see a movie with him, she, at first, refused, but then thought about how much he had helped her and agreed. To her surprise she enjoyed herself. She felt a brief happiness, similar to the snatches of happiness she had on the farm while playing with her cat, Big Ells.

When they were in the car, ready to go home, she turned a face lit with a broad smile up to Hank and said, "I thank you so-o-o" but she didn't finish. She was pulled into Hank's arms and kissed. She jerked away in alarm.

"Why did you do that? I don't want you to kiss me," said Margie.

Hank looked bewildered. "Am I that ugly? I thought you liked me."

"I do like you. You're the first, uh, man friend I've ever had, but, I . . . I'm just not ready for that yet," said Margie.

"I had only planned to kiss you. What did you think I was going to do, Margie?" asked Hank.

Margie closed her eyes and saw herself and Rick and suddenly felt she would be betraying Rick if she allowed another man to kiss her. She opened her eyes, which were now dimmed by tears.

"I'm sorry, Hank. I guess I'm just not ready for anything except friendship. I didn't mean to leave the impression I wanted anything else."

Seeing her puzzlement, Hank put his hand on her shoulder. "I didn't realize you thought kissing was wrong. It isn't, you know."

He sighed. "Margie. We've been seeing each other since January and now it is April. You seem to enjoy being with me and I assumed you knew how I felt."

"Can't we just be friends, Hank? I do really like you, but I still have things that I have to deal with. I thought I had overcome some of it, but I don't think I have. I don't want to lose your friendship. Could you give me a little more time?

Hank had such a sad look on his face, but he nodded. "Sure. We're still friends, but I don't want to wait forever to know where I stand, Margie. I really care for you, and not just as a friend."

Margie hesitantly put out her hand and touched his arm. "I'm so sorry, Hank. I don't want to disappoint you, and I do really like you, and if you'd rather not see me anymore I'll understand. I wish I didn't have so much doubt or fear about life, but I do."

"May I give you a hug, Margie? I think you need a good hug," said Hank.

Margie nodded and felt such comfort when she was nestled close to his chest. She sighed and looked up at Hank. "This feels so good . . . I feel safe, or something."

Hank laughed. "Okay, little girl, hugs it will be until Easter, but after that, I'm making no promises."

Now, instead of just once each week, she found herself attending a movie, a music concert, or a church event almost every Saturday, but other than an arm around her shoulders or holding her hand, Hank kept his promise.

Margie really liked Hank, but she kept having these almost identical dreams about a baby. In her dreams Margie had lost her baby, but she kept hunting and finally found it. Still dreaming, Margie would be so happy until she found that she could not reach her baby. She always woke with a start and had tears drenching her face.

She again lost her appetite and lost weight, but before Hank or Mrs. Duke began to question her she received a call from her friend, Jennifer Jacobs.

"Margie, when does your Easter break start? Mom and Dad wanted me to call early to make sure you didn't go somewhere else for Easter," said Jennifer. When Margie didn't immediately answer, Jennifer blurted, "You haven't already made other plans have you?"

Margie laughed. "No, I haven't made other plans, Jenns. In fact, I was going to call you to see if I could come early. I'm free the week before Easter and the week after Easter and I didn't want to stay in Seattle."

"Oh great! Our family will be complete this Easter and the extra days will be a good time for us to catch up on old times. We may even allow you to make biscuits," said Jennifer and laughed as they both remembered Mr. Jacobs' love of Margie's biscuits.

"Believe it or not, I get to cook lots of things, now. Mrs. Duke gives me free reign in her kitchen," said Margie.

"I'm glad since we don't want you to get out of practice. Dad wants you home so he can have biscuits and gravy every morning," said Jennifer.

"Okay, I'll come. Come for me the week before Easter on Friday evening? That's when my break begins," said Margie and the call ended. However, as soon as she cradled the receiver Margie realized that Hank had said something about a special surprise he had in store for her at Easter.

Margie hadn't been paying much attention when Hank had mentioned Easter and really didn't know what he was talking about, so she just put it out of her mind. She was eager to get away anyway. *I wish he'd forget all about dating. I don't want to date him, but I would like to keep him as a friend,* she thought.

Margie knew that Hank understood how she felt about the Jacobs family so she forgot all about it and spent the rest of that evening in a pleasant daydream of being with that precious family again.

However, when Hank called on Friday evening, everything seemed to blow-up when she told Hank her plans. Hank's voice was angry and Margie knew he was very upset.

"Going away! But Margie, you can't. We had plans. You know I told you I had a special surprise for you at Easter."

Margie was puzzled. "Hank, I didn't think you were talking about anything serious. Anyway, I promised the Jacobs' I'd spend the next holiday with them, since I spent Christmas with Jane Lewis and her family."

Now, Hank wasn't just upset he was furious. "This proves that you don't care about me and never have."

Hank's voice sounded not only angry but embarrassed. "I've been an old fool, but not anymore." Margie heard the phone slam down and shivered.

With tears streaming down her face she whispered, "Good-bye Hank and thanks for all you've done for me. I wish to God, we'd never met. I didn't mean to hurt you."

CHAPTER 20

Margie would have loved to talk to someone about this problem with Hank, but Mrs. Duke had gone to bed. More than that, nobody would understand unless they knew her story and she didn't want to tell that to anyone. *Jennifer knows I had a baby, but she knows none of the details about that,* she thought as she slowly mounted the stairs to her room.

All night she twisted and turned and fitfully slept until early morning and then fell into a deep sleep. Soon the same dream came again except this time she dreamed she saw her baby and it was a boy.

Margie sat up in bed, wide awake. She stared wildly around until she saw her reflection in the dresser mirror and slumped back on her pillow.

"Oh God, why are these dreams recurring over and over and this time more real than ever before. Did I really see my baby?" Margie whispered this aloud and then mumbled, "But, I'm sure Dad said it was dead. I know I heard him say that."

She lay pondering this until her clock alarmed and she slowly slipped from the bed and went in to take her shower. She knew that Jennifer would be coming for her and she wanted to be ready, but in the back of her mind was, "I should call Hank. I know he is hurt, but I don't know if I love him the way he wants me too."

When she went downstairs, Mrs. Duke was already at the table with breakfast prepared. Margie was surprised. "Mrs. Duke! This is wonderful, but you never get up this early. Couldn't you sleep?"

"No, Margie, I don't usually get up early, but I couldn't sleep, so I decided to make breakfast," said Mrs. Duke as she poured coffee into two cups.

A Fatal Beginning

"I heard you come back in last night, no more than twenty minutes after you went out the door. I thought you were going to a movie. Did you change your mind?"

Margie pulled out a chair and sat down. "We decided not to go, Mrs. Duke." Margie sighed.

"Mrs. Duke, Hank is very angry with me. He doesn't want me to stay with the Jacobs family for Easter. I told him that they had wanted me to spend Christmas with them and I hadn't, but had promised I would visit on my next holiday."

"Yes, I remember you telling me that you had promised. I don't think that should have made him angry. There must be something else, for I know that Hank Jenkins cares a lot for you," said Mrs. Duke.

Margie stirred her food and then looked up. "Mrs. Duke, I think Hank likes me a lot and he had something special planned for Easter. He had mentioned it, about two months ago and at the time I didn't pay any attention and actually forgot about it."

Now Margie swallowed the threatening tears and said, "He says he is tired of waiting for me to grow up and I don't blame him, but I don't want to be a hypocrite either. I can't pretend to love him when I don't know what love is."

Neither of them spoke for several minutes. "You do really like Hank, don't you, Margie?" asked Mrs. Duke.

"Yes, I do. He's been the best man friend, in fact the only man friend I've ever had. I'd love to stay just as we are, but he wants more than that, Mrs. Duke, and he said he was through being a friend," said Margie.

Mrs. Duke nodded her head knowingly. "Margie, Hank is a grown man who was married and I guess he's at the place where he wants a wife. Don't you think you could be a wife to a kind man like Hank?"

Margie shivered. "No, no, Mrs. Duke. I can't be a wife to anybody right now. I really can't." Margie jumped up and ran from the room.

Mrs. Duke sat on at the table until the doorbell chimed and she rose to answer it. Jennifer Jacobs and her father were at the door.

Mrs. Duke opened the door wider and said, "Good Morning! You must have gotten up before daylight. Come on in. I think Margie is packed and ready. I'll call her." She turned to leave the room but stopped. "Find a seat or would you like some coffee? There's plenty left. Margie and I just had breakfast."

The coffee was refused, but seats were taken and Mrs. Duke hurried from the room. She took the stairs slowly as she wondered if she should try to talk to Margie, but before she reached the top she had decided not to intervene. *This is the Lord's business and I shouldn't be meddling. Besides I don't know Margie's story and I wish I did,* she thought as she tapped on Margie's door.

Margie called, "Yes," through the closed door.

"Jennifer and her father are here, Margie. They're waiting in the living room," said Mrs. Duke.

"Tell them I'll be right down. I just need to brush my teeth," replied Margie and Mrs. Duke went back down the stairs, but at a faster pace. She was no longer troubled since she always left her worries with the Lord who always worked things out for the best.

Margie hurriedly finished up and left the room in pristine order, as she always did, and quietly closed the door behind her.

When she stepped into the doorway of the living room Jennifer rose to her feet. "So, you really are going. We were afraid you'd change your mind and I brought Dad so he could tell you how much he wanted some biscuits."

"Biscuits" questioned Mrs. Duke.

"Oh yes. When she stayed with us, she made biscuits for Dad every morning and sometimes at night, especially when we had chicken and gravy," said Jennifer. "Hasn't she made biscuits for you, Mrs. Duke?"

"No, she hasn't. I didn't even know she could make biscuits," replied Mrs. Duke.

"You told me the first day I came here that you didn't get up early and to fix whatever I wanted for breakfast," said Margie.

Mrs. Duke grinned. "So, I did, but I didn't know you could make biscuits. When you come back I may change my schedule."

They all laughed and Uncle James said, "Margie's biscuits will make an early riser out of you. That's for certain."

They talked for a few minutes and then Jennifer said, "I'm sorry to cut this visit short, but I'm on the evening shift at the hospital and need to be on the road."

The two girls hugged Mrs. Duke and Uncle James shook hands before picking up Margie's suitcase and following the two girls out to the car.

When they reached the car, Margie stopped and said, "Jenns, wait a few minutes will you. There's something I want to tell Mrs. Duke."

"Sure, I'll wait, but I really don't have a lot of time to spare. The hospital is under new management and they're being very strict at present." Jennifer opened her door and got into the car.

Margie hurried back into the house calling, "Mrs. Duke, Mrs. Duke."

"What is it, Margie? Did you forget something?" asked Mrs. Duke, coming in from the kitchen.

"Will you please try to explain what I told you to Hank? I don't want to hurt him, Mrs. Duke, but I'm just so mixed up." Margie's voice had a pleading tone and Mrs. Duke could tell she was truly sincere.

"Margie, I'll try to make him understand, but I really think you're going to have to explain your reasons in more detail. I don't really understand and I'm sure Hank doesn't either."

Seeing Margie's crestfallen look, Mrs. Duke gave her a hug and said, "Go on with your friends, Margie. If anything is meant to work out with you and Hank, you'll have to give it time. God works in his time not ours.

A Fatal Beginning

CHAPTER 21

Margie rode along, deep in thought. She hadn't even noticed that Jennifer had a new car until James Jacobs looked back and asked, "How do you like Jen's new car, Margie?"

Margie suddenly realized she hadn't even looked at the car. She had automatically taken the back seat, since Uncle James always rode in the front passenger seat, when he rode with Jennifer. Now, she gave the car her attention.

"It's a station wagon! Geez Jenns, when did you win the lottery?" asked Margie.

Before Jennifer could answer, Uncle James looked back with a big grin on his face. "It's a Ford Escort station wagon, Margie. She got a real good deal too."

He frowned as he continued. "That might be because of that feller who keeps calling her every five minutes. He works at the Ford place in Port Angeles."

Jennifer jerked her head sideways to give her father a scowl. "Dad, I wanted to tell Margie myself."

Uncle James quickly put his hand over his mouth and rolling his eyes looked back at Margie. "Okay! Okay, keep your shirt on. I didn't know it was that important."

When Jennifer turned to look at him again, Uncle James blurted, "Keep your eyes on the road, girl. You don't want to wreck before you tell Margie your secret, do you?"

From the back Margie laughed. "Okay, you two. You can be friends again. I know Jennifer has a new car and I know someone is interested in her, but I also know Uncle James is a wee bit envious as well as dreading the thought of losing his daughter to some man. Am I right?"

At first there was silence from the front seat then Jennifer spoke up. "How come you're so smart? I had never thought about this in that light, but I think you may be right."

"Of course, she's right. This is the first time I've seen my Jennifer act serious about any man except her good old dad, and I, well it makes me sad, I guess," said Uncle James.

Jennifer grinned as she reached over and patted his arm. "Aw, come on now, Dad. You know you just want to keep me around to chauffer you in my new car."

Uncle James chuckled. "Well, since I've never had a new car in my life I do feel right proud to be riding all over the country with a 'chauffer' or whatever you call it."

They rode on for several miles talking about the car, but without Margie really finding out too much about Alexander Stafford, the Ford salesman, who liked Jennifer.

Finally, the talk subsided and once again Margie became involved in her problem of how she really felt about Hank Jenkins. *Does feeling comfortable around someone mean the same as love,* she thought, but had no answer.

They passed a farm house settled among trees on the side of the road and a picture of her mother working at the many flowers that she had tended so lovingly floated through her mind. *Mommy always prayed when she was troubled. It didn't help her when Dad was beating on us, but I still heard her mumbling*, thought Margie as tears welled up in her eyes. Then a thought came unbidden into the forefront of her mind. *Margie, I was praying for you and you survived.* Margie gaped in surprise.

Mommy just sent me a message, she thought and trembled since the voice she'd heard in her mind was definitely her mother's.

The rest of the way Margie silently begged the Lord to give her some sign as to whether she should marry Hank Jenkins or not. He hadn't asked her yet, but she felt sure that was his intent.

She was relieved when Jennifer pulled into the parking spot before the Jacobs' farmhouse. From then on until bed time she didn't have a moment alone to think, pray, or anything else. By the time she went to bed she was too tired to even try to pray, but she slept the best she had in several nights. She awoke, wishing she had dreamed of an answer to her problem, but shook her head in doubt that the Lord even heard prayers.

Before she started to get up Jennifer tapped on the door then opened it and walked in. "Good, you're awake. I can't wait to tell you. Margie, I'm in love."

Margie grinned. "Well, duh. I surmised as much from what Uncle James said, but now tell me how all this happened."

Jennifer sat on the bed and tucked her feet under her before telling of meeting this wonderful man when she went car shopping. "I was waiting for a salesman when Alex came around the corner and looked at me. When he said Miss Jacobs, I fell in love. Wait until you meet him and hear him speak. He has this sexy, gravelly voice, and Oh, Margie, he is so good looking."

"Is that all love is? I mean, aren't there lots of men that could fit that description?" asked Margie.

"No, it isn't like that. We both felt the same when we first saw each other. It was like we'd always known each other, but had been separated, and had now found each other again," explained Jennifer.

Margie sat up and swung her feet over the side of the bed. She gave Jennifer a serious look. "But how do you know that is love? Jenms, what is love?"

Jennifer took on a dreamy-eyed look. "When you know you want to spend the rest of your life with that person and every minute seems like hours when you're away from them."

Margie grinned, thinking, *There's my sign. Thank you, Lord.* Then she said, "Well, I'm not in love, that's for certain, but I hope whatever you have lasts for life. You've got it bad, Little Sis."

Jennifer arose from the bed and stretched. "I'll have to go to work in another hour, but I'll be home at five today. I guess you'll end up cooking or, at least, making a huge pan of biscuits."

Margie turned toward the bathroom, but stopped and turned. "Jenns, can we get away from everybody, for a while, this evening? There's something I need to talk over with you. I've been having dreams about my baby and they are so real that sometimes, I think I'm losing my mind."

Jennifer caught her breath. "Dreams! What kind of dreams?"

Margie crimped her lips together. "The last one I had was this week and I awoke crying. In the dream I thought my baby was alive and I saw him."

"Him? How did you know it was a boy?" asked Jennifer.

In a tear-choked voice, Margie said, "I didn't until I saw him in that dream."

Jennifer grabbed Margie's arm and pulled her toward the bed. They both sat and then Jennifer grabbed Margie's shoulders. "Margie, I want a promise from you that you will never tell what I'm about to tell you. If you tell, it can cause me a lot of trouble and perhaps trouble for others as well. Do you promise?"

Margie saw that Jennifer was dead serious and yet she felt that whatever Jennifer had to tell involved herself. She sat for a minute and then realized she didn't want to ever do anything to cause Jennifer a problem. She nodded her head. "Okay, Jenns. I promise never to tell. What is it?"

CHAPTER 22

Jennifer reached over and clasped both of Margie's hands. "I'm afraid of your reaction, but I know you haven't been well and when Mrs. Duke called me . . . "

Margie interrupted. "Mrs. Duke called you? When?"

"About two weeks ago," said Jennifer. "She said you had stopped eating and had lost weight. She also said you hadn't been sleeping for she heard you moaning in the night. Now you tell me you dreamed of your baby, and I know I can't wait any longer."

Margie's browed furrowed. "What are you . . . Jenns, do you know something about my baby?"

Jennifer was very pale and through trembling lips she whispered, "Margie, . . . your baby didn't die."

Margie sat in wide-eyed shock with wild staring eyes. Her mouth hung open and her eyes were large in her pale face. She sat this way so long that Jennifer said, "Margie, Margie! Oh God, this is what I was afraid would happen."

Jennifer jumped to her feet and started for the door, but Margie stopped her. "No, don't leave me." Jennifer turned to see trembling hands reaching for her and Margie was as pale as a corpse

Jennifer sat down and put her arms around Margie whose body was shaking like a leaf."Margie, you have to be strong. Take a few slow, deep breaths. I can't tell you anything else until you are in a better shape."

Margie obeyed and finally seemed to be calmer, but Jennifer still held her and rocked to and fro as her own mother had comforted her when she was a child. After one last long breath Margie pushed back from Jennifer and clasped her hands in her lap.

"Oh Jenns. I've thought all this time my baby was dead. When I first became aware there in the hospital I didn't ask about my baby because I thought my dad told me it was dead." Margie shivered convulsively.

"I guess it was a nightmare, but my Dad came into my room in the hospital. I remember him standing over me and whispering into my ear. He told me my mother was dead and so was my baby, but he called it a bastard," Margie broke into soft sobs again and once again Jennifer gathered her into her arms.

"Jenns, I know the doctors said I was in a coma, but I can still hear that evil, hateful voice. It was so real that I smelt his sour breath as he bent over me. I was terrified, but I couldn't get away. I thought some noise scared him and he left, but I didn't want to wake up and see him again."

Jennifer was crying now. "Oh, Margie how awful! He must have been a mad man. He had to have been for you to have such a vivid nightmare, if that's what it was."

Margie became calmer. "It seemed so real, but later when nobody mentioned my baby I thought it had died and I just accepted it, but all these months I've kept having these dreams about my baby and now you say that he's alive."

Margie suddenly jumped to her feet. "Is this real? Is my baby alive? How do you know, Jenns?" Margie began rubbing her arms, clasping and unclasping her hands.

"Oh my God! My baby didn't die. My baby is alive. Oh God, thank you, thank you," Margie kept repeating.

Jennifer jumped to her feet. "Stop it, Margie. If you're going to carry on like this you'll end up in the hospital and I'll get in trouble," said Jennifer in an effort to calm her. That seemed to have an effect and Margie slumped to the bed again.

"Margie, your Dad signed the adoption papers and was paid three hundred dollars for your baby when he was a week old."

"Why wasn't I told?" It was my baby. He had no right to do that and the hospital had no right to do that," stormed Margie who now had more tears streaming down her cheeks.

Jennifer was crying again as well, but still wanted to comfort Margie. She put out her hand and clasped Margie's arm. "Margie, you were in a coma and not expected to live. A young couple had registered with the hospital asking to be told of the first newborn that became available."

With trembling lips Jennifer continued, "I wasn't there, but I was told that your baby was premature and might not live and your dad said you had been raped and didn't want the baby. He said you wanted to do away with the baby, but that he and your mother wouldn't let you. He signed the release and took the money, so I guess the hospital thought what he said was true."

Margie started shaking and Jennifer again put her arm around her. "Margie, the young couple was told that the baby might not live but they still gave your dad the three hundred dollars. They wanted a baby so badly that they were willing to take the chance. I saw the adoption paper where your dad signed it with an X."

With an X! Then daddy couldn't read and write, thought Margie as she remembered him not wanting to read the newspaper about the job offers. He'd said his eyes were bad. Margie shook her head, wondering why she'd even remember anything about her dad.

Jennifer, thinking that Margie was still in shock, patted Margie's shoulder. "You do know why I made you promise not to tell, don't you?"

Margie let out a slow sigh. "Yes, and I'll keep my promise, but why didn't you tell me about my baby before? I wish I knew who adopted him and where he lives."

"That's just it, Margie. I do know most of that, but I didn't know whether he was still alive or not, nor where he lived until several weeks ago," said Jennifer.

A Fatal Beginning

Margie's eyes lit up and she grabbed Jennifer in a big hug. "Jenns, have you seen him?"

"No, I haven't seen him, but I knew when he was first adopted that a family by the name of Larkin had adopted him. After you and I became friends, I started trying to get more information. It wasn't until just before Christmas that I overheard the doctor and a nurse talking about the family who adopted Elaine Archer's baby," said Jennifer.

"What were they saying?" Margie said in a voice full of dread.

Jennifer grinned. "Well, according to what I heard, he is a fine little boy, who is six months old and much loved by his adoptive parents."

"Do you know where they live?" asked Margie with a catch in her voice.

"Margie, you promised," said Jennifer.

"Oh, I'm not going to go up and knock on the door. I'll keep my promise, but Jenns, don't you see? If I know where he lives, I might have a chance to at least get a glimpse of him."

"No, don't even go near him, Margie. Somebody will notice you watching him and get suspicious."

"Jenns, I promise you that I won't go every day and when I do, I'll wear dark glasses on some days and not on other days. I'll not go often, but Jenns, I just have to see him. Don't you realize that this is almost like the story of Lazarus who Jesus raised from the dead. I thought my baby had died and now he's alive. Oh Jenns, I'll never doubt Jesus again," said Margie as she dropped to her knees beside the bed and wept as she prayed, "Please forgive me, Jesus. Please, please."

Jennifer dropped to her knees beside Margie and she too prayed, but silently. Her prayer was that she hadn't done the wrong thing in telling Margie.

Both girls finally rose to their feet again; Jennifer with a worried look and Margie with the most glorious smile Jennifer had ever seen on anyone. Looking at Margie, she thought, *to bring that much joy to another can't be wrong.*

They hugged each other and turned to leave the room, but Margie stopped at the door. "Jenns, if I promise you that I will only drive by the house occasionally, in a taxi, or perhaps attend the church they go to and sit in the back just to get a glimpse of him, will you show me where they live?"

Jennifer nodded. "All right, I will, Margie, but always remember that if this is found out you will have destroyed my chances of ever having a nursing job again and I may even go to jail."

"I promise that I'll never do anything to get you in trouble, Jenns and now I think we'd better get downstairs before someone comes looking for us," said Margie.

Jennifer looked at her watch. "Yeah, and I'm going to be late for work if I don't get a move on."

Together they went trooping down the stairs to be met by Aunt Amy at the foot of the stairs. "Jennifer, I thought you were going to be late for work. I was just starting up to remind you. What on earth were you girls doing?"

Margie, with glowing face, smiled. "She's been telling me some of the most glorious news I've ever heard." Jennifer gasped and gave Margie a hard look.

Margie winked and said, "Don't look at me like that, Jenns. I think it's great that you've found the man of your dreams and I'll get to be your bridesmaid. Did you know your daughter is practically engaged?

Margie gasped when she saw the amazed look on Aunt Amy' face and the disgruntled look on Jennifer's. "Oh, my gosh! Don't look so serious, I was only joking. She didn't tell me anything like that, Aunt Amy. I made that all up. Actually, we were talking about some awful dreams I've been having, and I thought Jenns may be able to understand why, since she's a nurse."

Amy smiled in relief. "You scamp. You had me startled. Jennifer better not keep something like that a secret from me."

Amy turned to Jennifer. "Will you have time to eat? I hate for you to go to work without eating breakfast and don't you be driving too fast either."

Jennifer hugged her mother. "Nope, gotta run, but I'll eat at the hospital." She darted out the door and soon they heard her car go down the drive.

Amy looked at Margie and turned to the kitchen. "I guess we'd better fix your uncle some breakfast or we'll hear from him."

CHAPTER 23

Margie started to make biscuits for James while Amy cooked apples and fried eggs, but her mind wasn't really on her cooking. Instead she stood thinking. *Is he black-headed like Rick? Is he chubby? Does he cry a lot?* Her mind ran around and around like a kaleidoscope of color.

The kitchen door opened and James came in with his basket of eggs and placed it on the table. Aunt Amy stopped stirring apples and stood glaring in unbelief.

"James Jacobs, what are you about? Don't put that nasty basket down on my eating table. We're trying to get breakfast ready and now I'll have to scrub the table." Amy reached out to pick up the basket.

"Just look at the mess you've made," she scolded as she grabbed a dishcloth from the sink of soapy water and turned to scrub the table free of dirt and straw.

James grabbed the basket. "Jest you hold on a minute. I've got something I want you to see." From the top of the heap of eggs he selected a huge egg and held it in his open palm.

"I got that from 'neath that big Rhode Island Red hen we got from Jerry Slater last fall, but that biddy didn't lay no egg this size. I believe it's a goose egg, but if it is, how did it get in her nest?"

Both Margie and Amy stood staring at the oversized egg with puzzled expressions. Then Margie grinned, "Maybe the Easter Bunny brought it."

Amy chuckled. "Well tomorrow is Easter Sunday, so I'll bet Mr. Bunny came early to leave you his prize egg."

James' eyes took on a gimlet look. "Yeah, and I'll bet Jerry Slater wore his rabbit suit when he left it too. That'd be just like him, to sneak over here and try to fool me so he'll have some big tale to tell down at the store."

A Fatal Beginning

James placed the basket on the floor beside the sink. He rose back to standing position and said, "If that little leprechaun shows up over here don't neither one of you mention that egg. I'm going to 'figger' some way to turn this around on him."

"Well, while you're doing your figuring you can wash those eggs and put them in this clean basket," said Amy as she handed her husband a clean, lined basket.

Soon the three of them were busy, Amy frying sausage and eggs, Margie placing her biscuits in the oven, and James carefully washing each egg as he hummed 'Here Comes Peter Cottontail.'

James finished first, and now softly whistling Peter Cottontail, he carried the basket of eggs to the scullery and placed them in the cooler.

When he stepped back into the kitchen he sniffed in appreciation. Then taking his usual seat at the head of the table he said, "You must love us a lot Margie. Those biscuits were made with love. Smelling like that, they have to be."

Margie, whose mind was still on her baby, stirred the gravy she had decided to make while the biscuits baked, and made no comment. James gave her a curious look.

"Hey, Margie, snap out of it. I'm bragging on your biscuits and you didn't even hear me. You should listen when I talk. I'm important. I won the prize Easter egg. You said so yourself."

On hearing her name, Margie jerked around with a spoon dripping gravy in her hand. "What? Did I do something wrong? Did I mess up the biscuits?"

James shook his head. "Nope you didn't mess up the biscuits, but you're messin' up the floor with that gravy spoon. I don't know what you are dreaming about? You didn't hear me praising these biscuits and wondering if you loved us so much that it made your biscuits better."

Margie looked at her hand with the spoon and then down at the floor and gasped in surprise. "Oh my God! What a mess." She turned red and immediately put the spoon back in the pan of gravy before grabbing paper towels to clean up the now gravy-dotted floor.

"I'm so sorry. I do have something on my mind, but it doesn't keep me from loving you and all the Jacobs family. If I could season my biscuits with love, I'd do that too and wouldn't drop gravy all over the floor either."

When James let out a peal of laughter and Amy smiled as well, Margie grinned also. "My mother always told me to keep my mind on the job at hand. I guess I forgot."

Amy, still seated at the table, sat looking at Margie. "Margie, I don't mean to pry, but is there any way I can help with whatever is bothering you?"

Margie looked at this wonderful woman, who she called Aunt Amy and wished she could talk to her, but it was all too new and raw. Besides that, she had promised Jennifer that she would never tell anyone.

"Thanks, Aunt Amy. I know you would help me if you could, but this will take time and right now the best thing you can do for me is pray."

"I'll certainly do that, dear, and so will your uncle James. We both know that the Lord works out things for the best, even though we sometimes think he is slow in the working." Amy looked at her husband who nodded and rose from the table.

After breakfast was over both women cleared the table and started on the dishes, but Amy suddenly stopped. . "Margie, I'll finish these if you'll walk down to the mail box. I'm expecting a package from Sears and Roebuck."

Margie dried her hands and went out the kitchen door and started around the side of the house, but stopped stock still and stood staring as two men walked up the path toward the front door.

A Fatal Beginning

The man in front was a small, wiry-looking man with bright red hair. *The leprechaun,* thought Margie, but when the other one came into view she gasped and turned pale. *Rick!* she thought, but sighed as he came closer. His hair was dark, but not black and curly like Rick's and when he said hello to James his voice had a low gravelly sound, which was nothing like Rick's youthful gentle voice.

Margie stood still, hidden from their view, until they went into the house. She then continued her journey to the mailbox.

Sure enough, Amy had a package from Sears and Roebuck and Margie had quite a tug getting it out of the mailbox. *It must be clothing or something soft,* she thought since any hard material would have made it impossible to get it into the mailbox.

She reached the house just as she heard the kitchen door slam and male voices, talking in laughing banter, coming from the chicken lot and woodshed direction.

I don't think Uncle James has had time to set up his own 'goose egg' thought Margie as she went up the steps onto the front porch.

She met Amy coming from the kitchen. "Don't be surprised if you hear loud laughter and some men coming back to the house in a few minutes. If your uncle has had time, he's set a trap or something for Jerry Slater."

Amy took the package and laid it on the kitchen table just as Skip, the nearly blind Collie dog began barking furiously. Then, sure enough, running feet and cursing was heard. They ran to the window and saw two men running through the yard with their arms flailing the air trying to keep bees away from their arms and heads with Skip nipping at their hills. Margie didn't hear a gravelly voice this time, and she thought *maybe one didn't curse in a gravelly voice.*

James came through the kitchen door. "Did you see them two men running through the yard? I've never seen the beat in my whole life."

Amy had been laughing too, but suddenly stopped. "James, what if one of them is allergic to bee stings?"

"I hope they ain't, but if they are I didn't tell them to get so close to Skip nor the bee hives as they went to see my Easter Eggs," said James with a broad smile.

"Why James, Skip couldn't see them well enough to bite. Jerry Slater knows how blind he is," said Aunt Amy.

James let out another peal of laughter. "Yeah, Jerry knows Skip's purt near blind, but if anybody gets too close to him he's ready to attack. He run smack into that new beehive and turned it over. I guess the bees thought Jerry Slater had upset their home."

"Who was that other man? I've not seen him around here before, have you?" asked Amy.

"Nope, I ain't see him before, and to tell the truth I didn't think to ask either. I had me a pay-back trick figgered out to play on Jerry, but he never even got to the chicken house," said James, still laughing.

"Well, I hope they aren't allergic to bee stings or we'll never hear the last of it. Jerry Slater likes to always be the winner and you know it," said Amy.

A Fatal Beginning

CHAPTER 24

Margie thought about the man who looked like Rick, and wondered who he was. She finally decided that he must be related to the Slaters and forgot all about him as she hurried to help Aunt Amy boil and color eggs for the children's egg hunt at church the following day. The two women spent the entire day preparing for the events on Easter Sunday.

Wanting to be there for Jennifer's reaction to the cake she had spent so much time making, Margie didn't look at the time until she was ready to get in the shower. Taking a very quick shower she hurriedly dried off, but still did not hear Jennifer's car as she arrived home from work.

Jennifer pulled into her usual parking place beside the house and opened the door to be assailed by delicious smells wafting from the open kitchen windows. She crossed the lawn in a trot, sniffing all the way. As she stepped through the kitchen door the wonderful smell of strawberries and cake caused her to stop, before following the smell on into the kitchen. There in the middle of the table stood the most beautiful cake Jennifer had ever seen.

"Oh my God! Where did this cake come from? It's beautiful," breathed Jennifer as she leaned close to get a good whiff.

"Don't you dare touch that cake, Jennifer Jacobs," said her mother, coming through the hall into the kitchen. That's going to be the center piece of the table in the church basement. We're preparing an Easter dinner for all the soldiers and veterans in this area.

"Evelyn Slater called and asked if we knew of anyone who she could get to make a special cake for this event and Margie volunteered," explained Amy. At Jennifer's open-mouthed gaze she continued, "Evelyn and I were just as surprised as you are. We both knew that

Margie could cook, but had no idea she could bake things like this," said Amy, beaming in appreciation.

The two women stood back admiring this baking wonder. "It's so pretty. I don't think I could cut it," said Jennifer. "Is the cake white or chocolate?"

Margie walked into the room at that moment. "It's all white, but there will be a choice of vanilla or chocolate ice cream to go with it."

"It did turn out good, didn't it? I was scared to death it would sag in the middle or be crumbly; well you know how it is with baking."

"No, I don't know about that kind of baking. I just know about the ordinary stuff," said Jennifer looking at Margie. "How did you learn to bake and cook the way you do? Did you learn it in school?"

"No, I took all business classes in school, but Mom let me help her from the time I could stand on a chair and stir things in a bowl."

Margie's eyes dimmed with tears as she said, "Mom was a really good cook and I never understood how she could make such good meals with the meager supplies she was allowed to buy. Mom could make a feast out of salmon, caught fresh from the river."

Jennifer reached over and hugged Margie. "I'm glad you have such good memories of your mother. She had to be a wonderful person."

Margie swiped her hand across her eyes and smiled. "She was wonderful, but she shouldn't have stayed with Dad. I lay awake at night and wonder why she stayed with him. I wish she hadn't."

James Jacobs came through the door and stopped. Like Jennifer, his eyes became locked on that cake, before he turned to his wife. "I'll bet you spent all my egg money to buy that. You know we can't afford fancy fixin's like that."

Amy chuckled. "Take a good look at it, James. Ain't it pretty? It only cost twenty-five dollars."

"Twenty-five dollars! I'll bet it cost more than that. Where did you get it anyway?"

Jennifer grinned. "It came from the M&M Bakery, and Dad, it's worth every cent you paid for it."

James Jacobs frowned. "M&M Bakery . . . There ain't no such place in our town."

Jennifer grinned mischievously. "Did I say bakery? Well I meant baker for our Margie is the baker . . . Margie Meadows, the baker."

"Good Lord, Margie, why are you wasting your time going to college when you can bake like that. Why, I ain't never seen a cake that pretty, even in a bakery," said James, giving Margie a serious look.

Margie laughed. "Uncle James, stop kidding and tell me what you really think."

"What I really think! . . . Just what I said. You could make a fortune and name your own price. Your biscuits and gravy can't be beat, but they ain't purty like this cake." He stood there as if bereft of speech.

The recently installed phone's shrill ring startled them all. "Now who could that be? I ain't never told them down at the store that we have a telephone."

Jennifer, who was closest to the phone, picked up the receiver. "Hello! Oh Evelyn, how are you?"

She stood listening. "Yes, we do plan to come. No, we didn't know it was a surprise, or at least I didn't." Jennifer turned to her mother.

"Mom, did you know this event for the vets was to be a surprise?" Amy nodded and pointed to the cake.

Jennifer handed the phone to her mother. "Evelyn wants to talk to you."

The two girls carefully moved the cake to a card table they had put up in a corner of the kitchen. "We'll never get this in the car. We'll have to make a tent to cover it." said Jennifer.

"I have a box for it, but let's wait until supper is over so we'll have plenty of room to work," said Margie.

CHAPTER 25

The telephone was on the wall leading into the living room, and Amy was still engrossed in conversation, so Margie and Jennifer worked on supper from the other end of the kitchen where the sink, stove, and cabinets were.

Before Amy ended the call, the table was covered with bowls of green beans, corn, creamed potatoes, and beef tips smothered in rich brown gravy, as well as dishes of sliced cucumbers, onions, and green peppers. Just as Amy hung up the phone, Margie brought a serving plate holding squares of thick corn bread to the table and Jennifer followed with a tub of butter and a small pitcher of honey.

James stuck his head around the edge of the door and sniffed. "Smells good in here so I'm guessing supper is ready."

He grabbed Aunt Amy by the arm. "May I escort you to the table, Ma'am?" and almost dragging his wife, he strutted across the room, jerked out a chair, and plopped Aunt Amy into it, none too gently.

He turned to look at the girls. "You fellers didn't think I had good manners, did you? Well, I do and I just proved it," he said with a satisfied smirk.

Margie and Jennifer broke out laughing when Aunt Amy said, "You call that manners, James Jacobs. You bed down your goats better than that. You shoved me into this chair so fast and hard that it nigh jarred my teeth out."

Mr. Jacobs grinned. "Oh well, sorry about that, but if you didn't have store-bought teeth they wouldn't jar around. Mine don't."

Aunt Amy glared at him. "Don't start on that again. I know you had a proper up-bringin', you had a tooth brush too and a mama to see that you brushed your teeth."

The three observers knew that Aunt Amy was upset, but they also heard the longing in her voice when she mentioned his having a mama. James Jacobs' face fell and he put his hand on her shoulder. "Amy, I'm sorry. I get carried away with my foolishness, but I never meant to hurt you."

Amy smiled and put her hand over her husband's as it lay on her shoulder. "It's all right, James. I know you meant no hurt, but some hurts go so deep that I don't think one ever truly gets over them."

Behind her Margie gasped and then hurriedly left the room.

James Jacobs' eyes followed her flight. "That girl is carrying around a deep hurt and if she don't get rid of it she'll have a breakdown."

Amy Jacobs nodded. "I always felt that nobody had a deeper hurt than my own, but I feel that Margie's is deeper. Something needs to be done, but I don't know what."

Jennifer's eyes had followed Margie's flight and with a worried frown she said, "I'll go see if I can talk to her. Go ahead and start your suppers."

When Jennifer reached the top of the stairs she heard Margie's muffled sobs. She quietly pushed the door open and knelt beside of Margie at the bed side. "Margie, would you like to drive by the Larkin home tomorrow?"

Margie turned startled eyes toward Jennifer. "I thought you didn't know where they lived?"

Jennifer smiled. "I knew what area they lived in, but I'd never really seen the house and I still haven't, but I know it is number 23 McKinley Drive in Sequim. That shouldn't be too hard to find, but you'll have to help me look as I drive."

Margie got to her feet and so did Jennifer and then Margie's put her hands on each side of Jennifer's face. "Jenns, you're the best sister anybody could ever have."

Jennifer grinned. "I know it and if you'll wash your face I'll go with you to eat that delicious supper waiting for us."

When they again entered the kitchen, Amy Jacobs thought she had never seen two prettier or happier looking girls. *I don't know what Jennifer said, but it sure changed a weeping girl to a smiling one.*

This happy attitude lasted through supper and all the clean-up after supper and when Amy went to bed she still heard muted laughter coming from Margie's bedroom.

When Amy walked into the kitchen the next morning she found a huge breakfast waiting to be put on the table. She stood looking in amazement as Margie came through the door with a basket of eggs.

"Margie, you're going to spoil me if you keep this up. How long have you been up?"

Margie turned a smiling face toward her. "I've been up long enough to drink two cups of coffee and cook breakfast."

Just then James came through the door followed by Jennifer. Both spoke at the same time. "What's that wonderful smell?"

"I made French cinnamon toast with eggs and sausage. Sorry, Uncle James, but I didn't make biscuits this morning. I hope you won't be too upset."

"Well, since it all smells so good, I reckon I could forgive you this once," replied Uncle James.

Soon everybody had their plates filled and a cup of coffee beside each plate. Margie looked around the table. "Did I leave anything out?"

Jennifer giggled. "You left you out. Where's your plate?

Margie shook her head. "I don't believe I can eat this morning. I'm too excited."

"Too excited to eat! All the veterans in the world ain't that important." James motioned for Margie to take her seat at the table.

"You set yourself down there, my girl. You're not leaving this house 'til you've eat your breakfast." James

A Fatal Beginning

jumped to his feet and got a plate, napkin, and silverware and placed it at Margie's usual seat. "Now, you eat and don't you leave this table 'til you do."

Jennifer and her mother broke into gales of laughter at the surprised look on Margie's face. James looked at them both and grinned.

"Aw shucks! I had her convinced, but you two had to ruin it. I do want you to eat, Margie."

Margie grinned. "Okay, Uncle James, I'll eat a little, but I won't promise it will stay down."

"Stay down! Course it will. Grub like that is fit for a king. You just relax and take your time. You'll fill better with your stomach full," encouraged Uncle James.

Margie smiled as she took her first bite and to her surprise it not only stayed down, she enjoyed it. *I just need to relax, but how can I when I get to see where my baby lives this morning,* she thought.

The rest of the family had eaten, but slanted glances in Margie's direction fearing she would have to leave the table. When she seemed to be enjoying her food, James said, "See there! I told you it was good. You just need to relax more, Margie."

Margie looked at these kind, caring, people and smiled widely. "I think eating with a family that loves you gives everything a better taste."

James Jacobs' kind heart almost had him in tears, but he swallowed before saying, "Well, we do love you, and it ain't got nothing to do with your biscuits."

Sensing that he was trying to hide his emotions Margie grinned and raised her eyebrows. "Oh great! No more biscuits on this visit."

James' eyes blared. "Here now. We don't want to be rash in our actions. It won't hurt to maybe make biscuits at least once more."

CHAPTER 26

Using the excuse that they needed some personal items, Jennifer told her mother that she and Margie were going to town, but would be back by eleven o'clock to help take the food to the church basement.

"No, don't stay away that long. We may have to make two trips to the church since there are four of us to ride in the car as well as all this food," said Mrs. Jacobs.

"Okay, Mom. Don't fret. We'll try to get back by ten-thirty. I know how nervous you get if everything isn't just right. Besides, we may need to make one trip just for Margie's cake," said Jennifer as she and Margie walked to the car.

Jennifer drove at a steady sixty miles an hour since their section of Highway 101 was almost empty of traffic at that time on Sunday mornings. As they entered the town of Sequim, Jennifer slowed down and both girls looked at every street sign in an effort to find 23 McKinley Drive. After about twenty minutes Jennifer pulled into a gas station and bought gas, which she really didn't need, in order to get information from the attendant.

Jennifer got out of the car while her tank was being filled. "We're looking for 23 McKinley Drive. Do you know in what direction we need to go?"

"That's the Larkin place. Are you kin to them?" asked the attendant.

"No, but we need to see them. Can you give us directions, please?" Jennifer asked of the young attendant.

He pointed with his left arm as he pumped gas with his right arm. "This is Vermillion Street so go through three stop signs and turn right onto McKinley Drive. Their place is the fourth on the right, a white house with green shingles on the roof and green shutters at the windows."

Jennifer thanked him and went inside to pay. The attendant looked through the open window and smiled at

A Fatal Beginning

Margie. "You're about the prettiest girl I've ever seen. Do you live around here?"

"No sir, I don't," said Margie from a very red face.

"I wish you did," he said with a smile and started to say something else, but stopped when Jennifer returned. She wondered at the big smile pasted on his face until she opened the car door and saw Margie's red face.

"What's happened? Your face is as red as a beet. Did that jerk say something to you?" Jennifer got in and Margie muttered, "Let's go."

Jennifer pulled out following the attendant's directions. "Did he ask you out, Margie?"

"No, but I think he would have. He wanted to know if I lived around here and he said he wished I did," said Margie.

Jennifer laughed. "I told you what would happen when you got that haircut. Now, I guess you believe me."

Suddenly she slowed. "Here's McKinley Drive, so start looking for Number 23 and a white house with a green roof and shutters." Margie's eyes became riveted on the street and when she saw it she gasped.

"There it is, Jenns, 23 McKinley Drive. It's a pretty house isn't it? My baby is just inside. Oh Jenns, to be so close and yet not be able to see him," Margie dropped her face into her palms and sobbed.

Jennifer sped past the house and turned right to get back to Main Street. "Margie, I just knew this would happen, but you promised. I'm wondering now if you can refrain from trying to contact him."

Margie lifted her head and mumbled, "Jenns, I promised and I won't cause you any trouble. Besides, I couldn't take care of my baby now. I don't have a home nor a job . . . No, I want to see him . . . I'd love to hold him just one time, but that's being selfish. I just hope they are good to him."

Jennifer reached over and patted her arm. "I'm so sorry, Margie, but you are right. You have no way of caring for him right now and from all I've heard the Larkins' are really good to him. I'll try to find out more."

They rode along in silence for several miles and then Margie said, "I'm going to get my education and a good job, but I'm going to always stay close to where he is. Anything can happen. Someday he may need me and if I have a good job with some money then I can help him."

They quickly made their purchases in town and pulled into the Jacob's driveway right at ten-thirty. As they got out of the car Jennifer looked down at her watch. She held out her arm toward Margie. "Look at the time. Mom will be so proud of us."

Margie grinned. "Gosh, I'd forgotten all about your promise to be back by ten-thirty. I'm glad we made it through since getting that cake to the church in secret will take some doing."

"I believe we should take the cake first, don't you? That or all of us go with the other food and then you and I come back for the cake. What do you think?" asked Jennifer.

Margie stood deep in thought until Amy came to the door. "Girls, I think we need to get that cake down there first, if it's supposed to be a surprise."

The decision was made and after taking out all the jacks, spare tire, and pumps, the cake was carefully settled into a huge box and loaded into the trunk of the station wagon. Jennifer drove at a much slower pace fearing that the cake would be jostled and tilt to the side. They arrived at the church with no mishaps and thankfully took it inside to find only Evelyn Slater and two other women.

Jennifer and Margie carefully made their way to a table in front of the room. "Here's the cake and wait until you see it. It will be the biggest surprise anyone around here has ever had. Where do you want us to put it?"

A Fatal Beginning

Jennifer was looking at Evelyn Slater who had a surprised look in her eyes as she looked at the size of the box.

"Jennifer saw how serious she looked and put her hand on Evelyn's shoulder. "I know it looks big, but Margie did make it and you, and everyone else will love it. I hope you have ice cream."

Mary Kincaid, one of the other women, spoke up. "We have vanilla, chocolate, and strawberry. Will that be all right? Janie and I bought it," she said nodding toward the third woman in the room.

Margie smiled. "It is a white cake so any of those flavors will work well."

Evelyn Slater stood studying the box. "I don't know where we should put it. It must be a giant cake if it fills that whole box. Does it?"

Jennifer laughed. "Well it is round and so the corners aren't filled but it took that size box to fit without disturbing this masterpiece. I can't wait for everybody to see it. You'll all be begging Margie to open a bakery here in town."

Everybody in town knew about Margie being sort of adopted by the Jacobs family, but they hadn't had the opportunity to really become acquainted with her. The women smiled and Evelyn said, "I sure do appreciate you doing this Miss, uh Margie." Margie was given a questioning look.

"Yes, please call me Margie, Mrs. Slater since Jennifer is like a sister to me and I hope you will allow me to be a part of your community," said Margie.

Evelyn and the other women smiled, but the woman called Janie said, "You are most welcome to be a part of our town. We hope to see more of you."

"We have to go back and get the food and Mom and Dad, of course, but I dare either of you or anyone else to open that cake until we are here," said Jennifer, looking from one woman to the other.

"We won't bother it, and I'll make sure nobody else does, but hurry. I'm getting excited myself," said Evelyn.

Jennifer and Margie hurried back to the car and soon returned with Mr. and Mrs. Jacobs as well as enough food for the entire town, or so James Jacobs had said as he helped to carry the numerous containers from the house to the car.

A Fatal Beginning

CHAPTER 27

By the time they returned, the church yard was filled with parked cars and people meandering around to chat with their neighbors. Uncle James looked disgruntled, "Why this big a crowd don't show up for a funeral. I hope they're not all big eaters."

"James Jacobs, you sound like you don't want to feed veterans. What's wrong with you? They're your buddies," said Amy Jacobs as she got out of the car.

"Oh yeah! That's right. This big crowd is for the veterans, ain't it? I'm glad Jerry Slater ain't a veteran or he'd brag from now on about how many people showed up to see him," said James.

"Sh-h, it's supposed to be a surprise, and if you don't quit talking so loud he'll certainly know," cautioned Jennifer as she and Margie began taking containers from the car.

Soon several young men were there, eager to help. They seemed especially eager to help Margie. One young man, however, was Alex Stafford, the man from the Ford dealership. Margie knew he was there because of Jennifer. She assumed that all the others that were so willing to help must be his friends and she smiled at their antics in trying to be first in line to help her. However, she was glad when all the food was inside and she could slip away to the restroom. She had never been around people socially and even though she was trying to learn to adjust to social gatherings, it was still very difficult.

Jennifer came looking for her. "Margie, are you ill?" Then she saw Margie's white face and troubled eyes.

"You're scared to death. Why?" Jennifer, being raised in a large family, had no idea what could have scared her.

Margie dropped her head. "I don't know how to act, Jennifer. I've never been in a social gathering before."

A Fatal Beginning

"Didn't you go to church?" Jennifer asked in an amazed voice.

Margie looked like she was ready to cry. "I've never been to a church service in my entire life."

"I thought you said your mother prayed all the time," said Jennifer.

Margie wiped her eyes on a paper towel. "She did and she read the Bible to me, but not when Dad was at home. Mom and I were never allowed to go to church nor anywhere else."

Jennifer stood hesitant for a moment then she smiled. "You come with me little sister. I'll stay with you through your first social adventure."

Jennifer took Margie's arm and they went back through the kitchen and on into the main part of the basement, called Fellowship Hall by the members. Long tables with chairs had been set up and most of the people already seated when they walked through the door. Alex Stafford raised his arm and waved until Jennifer noticed him. He motioned the two girls to sit beside of him.

They found their seats just as a band struck up The Marine Hymn and a short procession of veteran marines marched into the hall and took their appointed seats. Next four veteran sailors marched in as Anchors Aweigh was played. Margie thought that was all until a young man, wearing a uniform with the Air Force insignia showing on his sleeve, came as a few strands of the Air Force theme, 'Off we go into the wild blue yonder,' was played.

When that man stepped through the door, Margie felt like she was seeing a ghost. She had trouble breathing as she clinched her hands together. *It's Rick, but how*, she thought as she tried to breathe. The man marched to the seat appointed for him at the head of the table of veterans, which gave Margie a clear view of him. It wasn't Rick, but from a distance he did look like Rick. *That's the man who got into the bee hive with Jerry Slater*, she thought, but still couldn't take her eyes off him.

Another man in military uniform came marching in to the same tune. This man, however, did not take a seat, but stepped to the podium where a microphone was placed.

"Good morning, ladies and gentlemen. I am Colonel Alan Reedy of the United States Air Force, stationed at Fort Ord. I'm here today to honor these veterans who have served our country and kept us safe. We would not be allowed to gather here today had they not served our country in World War II, but I'm also here to present a medal to a young Air Force officer who has gone beyond the call of duty to save his fellow airmen. I ask Lieutenant Stephen Crandall Hammer to please come to the front."

Every eye was fastened on the tall young officer who rose from his seat and stepped forward to salute his superior. He continued to stand at attention while Colonel Reedy pinned a medal to his chest.

Margie felt like she would explode with pride as the colonel went on to tell how Lieutenant Hammer had stayed with his plane until all of his men had parachuted out. Though injured and endangering his own life in doing so, he only jettisoned out just as the plane exploded.

"Oohs and aahs were heard throughout the room as this story was related and when Lieutenant Hammer turned to face the crowd, the first face he saw was the tear-drenched face of Margie Meadows. He knew that his life was somehow connected with hers, but also knew he had never met her. He drew in a long breath and promised himself that he would become acquainted before he left this event.

Soon everyone was urged to be seated and the Reverend John Hale, pastor of the church, gave a rousing patriotic talk before asking the blessing. Once this was done the pastor's wife stepped to the podium. "Before we begin our meal, we have a special surprise for all veterans that are here today."

She motioned to two young men near the doors to the kitchen and soon the doors were held open as the men returned bearing a huge box which they placed on a table in the center of the room.

Mrs. Hale then turned to the microphone and said, "Jennifer Jacobs and Margie Meadows will you please show us what is in this mysterious box?"

"No," whispered Margie, but Jennifer grasped her arm. "Come on, I'll be right beside you."

The two girls made their way to the table where Amy Jacobs and Evelyn Slater stood waiting. The women hid the girls from view as they carefully cut the box away and then stood back, as did the two women and the cake was seen in all its glory.

The whole room seemed to be stunned by this amazing confection, but Evelyn Slater didn't wait. She held up her hand.

"This cake was made to honor all the veterans here today, so please remain standing while our high school band plays 'God Bless America.'" When the band finished, to thunderous applause, Evelyn Slater said, "Now, after you have eaten your meal each of you can pass your plate to be served cake and ice cream."

Somebody from the back of the room yelled, "Who made a cake like that? We don't have a bakery in this town."

James Jacobs said, "No, but we have a baker visiting. It is Miss Margie Meadows." He pointed to Margie whose face was flaming red as she ducked behind Jennifer and then quickly left the room.

Seeing her fleeing back, the crowd was astonished by her actions. "Most people would be walking proud for that kind of attention. What'd she run for," said an older man at the front table.

James Jacobs stood up. "Now don't get all upset. Miss Meadows is new to the area and she ain't used to being in crowds. We need to give her time to get to know everybody."

This seemed to please everybody and soon they were all in line to get their plates filled before returning to their tables. There was one person who wasn't pleased, however. Lieutenant Steven Hammer wanted to leave all the food and go find this girl who had caught his attention. He started to get out of line, but was halted by Colonel Reedy's quip, "She'll be around, lieutenant. Come on, let's eat".

A Fatal Beginning

CHAPTER 28

Jennifer waited for twenty minutes and when Margie didn't return she went looking for her. She wasn't in the building and Jennifer was beginning to get concerned as she went out of the building to walk around to the arbor in back. As she neared the car parking lot she saw Margie waving to her from the car. She hurried to the car. "Margie, you can't stay out here. Come on back inside," said Jennifer.

Margie was pale as a ghost. "I can't, Jenns. Honest, I can't. I'll just lie down in the back seat until this is over, unless you can take me home now."

Jennifer could see that Margie was really sick, but didn't know what to do. Suddenly she thought of Alex Stafford and poking her head through the open window, she smiled at Margie. "Will you let Alex drive me and you home?"

"Alex!" gasped Margie and then remembered who he was and nodded in agreement and Jennifer hurried back into the building.

As Jennifer walked back her thoughts were troubled. *She'll never make it in this world if she doesn't overcome her fear of crowds*, she thought as she reached the basement door. Once inside she went to her seat beside Alex and told him about Margie's dilemma. Alex quickly suggested that he and Jennifer should take Margie back to the farm. Since this is exactly what Jennifer had hoped for she smiled and patted his arm as she arose from her seat.

"I'll need to tell Mom what we are going to do. You go on outside and wait for me. I won't be but a minute," whispered Jennifer as she turned away, but Alex grabbed her arm.

He grinned as he said, "Let's get a piece of that cake first. Can you wait that long?"

A Fatal Beginning

Knowing that her dad would be eager to go home as soon as the cake was, Jennifer whispered. "No, but I'll tell Mom to save a big piece and ice cream for the two of us." Alex nodded and went toward the exit as Jennifer left the dining hall and headed for the kitchen.

Steve Hammer, however, who had been listening to this conversation, did not hurry away. He quietly followed Alex out of the room.

Alex stopped when he heard footsteps behind him and turned. He waited until Steve came up to him. "Can I help you?" He asked just as Jennifer came up the ramp from the kitchen.

Jennifer gave Steve a questioning look and asked, "Are you leaving, lieutenant?"

"No. I was hoping you would introduce me to your friend. Will you do that?" Steve asked, but Jennifer looked worried.

She shook her head. "I don't think right now is a good time. She's not feeling well. Alex and I came to take her home."

Steve put out his hands in an imploring manner. "I won't try to talk to her, but I would like to at least meet her."

Jennifer looked at Alex and he said, "Let's introduce him and if she doesn't want to talk that's all we can do."

He looked at Lieutenant Hammer, "That's the best we can promise right now."

Steve nodded and they walked to the car. When Jennifer opened the door, Margie raised to sitting position. "Are you going to take me . . .," Margie stopped with a gasp as she saw Steve Hammer standing there.

Fearing Margie would get more upset and start vomiting, Jennifer quickly spoke up. "Margie Meadows this is Lieutenant Steve Hammer who wanted to be introduced to you."

Margie looked at Steve and at first turned red and then deathly white as she mumbled, "Hello lieutenant," before hanging her head out the door and gagging.

Jennifer looked at Steve Hammer and shook her head. "We'll need to go she's really not feeling well. Please excuse us." Jennifer pushed Margie back and rushed around to the passenger side of the car and jumped in.

Alex gave Steve Hammer a tight-lipped grin as he threw up his hand and started the engine. He pulled out, leaving the lieutenant standing with a look of astonishment on his face.

Once back at the farm, Jennifer went with Margie upstairs and waited until she was lying down before she asked if she wanted water or anything.

"No, Jenns. I'll be all right now. I'm sorry. You go on back. I'll try to take a nap," said Margie and Jennifer sped down the stairs and out to the car.

Alex Stafford had waited in a very puzzled frame of mind. *Margie is a beautiful girl. I wonder why she is terrified around strangers. I don't know how she is attending college*, he thought.

So as soon as Jennifer got in and closed the car door he spoke up. "How is that girl attending college if she can't be around strangers or in a crowd?"

Jennifer drew in a long breath. "Start the car and I'll try to explain what I know." During the ride back to the church Jennifer told of her meeting with Margie and everything that happened except about Margie's baby. Alex did not interrupt and Jennifer had just finished when they pulled into the church parking lot.

"Is that monster, her father, in jail? Poor girl! I'll bet she hasn't told the half of it. No wonder she's afraid. If one's own father tries to kill them, I can see why anyone would be wary around people, but she needs some help. Maybe you can get her to see a psychiatrist. Do you think she would listen to you?"

A Fatal Beginning

"Her father is dead. He was found beaten almost to a pulp in a seedy part of Port Angeles about three weeks after he killed her mother and beat her up so badly," said Jennifer.

"Well he sure deserved that, but it has left his daughter in a very mixed- up state of mind." Alex was upset, but he turned to Jennifer and smiled.

"That's what I like about you, Jennifer. You and your family didn't really know Margie, but you accepted her into your family and became her friends. It takes special people to do something like that." Alex reached over and kissed her cheek before opening the door.

"Let's go get that cake and ice cream," he said as he saw how red she had become as she exited the car and came around to his side.

Jennifer took his offered arm and with an 'almost walking on air' feeling walked proudly back into the church basement.

A worried Amy Jacobs came to meet her as soon as Jennifer walked in the door. Jennifer, noting the concern on her face, smiled and said, "She's at home lying down. She just had one of her stomach upsets like she gets in crowds."

Amy grimaced and shook her head sadly. "I wish there was some way to help her. Jennifer, could you ask some of the doctors there at the hospital if there is some way to help her?"

Seeing other people coming toward them, Jennifer said, "We'll talk about it when we get home, Mom." Amy nodded and left it to Jennifer to explain Margie's absence.

When Jennifer was through explaining Amy touched her arm. ""I saved you and Alex that cake you asked for as well as ice cream, but you'd better hurry. You know how your dad is when he wants to go home."

Taking Jennifer's hand, Alex followed Amy Jacobs into the kitchen as she reached into an overhead cabinet and took out the two plates. "Sit down and I'll go get the ice cream," said Amy..

They had just gotten seated when Lieutenant Hammer came through the door. He glanced around the room and then seeing them at the table headed their way. He warily pulled out a chair at the end and sat down.

"I know I'm being a pest, but Miss Meadows is the most beautiful girl I've ever met and I'd like to know more about her. Does she have some kind of disease?"

"Disease?" gasped Jennifer. "No, she doesn't have a disease, but she is in need of seeing a good doctor. I can't tell . . . ." The door swung open again and Colonel Reedy stepped through.

"Lieutenant, we have forty minutes to get back to base. Had you forgotten the time?"

Steve snapped to his feet with a salute and said, "I'm sorry, sir. I'm ready to leave, but please give me another minute."

The Colonel nodded and turned away. Steve leaned close to Jennifer and said, "May I phone you, Miss Jacobs. I want to know about Margie."

Alex quickly spoke up. "Here, take my card and call me. Jennifer has told me what she knows."

Lieutenant Hammer grabbed the card and thanked Alex before following his superior officer from the room. This left Alex wondering why this man wanted to know so much after having just met Margie.

A Fatal Beginning

CHAPTER 29

Back at the farm, Margie lay dreading the Jacobs's return. *I know they think I'm silly, and probably I am, but I get into a terrible shape inside . . . I can hardly breathe, I want to cry, and then I shake, before I start vomiting,* thought Margie, but she knew it had been worse this time . . . *he looked so much like Rick and I felt I would faint if I couldn't get away,* she thought as tears seeped from beneath her closed eyelids. She was still pondering her problem when she heard the car pull into the parking space at the side of the house.

Soon Jennifer's steps were heard on the stairs and then Margie's door swung open. "Did you go to sleep? You don't look much better," said Jennifer.

Margie sat up and swung her feet over the side of the bed. "Jenns, I know I embarrassed your whole family and I'm so sorry, but honestly, I couldn't help it."

Jennifer sat down beside her. "I know you can't, Margie, but we both know that you can't go on this way. You need some help. I mean professional help, like a psychiatrist."

Margie shivered. "I can't do that Jenns. There are things I can't tell anyone or I'd end up in a psyche ward in some hospital."

Jennifer put her arm around Margie's shoulder. "If you were assured that you would not be sent to a psyche ward, would you be willing to go to that kind of doctor?"

Margie could see the concern in Jennifer's face, but she still feared seeing a doctor. "Jenns, I think I will eventually learn to meet people and when I get to see my baby once, I think I'll be all right."

Jennifer sighed. "Margie, that Lieutenant Hammer was very interested in you, but you actually became worse when he was introduced. You know that isn't normal. Most girls would be excited to have a handsome man going to such lengths to be introduced."

Margie's eyes misted over again, but she angrily brushed them aside. "Jenns, I don't want to meet any men or anyone else until I get to see my baby. In fact, I don't want to do anything but get through college, get a good job, and then stay close to my baby. He may need some help and if I'm all tangled up with some man I might not be able to do that."

Jennifer wrapped her arm around Margie's shoulder. "Okay, I hear you, but if you don't take care of your health you won't be able to do any of that. Little Sis, if you can't be in crowds how do you think you can get a good job. Please let me check around. I promise that I won't do anything until you approve, but I promise that you will not be sent to a psyche ward in some hospital."

Margie sat thinking of having to again tell Hank she couldn't be more than a friend and her stomach heaved again. She turned anguished eyes to Jennifer.

"Okay, Jenns, but promise that I won't have to go if it gets to be more than I can handle."

At this Jennifer threw both arms around Margie. "Okay, little sister, from here on in it'll be 'Jennifer to the rescue' with you." She released her hold on Margie and stood up.

"Let's go down and tell Mom and Dad about your decision. They have been so worried."

Margie followed Jennifer slowly down the stairs, but stopped about halfway down. "Jenns, do you think it will be all right if I take that medicine Dr. Samuels gave me before I came down here. I really don't think I can cope with the Hank Jenkins meeting without something."

Jennifer had stopped and turned. "I think it will be all right, but I'll look at the bottle and then check with the doctor and let you know in the morning."

They started on down the stairs when Margie said, "Oh Lord, I wish there was a good business college closer and I could leave the University."

When they walked into the kitchen, James and Amy were sitting side by side, but turned an interest look their way when the girls stepped through the door. Margie walked up to stand in front of her 'pseudo-adoptive' parents and put out both her hands, one to each parent. When James and Amy clasped the extended hands, she said, "You two can stop worrying. I told Jenns to find me a good doctor."

Suddenly she swung around to face Jennifer. "Get a woman doctor, Jenns. I don't think I could ever really talk to a man. I promise all of you that I'll try. I want to be able to cope and I know I'm not doing a very good job right now," said Margie.

Amy jumped up and encircled Margie in her arms. "Oh, Margie, thank you. We've all been worried to death. We know you can't go on like you are now. In fact, I worry that you'll have a breakdown when you have to stop seeing that pharmacist."

Margie's eyes misted over. "I dread going back to the university, for that very reason. I just told Jenns that I wished there was a good business school in some other town that I could transfer to and still get a business degree."

James Jacobs still held the hand he had been holding and when Amy released her hold on Margie he squeezed her hand. "Margie, you know I'd like to have you here running a bakery, but if you can't then I think seeing this doctor is what you need to do more than anything else right now."

Margie leaned up and hugged James. "Okay, Papa, I'll do it." She stepped back and they all laughed.

Amy suddenly stopped laughing. "Guess what I did? I sneaked in when nobody was looking and cut enough cake for all of us, so if you girls will help me get supper we can have ice cream and cake for dessert."

Nothing else was mentioned about Margie's health or doctors. The conversation was all about the cake and the dinner for the veterans. "I was right proud of that young air force man. He's awfully young to be getting an honor like that," said James.

Amy reached for the green beans. "Did he go with you and Alex to bring Margie home, Jennifer?"

Jennifer looked at Margie who had turned red. "No, he just wanted to meet Margie and I introduced them, but I don't think Margie wanted to meet him. I thought she was going to vomit on him."

Both James and Amy stared in open-mouthed amazement. Finally, Amy said, "She didn't, did she?"

Jennifer laughed. "No, but he certainly looked stunned. Alex said he felt sorry for him and to be honest, I did too, but I did tell him Margie was sick. He still insisted though, so I introduced him."

James sighed. "Well, if he knowed she was already sick, I guess that wouldn't too bad. I don't figure a young feller would like to be introduced to a girl and get vomited on. If it was me I know I'd feel downright insulted."

Seeing the twinkle in his eyes, Amy slapped his arm. "It'd take more than that to insult you, James Jacobs. You're the most persistent man I ever met."

James grinned and gave Amy a lascivious look. "Well, when a man sees something he wants he ort to have the gumption to pursue it. Paid off for me, didn't it?"

CHAPTER 30

Later when the girls met in Margie's bedroom, Jennifer said, "Well, Little Sis, you only have one more day and I have to work tomorrow. I wish I didn't since we've never really talked about your dilemma with Hank."

Margie grimaced. "I know. I've been avoiding it, but I really don't know how to handle it. Hank says that I led him on, but I don't know how, if I did. However, after seeing you and Alex together and talking to you, I do know I would not want to spend the rest of my life with him. I like him, but I know I don't love him and never could. He is a really good person, though."

Jennifer shook her head. "Well, I don't think he's the man for you. You can't make yourself love him. You'll just have to tell him you're not ready and never will be."

Margie nodded. "I know, but it will be hard. If there was a college or even just a good business school nearer here, I wouldn't even have to go back. I could just leave him a letter."

Jennifer started to protest, but Margie said, "I know, Jenns. That's the cowardly way out, isn't it? But, I really don't want to hurt him. He is a nice man and he did help me a lot. Life isn't fair, Jenns, or at least, I don't think it is."

Jennifer looked solemn for a moment. "I don't know about fair, Little Sis. I think we were given life and as we live and grow we will encounter thorns and thistles, like the Lord told Adam when he was driven from the Garden of Eden. If we think about it, aren't we all given the tools needed to combat all the things we encounter? In new situations we worry about it and then act too quickly which ends up not being a solution to our problems, or so it seems to me."

"Jenns, when I was little I was scared to death. I guess I was cowardly then too. I could have run away, but I

A Fatal Beginning

thought if I did, Dad would kill my mother ". . . Margie halted in amazed realization. "I stayed and he not only killed her, but almost killed me and my baby. I guess I wasn't very wise, was I?."

"No, Margie, it wasn't that you weren't wise, but you were just a child who had no coping skills and had a very poor self-image. Look at you now. You have overcome more in your short life than lots of people ever have to face."

Margie grinned wryly. "I haven't been coping very well or I wouldn't be in need of a psychiatrist. I don't know if I'm strong enough to do that, either."

Jennifer grabbed her shoulders and gave her a gentle shake. "Yes, you are. You want to be strong for your baby. He doesn't deserve a wimp for a mother."

Margie jumped to her feet with a martial gleam in her eyes. "He'll not have a coward for a mother. You find that doctor, Jenns, and make the appointment as quick as you can get one. I'll do anything for my baby, even if he never knows it."

Jennifer grinned. "That's my girl. I'll see about it tomorrow." They hugged each other and Jennifer left, but Margie still sat on the side of her bed for a long time. *God, why did Rick have to die? If he had lived Mom wouldn't be dead because Rick and I would have taken her with us when we married*, thought Margie.

Finally, she got to her feet realizing that fate had taken a different turn and she couldn't change it. *I wonder if our lives are predetermined, but Mom always said that God was a God of love and surely I wasn't fated to lose my mother and my baby at the same time. Maybe Dad knew Mom and I were afraid of him and bullies, like him, always abuse those weaker than themselves,* she mused as she donned her pajamas and climbed into bed.

She didn't think she would go to sleep, but when she thought about seeing her baby again she began to fantasize about holding her baby in her arms and her fantasies soon faded into sleep. Soon dreams took over and she dreamed about seeing her little boy, but he was always at a distance, preventing her from a full view of his face.

In one dream there were things that she didn't remember clearly, but she knew she was in a crowd. In the dream she kept trying to get closer to her baby, yet stay out of his sight. As she struggled through the crowd she was getting very frustrated. She awoke with a start when a rooster crowed. She sighed and turned over hoping to go back to sleep, but then she smelled bacon frying and swung her feet to the floor.

Her first thought was that she wanted to see Jennifer, so she jumped to her feet, grabbed her robe, and started for the door, but suddenly she heard Jennifer's car start. She dashed to the window and saw the back of the car going through the open gate at the end of the driveway. She sighed, *Oh well, I don't know why I wanted to see her anyway*, she thought.

Thinking that she could help with the jelly-making that Aunt Amy had planned, she hurried to make her bed and straighten the room before going down the stairs. At the foot of the stairs she stopped as somebody rang the front doorbell. Quickly she darted down the hall to the bathroom under the stairway, since she wasn't dressed for visitors. She listened quietly as she heard men's voices.

"Hello, Jerry, what brings you here so early this morning?" James's voice sounded puzzled.

The men must have gone back onto the porch for she couldn't hear them as well. However, she did hear Mr. Slater say "Steve made me promise to come over and see how Margie was and let him know. He had to go back to base last night and I promised I'd let him know, so here I am."

Margie shook her head. "Why, why, why do these men want to bother me? I don't want a man and I'm not going to get tangled up with another one. If I can get this mess with Hank straightened out I won't speak to another man except on business," she muttered to herself as she washed her face and hands. Then she opened the door and peeped out; not seeing or hearing anybody she dashed to the kitchen.

Amy was putting a plate of biscuits on the table. "Well, I'm glad you're up. I was going to come and wake you in a few minutes so your breakfast wouldn't get cold."

"I thought I heard somebody talking," said Margie.

"You did. Jerry Slater said that lieutenant that was at the party, told him to come over and check on you. I believe he was pretty taken with you, Margie."

"I don't want a man to be taken with me, Aunt Amy. I'm having a hard enough time learning to live with myself without being entangled with some man. I guess Jennifer told you about Hank, didn't she?"

Amy looked uneasy. "Don't look like that Aunt Amy. I don't mind if she told you. I don't know how to handle it. I dread having to go back and hurt Hank, but I'll have to. I've learned my lesson, though. I'll never get tangled up like that again," Margie stated firmly.

Amy grinned. "Well, Jennifer only told me since she wanted advice on what to tell you. I think you're wise, honey. Just remember that it would hurt him worse to continue when you don't have the kind of feelings he expects."

Margie nodded and took her place at the table. "It's one of those lessons I need to learn, I guess, but I'll be really wary about men from now on."

Amy took a seat across from Margie. "Of course, that lieutenant won't be bothering you since he's in the Air Force and it's hard to tell where he'll have to go as long as he's in service."

Or get killed, thought Margie and chided herself for even though he looked like Rick, he still wasn't Rick.

"That's right, Aunt Amy, when a man is in a branch of service he has to go wherever his commander orders him to, so I'll never see him again."

Aunt Amy grinned. "Probably not, but sometimes the Lord moves in mysterious ways."

A Fatal Beginning

CHAPTER 31

Jennifer came through the door a half hour early that evening. Her face was lit up with a wide grin. As soon as she stepped into the kitchen she met Margie and almost knocked the platter of cornbread out of Margie's hands as she flung her arms around her.

Margie managed to land the platter on the table with a thump and Jennifer said, "Oops! I think I'm too excited." She turned a beaming face to Margie.

"You're going to love me, Little Sis. I've found a business college for you and I also have an appointment for you with Dr. Angela Moses on May 29th at three in the evening."

Margie was so stunned that she stumbled and Jennifer caught her arm to steady her. She had suddenly remembered that a college had been part of one of the dreams she had forgotten from last night. Now the dream came back to her and she turned to Jennifer with a look of awed surprise on her face.

"Jenns, last night I dreamed about my baby, but I also dreamed of going to a business college. I thought it was a sprawling building with two floors. In my dream I was working in the office on the first floor, but I saw a set of stairs just outside the office door and someone was coming down. Then the dream became one of seeing my baby, but he was so far away that I couldn't see his face. I was pushing and shoving trying to get closer when the rooster crowed and woke me," said Margie, still staring in an awestruck manner.

Jennifer drew a brochure out of her purse and Margie gasped as she looked at the picture she had seen in her dream. She grabbed the brochure and stared in amazement. "This is the building in my dream, Jenns. Where's it located?"

Jennifer pointed to the writing below the picture. "It's in Port Angeles. See, it says Peninsula College, offering degrees in business and math as well as other subjects. Dr. Forbes told me about it. He says it is located on a hill overlooking Juan de Fuca Strait and that the campus is beautiful. See, the address is 1502 E. Lauridsen Blvd, Port Angeles," said Jennifer, quickly scanning the information. "Here's a phone number. You could call them . . . but not tonight."

Margie eagerly scanned through the brochure and then holding it to her heart she looked at Jennifer with tears in her eyes. "Jenns, how come you'd never heard about this place? Do you remember how scared I was about going to the university? I thought you would have known if there was another college close by. I don't know why you had never heard of this place."

Jennifer shook her head. "Little Sis, I swear that I'd never heard of this place before today. I guess I was just so excited about training to be a nurse and had no reason to inquire about any other place."

Margie sat holding the brochure. "Did that doctor say it was a good school? If it isn't widely known, then it probably isn't any good or perhaps businesses don't hire graduates from there. I probably couldn't transfer my credits here even if it is good."

Jennifer shook her head. "Let me see that brochure again." Margie passed it to her and she turned several pages and stopped. "Well, it says it is accredited so it must be a good school. Maybe it doesn't have a big budget that could support broad advertising."

Margie dropped her head. "I'll still have to go back and finish this semester at the university or I'll not have any credits to transfer."

"Margie, you only have about six more weeks to finish. That will give you time to check everything out and get transferred before the summer classes start. You do want to go to summer school, don't you?"

Everything she had hoped and prayed for seemed to be happening; first she learned that her baby didn't die and then finding this college had her locked in spell-binding wonder. Margie stood clasping her hands together. *I don't know how to act. I want to shout, sing, dance . . . God, I've never felt like this before,* just as the front door opened and the voices of Amy and James caused her to jump up and run out the kitchen door. This overwhelming joy was something she had no experience with and as tears of joy streamed from her eyes she ran down through the back yard and sank to the ground behind the big oak tree that sheltered the barn. *So, God does hear prayers or pleas or whatever it was called when I cried and begged for things to change,* she thought.

After a while she grew calmer and she went back to the house in a much different frame of mind than she'd had that morning. When she opened the door, she was met by Jennifer's smiling face.

"Little Sis, you'd better be glad you left me in the kitchen. This big dinner you had cooking would have burned to a crisp." Jennifer stepped back and Margie saw her cornbread, green beans, fried chicken, and coleslaw spread out on the table and everyone's plate was prepared.

Margie gasped, "Oh my goodness! I completely forgot that I was cooking dinner." She looked at Jennifer, Uncle James, and Aunt Amy as if expecting a scolding.

James grinned. "Well it looks good and smells better, so if some people wouldn't take off somewhere right at eating time, I could tell you how it tastes."

Amy slapped at his arm. "Hush James! You're not starving."

Margie laughed. "I guess I did act crazy, but Jennis brought the answer to all my problems" . . . she stopped. "Well almost all my problems and it made me so happy I

A Fatal Beginning

was about to jump up and down and knew that seeing me acting like that would really ruin everybody's dinner."

James grinned. "That would do it all right. You'd be acting like me and nobody wants that to happen."

During dinner the whole family discussed the best plans for making the move from Seattle to Port Angeles. "You could just move in and stay here with us, Margie. That way you wouldn't have to pay rent and live in some room by yourself," offered Amy.

"No, she can't, Amy. She ain't got no way to go there and back every day," said James.

Jennifer had been thinking the same as her mother, but realized that Margie couldn't ride with her since her hours were so erratic. Suddenly she broke in.

"Yes she could if she got her own car. I know my schedule is so changeable that I wouldn't be dependable, but if she had her own car she could live here. It's about fifty miles between here and Port Angeles, but I drive it every day myself and it isn't too bad."

"She can't drive so that's out unless you have an answer for that one, Miss Smart Aleck," jibed her father.

"She can learn to drive, Dad, but I don't want you trying to teach her," said Jennifer.

Amy rose to her feet. "Well, first things first and a car isn't one of them. I think, checking out this Peninsula College should be the first thing we need to do. You girls will have to do that, though, for I don't know one thing about stuff like that."

Margie rose as well and patted Amy's shoulder as she said, "Maybe not, Aunt Amy, but you know how to get the ball rolling and that has to be first."

CHAPTER 32

Margie didn't get much sleep that night with all the things that could go wrong running through her mind. Finally, at five o'clock she arose and made her bed, straightened her room, and started for the hall bathroom. When she opened the door, Jennifer was coming from her own room.

"Margie, it's only six forty-five, why are you up so early? You can't go back to Seattle until this evening," said Jennifer.

"I couldn't sleep, so I just got up. I have a lot to do and I wanted to talk to you before you left for work," said Margie.

Jennifer nodded. "Come on down and we'll make a list of what you can do while I'm gone today. What you can't get done we can probably do by phone."

Before Jennifer left for work the two girls had a list of things Margie could do that day. Jennifer promised to check further on the college as to ratings and also try to get the names of some people who had gone there.

Margie called Peninsula College and was told that they could accept any work she had done at the university and that their graduates were snapped up by businesses, not only local but state-wide as well. She also learned that they did not have dormitories, but there were good hotels near the college. The lady she spoke with said that sometimes they could help students find living quarters with local residents.

Jennifer came home early, as she'd promised. Margie and her adoptive parents were packed and ready. They stopped at a roadside diner outside of Seattle and ate supper and still made it back to Mrs. Duke's house at seven o'clock. Margie grew quieter and quieter as they drew closer.

A Fatal Beginning

James leaned over the back seat and tapped her on the shoulder. Margie turned to look back at him. Both Amy and James drew in their breath.

"Margie, are you sick? You're pale as a ghost," said Amy.

Jennifer couldn't get over to the outside lane and had to keep driving, but she glanced over at Margie. "Are you car sick again?"

Margie shook her head. "No, but I'm terrified that something will go wrong and I'll have to stay here until I graduate and I just know that Hank will be coming to Mrs. Duke's as soon as he knows I'm back."

"Don't tell him, you're back," said James.

"Mrs. Duke will tell him, Uncle James. She thinks I should marry him and she's been encouraging him," replied Margie.

"I'll tell her you haven't been well, which is the truth, and that she should let you rest a day or two before he is called," said Jennifer.

As it turned out that was one worry Margie didn't have to deal with, but she didn't know that until the following day. Margie had called Mrs. Duke and told her she would be returning that evening so as soon as the car lights shone on the windows of the house the door opened.

As soon as Margie stepped onto the porch, Mrs. Duke was there to meet her with open arms. "Oh Margie, I have missed you so much." She hugged her close again and then stepped back to look at her.

"You've lost weight! I thought you'd be back with some extra pounds on you and a rosy complexion. Have you been ill?" Mrs. Duke sounded anxious.

Margie hugged Mrs. Duke and then said, "Let's go inside so Uncle James can bring my stuff in. Okay?"

Mrs. Duke looked startled. "Oh my, I'm sorry I'm acting so foolish, but I've missed this girl something awful. I don't think I can let her go away again."

Amy Jacobs gasped and gave Jennifer and James a look of caution. "We know how you feel, Mrs. Duke. She's become our adopted daughter."

Mrs. Duke directed James and Jennifer to take Margie's bags upstairs and then led Margie and Amy into the living room. She pointed Amy to a chair opposite the sofa and pulled Margie to a seat beside her on the sofa. She sat for a second just looking at Margie.

"Margie, you were so sick when you left, but I thought that going back to be with your friends for a bit would make you feel better. You don't look better and you have lost weight. I believe you have something going on and I'm going to call Dr. Samuels and tell him to get you an appointment at the hospital," said Mrs Duke.

Margie smiled at her landlady, who had been so good to her. "You don't have to worry, Mrs. Duke. I have an appointment for next month, with a doctor that Jennifer knows through her work. It's back in Sequim, where they live though, but that's all right."

Amy spoke up. "We were concerned as well and Jennifer talked to some of the doctors there at her hospital and this doctor Margie will see is recommended highly."

Mrs. Duke seemed to relax and nodded as she continued. "That's good. I first thought she was having problems in her classes, but Hank helped her and she did well. Margie has told you about Hank, hasn't she?"

Amy glanced quickly at Margie. "Oh yes, we heard about how much he had helped her and . . . .. She stopped as Jennifer and James came into the room.

James looked at Margie. "I told Jennifer that we should take some of your stuff back with us so you won't have to get a U-Haul to move you back." Seeing the startled look on the faces of the women he stopped.

"What? You're going to move back ain't you?"

A Fatal Beginning

Jennifer looked at Margie's white face and said, "Don't get sick on us again, Margie. She has to be told." Jennifer turned to Mrs. Duke.

"Mrs. Duke, Margie has found a good business school in Port Angeles and has decided to move her credits from the university and finish her degree down there."

Mrs. Duke looked at Margie with tears in her eyes. "Haven't I been good to you?"

"Oh, Mrs. Duke . . . yes, you've been like a mother to me and I don't want to hurt you. I . . . I've struggled ever since I started at the university and my stomach doesn't seem to be getting any better. I think a smaller school would make it easier on me."

Seeing Margie's stricken look, Jennifer stooped down in front of Mrs. Duke and Margie. "If Margie doesn't get some help we fear she will have a nervous breakdown. She's had such a terrible life and she wanted to find a smaller school. I asked around and finally found a good school in Port Angeles. That will be close enough to us so she can stay with us. We couldn't and won't be any better to her than you have been, but she and I are the same age and she can talk to me easier than she can to other people. "

Mrs. Duke sat listening then started to argue, but Jennifer interrupted. "You see, Mrs. Duke, I met Margie in the hospital when she was very ill and when she left the hospital she came to stay with us. We're like home to her." Hearing a choking sound, all eyes turned to Margie who jumped to her feet and holding her hand over her mouth, ran from the room.

"I love Margie and want the best for her, but having her here has been so good for me," said Mrs. Duke from a very sad face. She sat like that for a moment and then said, "She saw Dr. Samuels and for a little while she seemed to be feeling better and I know she was doing better in her classes since Hank helped her. In fact, I think Hank wanted to marry her, but she couldn't make up her mind."

"Margie ain't in no state to be deciding something like that. She don't need to worry about nothing for a while," said James. "That girl can't stand to hurt nobody and when she thinks she has it gets her all upset. I thought she'd be sick before we got here 'cause she didn't want to hurt you, but she had to come and get everything fixed up at that university."

Mrs. Duke looked at Amy. "You know how I feel, don't you, Mrs. Jacobs?"

Amy got up and took her hand. "Yes, I do know, Mrs. Duke, but I think that right now, we need to all be concerned with what's best for Margie."

Jennifer left to check on Margie and Mrs. Duke rose from the sofa. "Would you all like something to drink or eat? I was waiting supper on Margie, but I doubt she'll be able to eat."

James turned from the window where he had gone to check on the traffic in the street. "We stopped at a restaurant on the way here, so we don't need nothing to eat." He turned back to the room. "Don't all that traffic keep you awake?"

"No, I'm used to it. Actually, it is quieter here than on most streets around the university. Margie couldn't sleep when she first came here, but I think she got used to it."

"Knowing Margie, she wouldn't have told anybody if she didn't sleep," said Amy.

Jennifer and Margie came back into the room and Margie went straight to Mrs. Duke. "I'm so sorry, Mrs. Duke, but I really do need to make this move. I've told Jennifer that I will see this doctor and I promise that I'll keep in touch with you. I'll have to stay here a few more weeks until this term ends, but I'll pay you."

"Margie, I'd be lying if I said I wanted you to go, but you're probably doing the best thing for yourself right now. So, we'll not say anything else about it and let you and these good people make any arrangements you need to," said Mrs. Duke as she turned toward the door to the hallway.

"I'm going to eat supper. I waited on you, but Mr. Jacobs said you had eaten. I'll do that while you gather what things you want to send back with them."

Margie gave her an impulsive hug. "Thanks so much, Mrs. Duke." The older woman smiled and left the room as Jennifer grabbed Margie's arm and hurried her back to her room.

CHAPTER 33

When the Jacobs car pulled away from Mrs. Duke's house it was filled with everything that Margie felt she could live without until the semester ended. James Jacob had made three trips up the stairs and on the last trip he stopped halfway down and looked back at Margie.

"Margie, you've not kept enough clothes or else you plan to wear the same clothes every day for the next month."

Margie chuckled. "Mrs. Duke will let me wash my clothes once each week, so I'll wash everything on the weekends and have them clean for the next week."

James had started on down, but they all stopped to look when he stumbled on the last step. He regained his balance and turned to look back up the stairs at Jennifer and Margie. "You don't aim to wear the same dress a whole week, I hope. I don't wear my clothes that long."

James sounded so serious that Amy said, "Aw James, she kept more than one dress, but if you don't quit stepping on the tail of that dress you're carrying, she'll have one less dress when she does comes home."

Jennifer helped her father rearrange his load and then ushered her parents through the door and into the car. Margie followed them to the car and stood on the driver's side until Jennifer was ready to get in. They hugged each other and Jennifer opened the door before turning to Margie. "Little Sis, Mrs. Duke now knows you're moving so that's one hurdle you won't have to worry about."

Margie nodded. "Yes, but the biggest one is still waiting for me. I just know Mrs. Duke will call Hank while I'm at school tomorrow."

"She probably will, but that may be good. Just think how much easier it will be to study for your finals if you don't have that worry on you. It's better to get it settled, even if it is painful," said Jennifer.

Margie smiled. "You're right, Jenns. I really want my grades to be good. I'd hate to transfer a bunch of Fs."

Jennifer patted the hand on the door frame. "Don't start worrying about that. Just take one step at a time. Get that secretary that you stayed with at Christmas to help you. You said she was nice."

Margie's face seemed to lose its worried look. "I've never discussed Hank with her, but I'm sure she'll know what I need to do. I'll ask her and you are right. I do worry over things I shouldn't." She stood back from the car. "Drive carefully, Jenns. I don't want to lose the only family I have."

Jennifer gave her a saucy look. "That's a nice way of telling me I'm not a good driver."

Margie gasped in surprise, but seeing Jennifer's look she laughed and so did the occupants of the car. Jennifer put up the window and waved as she pulled out of the driveway.

Mrs. Duke had finished eating and was waiting in the living room. "This doctor you plan to see, is he there at the hospital where Jennifer works?"

Margie looked puzzled. "Yes, I think so, but . . . really, I didn't ask since Jennifer will drive me to my appointment."

"Will you be allowed to work at this new college like you have here at the university? I've also heard that some classes won't transfer," said Mrs. Duke.

Margie assured her that she had checked all that out. "We've really been checking everything since Jennifer first heard of this college. It offers degrees in business, but I think it is a liberal arts college. The lady I spoke with did tell me that businesses seemed eager to hire their graduates."

They talked for a few more minutes until Mrs. Duke said, "Well, you look like a scared rabbit and I think you need to get a good night's sleep. Don't worry that I'm going to be upset with you, Margie. I want what's best for you, but I will miss you when you move."

Margie rose to her feet. "I'll miss you too, Mrs. Duke, but like I promised, I will write and keep in touch." With that Margie left the room and Mrs. Duke sat silently for a few minutes and then picked up the phone. There was no answer at Hank's house and Mrs. Duke also went to bed.

When Margie arrived at the university the next morning she had made up her mind that as soon as her classes were over and she got to the president's office she was going to talk to Jane Lewis. Her plans, however, did not prosper. Jane Lewis wasn't there and Beverly Tums, a secretary from the dean's office was filling in until she returned.

"Jane's been away for two weeks and I think she has a few more days to go. She's lucky getting to attend a seminar in Denver, Colorado. A lot of business people are attending since it is about how to solve problems in business. It may be problems in life also, but I don't know for sure, I'd go if it was a' pony and dog show' just to visit Denver," said Beverly when Margie wanted to know where Jane was.

Just as Margie was clearing her desk that evening, the phone rang. It was Jane. "Margie, I'm glad you're back. How do you feel?"

"I'm feeling better, Jane, but not well, yet. I have an appointment with a doctor in Port Angeles for next month, though. I have some news for you, so I'll be glad when you get back," said Margie.

Jane sounded younger than she usually did and excited, or so Margie thought when she said, "I have some news for you also. Oh Margie, I think I'm in love."

"Who with?" asked Margie.

"A man, of course, and you know him. You know the pharmacist that helped you with accounting, Hank

A Fatal Beginning

Jenkins. He is attending this conference as well and we've been seeing each other . . . Oh here he comes. I'll be back next week and tell you all about it. He's really nice, so wish me luck," said Jane and hung up.

Margie put down the phone trembling in amazement. *God, you really do answer prayers. Oh thank you, thank you so much. I didn't want to hurt Hank, but I didn't love him and Jane . . . Jane really wanted to meet some nice man and get married. She's just right for Hank.*

The walk back to Mrs. Duke's had never been so short for Margie. She walked into the house and could tell that Mrs. Duke was disturbed about something.

"You act agitated, Mrs. Duke. Is anything wrong?" asked Margie.

"No. There's really nothing wrong, I don't guess. Did you know that Hank is away? He's been gone almost three weeks, but he'll return Monday, or so Mary said. I guess you knew that, but I didn't. I haven't seen him since you left. I had no reason to call since you weren't here, but this morning I called the drugstore to tell him you're back," said Mrs. Duke.

Margie didn't know whether to tell Mrs. Duke about Hank and Jane Lewis or not, so she said, "I didn't know until today. Hank only wrote one letter while I was away, but Jane called the office to see if I was back. She told me about this conference she was attending and she said Hank was there as well."

Mrs. Duke smiled. "Well, that's nice. He, at least, had someone he knew to talk to. What kind of conference is it?"

Margie had started upstairs to put her books away, but stopped. "It was something to do with problem solving for businesses or something like that. Jane will tell me all about it when she returns." She went on up the stairs still thanking the Lord in her heart, until she remembered that

Jane had said she was in love, but she didn't say how Hank felt.

For the rest of that week Margie's life fell back into its usual pattern; awaking at six a.m., bathing, eating, going to classes, work, and then sleeping again. She hadn't tried to do any of the things needed to transfer her credits. She had planned on Jane's help and decided to wait until she returned.

In the evenings she told Mrs. Duke about all the things that had happened while she was with the Jacobs family. When she mentioned the lieutenant, Mrs. Duke gave her a searching look. "Was he a good-looking young man?"

Margie turned red. "I guess he was. I only saw him twice and one of those times he was running down the road flailing the air to knock the bees off him." Margie broke out in gales of laughter as she told about Jerry Slater and the bees.

Mrs. Duke laughed as well. "Sounds like he and Mr. Jacobs are both pranksters."

"Well, they do like to top each other when it comes to practical jokes, but I think they really like each other.

The phone rang and Mrs. Duke answered it and turned to Margie, "It's Jennifer."

Margie picked up the phone. "Hello, Jenns." She stood listening for a few minutes and then said, "No, I haven't yet. Jane Lewis is gone and I was waiting for her to come back. She'll be back on Monday."

She listened again and then said, "Well, I'll think about it, but you know how everything seems to upset me. Maybe we should wait until I see that doctor, but tell Alex I really appreciate him trying to help me."

Again, she listened and then said, "Sure that will be fine since he knows about things like that. Thanks, Jenns. I'll never be able to pay you."

When she hung up the phone Mrs. Duke was looking expectantly and Margie told her that she was thinking of learning to drive and buying a car.

"Jennifer and her boyfriend, Alex, are both trying to help me."

CHAPTER 34

With two of the major worries off her mind Margie was able to concentrate on her studies. On Saturday, however, she began to wonder if Hank would call or try to see her. She smiled and thought, *Perhaps I should let him fret about hurting me, like I did about hurting him.*

Since Margie had grown up with a pessimistic outlook on life, she now began to fear that perhaps Hank hadn't changed his mind. Her thoughts became worrisome. *Maybe he doesn't feel as Jane does. Oh Lord please let the loving be mutual. They are both such good people.*

As soon as she awoke on Monday morning her stomach began to feel queasy. She hurried to shower and go down stairs since eating something usually helped when she felt like this. Mrs. Duke had breakfast on the table and turned from pouring coffee as Margie entered the room. She stood gazing at Margie.

"Is your stomach bothering you again? It's probably because Hank is back and will be calling you," said Mrs. Duke as she took her seat at the table. "Come on and eat a bite or two. That usually helps doesn't it?"

Margie took her seat and taking a biscuit from the dish bit into it. She chewed slowly and the queasiness did ease up. She smiled across at Mrs. Duke.

"You're just like a mommy. You know what affects me and how to help. I'll miss that, Mrs. Duke," said Margie as she continued to slowly eat a few bites of egg and the rest of the biscuit to which she had added butter and jelly.

"I guess Hank is back, because Jane will be back in the office this morning as well. I do dread having to tell him that I can't marry him, Mrs. Duke, but I know it would be wrong. I'm not ready for marriage and may never be," said Margie softly.

Mrs. Duke sat looking at Margie. "Well, you know your feelings better than anyone else could. I just hope you're not ruining your chances for a good life. Hank Jenkins is a really good person and would provide a good living for you."

"Hank doesn't need to be burdened with someone who has all kinds of problems and also, I know that I don't feel for Hank what Jennifer does for her Alex," replied Margie.

Mrs. Duke arose from the table and seeing most of the food still on Margie's plate, she grinned. "Well, he couldn't a found a more economical wife. You don't eat enough to feed a bird."

Margie left for the university with lagging steps. She was eager to see Jane, but wondered if Jane knew about the Hank situation. *Nothing happened, so why am I worried*, she thought as she trudged up the steps to her first class.

Jane was waiting for her at one-thirty that evening. "There you are, Margie and my goodness, you've lost a lot of weight."

Margie walked into her open arms. They hugged each other and both stepped back. Margie smiled. "You look like the cat that found a pot of cream, Jane. I guess it must be love."

Jane rolled her eyes and gave a saucy grin. "You're right and I've got a double dose of it. Hank is the kindest, sweetest, and most generous man I've ever met, and he is handsome too. So, that's why I'm walking around on 'cloud nine.'"

"Does he feel the same way, Jane?" asked Margie.

"I think he does, God I sure hope he does," said Jane worriedly.

Noticing the worry, Margie said, "I'll bet he is as bad as you. He didn't seem like the kind of man to . . . 'lead a girl on.'"

"No, but he said, there's something he wants to tell me this evening, so maybe I'll find out. You pray for me, Margie," said Jane and then stopped.

"Margie, what do you want to tell me? I've been talking non-stop since you walked in, so out with it, girl."

Margie had taken a seat beside of Jane's desk and now she clasped her hands in her lap. "I'm moving to Port Angeles as soon as the semester ends," she blurted out.

"Oh no! Margie, you're not giving up on school, are you? I thought you had grown to like it here."

Margie shook her head. "No, I'm going on to school, but I'm transferring to Peninsula College in Port Angeles. Have you ever heard of it?"

"Peninsula College! Sure, I've heard of it. In fact, I took some summer classes there in order to get my secretarial degree faster. It's a good school," said Jane.

"Why did you decide to go there? I know you had trouble in accounting when you first started, but you've come out with really good grades at the end."

Seeing Margie's look of surprise Jane quickly added, "Oops! Don't tell anyone I told you, but unless you fail your exams I think you have a 4.0 GPA. Your student adviser mentioned it in while we were at the conference. She was very proud of you, so why the sudden desire to leave us?"

"Jane, you have been very good to me and I love having you as my friend, but I haven't been satisfied. My landlady is like a mother to me, and others have helped me so much, like Hank who helped me with accounting, and you taking me to your home for Christmas, but Jane, I have some unresolved issues," explained Margie.

Jane, who had been standing beside her desk, pulled a chair in front of Margie and picked up her hands. "Do you know what these issues are, Margie?"

Margie shivered and straightened up in her seat. "Yes, I know what some problems are and I know I need some help. My friend, Jennifer Jacobs, has gotten me an appointment with a doctor near her hospital, so maybe I will learn about some of the others."

Jane released her hands. "Okay, how can I help?"

Margie's eyes lit up. "I was hoping you'd offer to help me. I don't know how to go about transferring my credits to Peninsula and I don't know what program I need to be in when I get transferred."

Jane smiled. "You're in luck, girl. You need training for a private secretarial position and also training and knowledge of business management. I can't work on it right now, but by the time you come to work tomorrow I may have something for you. Is that soon enough?

Margie jumped to her feet and hugged Jane. "You bet it is. Thanks Jane."

CHAPTER 35

Margie walked back to Mrs. Duke's in a much better frame of mind than she'd been in that morning, but as she neared the house she suddenly thought, *Oh no. Hank will be here to talk to me. What am I going to say? Should I tell him that I know about him and Jane?*

Reaching the house, Margie took in a deep breath and decided she'd just tell Hank she still felt the same and he'd have to accept it. When she stepped through the living room door she could hear Mrs. Duke on the phone. "She just came in. Do you want to talk to her?" Mrs. Duke turned and motioned for her to come to the phone.

Margie didn't ask. She knew it was Hank and she turned pale as she took the receiver from Mrs. Duke. "Hello, oh, hello Hank, when did you get back?" She stood listening for a moment and then said, "Sure, but wait until about six o'clock, if that's all right."

She turned to Mrs. Duke. "He's coming over at six o'clock. He wants to talk to me. Mrs. Duke, I have to tell him that I can't marry him and that he should look for somebody else. That's what I've told him all the time, but he thought I was just too young to make up my mind."

Mrs. Duke grimaced. "If that's the way you feel, I think it is the only thing to do, but I hate to see him hurt. He's such a good man."

"I don't think he'll be hurt, Mrs. Duke. I think it made him feel good to be able to help me and he knew I needed him. Perhaps, when his wife died he hadn't felt needed and he saw that I was in need," said Margie and then wondered where that came from. *Lord, did you send that? I've never thought of the situation in that light before now,* she thought in amazement.

Mrs. Duke stood staring, as if she too had never thought about Hank's demeanor in that manner. "Margie, you may be right. I hope you are since we both really like Hank."

Hank arrived promptly at six and Margie walked down to the car with him. He opened the door and she got in. He got in and closed his door, but didn't start the engine since Margie said, "Hank, let's just sit here and talk. There's no point in going anywhere else for I haven't changed my mind. You are a very nice person and you deserve better than someone as mixed up as I am."

Hank looked pleased. He said, "Thanks, Margie," with a relieved sigh.

He smiled as he continued, "I feared you might have changed your mind, even though I'd been hoping you would before I went to this conference. Margie, while I was there I became much better acquainted with someone I already knew and . . . well, she is someone of my own age who shares a lifestyle similar to mine and I . . ."

Margie grabbed his hand. "Hank, I know. Jane told me, but I didn't tell her about the situation before you left. It is up to you about what you tell her, but from my point of view you saw how needy I was and your heart went out to me. You were lonely and wanted to help somebody, but it wasn't the right kind of love. I'm almost as happy as you are; having my two good friends find each other is an answer to my prayers."

Hank reached over and picked up her other hand and held both hands clasped in his. "Again, thanks, Margie. You are not only a beautiful young girl, but also a very wise one. You've made me very happy, and now I have to go see Jane." Hank sat back in his seat with an almost boyish smile on his face.

Margie opened her door. "I'm happy for you and Jane, Hank, and I think I'll sleep a lot better tonight. Oh, I forgot to tell you. I'm leaving the university. I'm moving to Port Angeles and will attend Peninsula College."

Hank had a relieved look on his face as he said, "Well, as long as you finish your education. I've heard that Peninsula College is a good school and I wish you the very best. Please keep in touch with me and Jane."

Margie promised she would and stood on the sidewalk until he went out of sight down the street. She turned with a jaunty step and ran up the two steps to the lawn before the house and on up three more steps to the porch humming, 'My God, how great thou art.'

After seeing Jane the next afternoon, she knew she was leaving two wonderful people who would always have a special reason for remembering her. Jane had met her at the door with a hug so strong that Margie for a moment thought she was angry, but Jane released her and stepped back. "Oops! I don't want to break the wings of our angel."

Margie looked puzzled for a moment. "Oh, you mean about Hank. Well, I'm no angel, but you two don't know how happy I am that you have met and fallen in love with each other . . . Two super people who deserve good people to love.

Jane leaned against her desk. "Hank told me about your relationship and what you told him yesterday evening is so right. You made him very happy and of course, I'm on 'cloud nine.'"

Margie grinned. "Geez, I like this feeling. Making other people happy makes me happy too."

Jane ran behind her desk and pulled a folder from a drawer. "Here you are my friend. These are all the papers you have to sign in order to have everything transferred." She proceeded to explain what was done on each sheet before telling her to take it to the admissions office.

"They'll be expecting you. I've already talked to Mary Seymour and it shouldn't take you more than twenty minutes, so go on over there now and get that much off your mind."

A Fatal Beginning

As Jane had said, Margie was finished with the transfers in a very short time, and discovered that a girl working there with Miss Seymour had gotten her degree from Peninsula College. Her enthusiasm about her time spent there made Margie very happy. Mrs. Duke watched her coming down the street and as soon as Margie walked through the door she said, "Well, you walked down the street like you've won a prize or something. What's made you so happy?"

Margie stood looking for a moment. "You know, Mrs. Duke, it just seems like everything is falling right into place and I feel so . . . carefree, as if the world is good."

Mrs. Duke grinned. "Well, you're not in love, so it must be something awfully special to make you feel like that and I'm glad. You've been so tormented and worried and now to be like this is a miracle.

Margie placed her books on the table behind the door and walked over to the sofa and took a seat. "My mother prayed all the time, but when she died I felt like prayer was a waste of time. I used to tell her that, but she'd say, "No, please don't say that. God hears us and He does answer prayers. It may not be right when we want it to happen, but He answers at His time."

Mrs. Duke nodded. "She was right, Margie. God works out of our sight, but anything good that comes your way is a blessing from our loving God.

CHAPTER 36

On the twentieth of May, Margie Elaine Meadows left Seattle with high expectations. She knew she had grown wiser while living there, but ahead of her was a chance of getting to watch her baby grow up. This move would bring her closer to where he and his adoptive parents lived, thus enhancing her chance to see him. She often visualized what it would be like to see him and each time a hard lump would form in her throat.

Riding along in the backseat of Jennifer's car she was left to hope and plan about the first time she would see him. *I probably won't have an opportunity until he is old enough to walk*, she thought and grew sad with that thought. All this was interrupted by Jennifer.

"Hey, Little Sis, I'm talking to you. I'll bet you're already worrying about your classes, aren't you? Alex and I are hungry and we think there's a truck stop about two miles ahead. We plan to stop there unless you object."

Margie laughed. "Me object! I've never been in a truck stop, but my stomach is beginning to hurt, so I need food. I've lost seven pounds this last month and I need to put a stop to that."

While Margie was saying 'good-bye' to Mrs. Duke, Alex and Jennifer had talked about how thin Margie had gotten in the last month. "Yes, you have and we both noticed it. That's why we're taking you to the first place we can find to eat even if it's a truck stop; they pile a plate high," said Jennifer and around the next curve was a Truck Stop nestled in front of a row of tall pines. Alex pulled in and stopped.

As Margie walked through the door, held open by Alex, every man at the bar turned to stare. Margie stopped in alarm and turned toward Jennifer, who was behind her with questioning eyes. Alex, right behind Jennifer, grinned and looked around the room before saying, "Okay, fellas

A Fatal Beginning

they're with me. You can finish your meals." He ushered Jennifer and Margie to a booth by the window.

Jennifer slid into a seat and Margie sat across from her. As Alex took his seat, Jennifer asked, "Do women not eat in here?"

Alex chuckled. "They don't without an escort. These men didn't see me behind you two beauties."

Margie dropped her eyes since she realized that all eyes were still turned their way. "Do they always stare at people that come in here?"

"Just ignore them. They'll stop soon since they are on schedules and don't have time to waste," said Alex as the waitress brought the menus.

Soon a large number of men did leave. Margie relaxed and ate the best meal she had eaten in a month. "Mrs. Duke would be insulted if she could see how much I've eaten. She's a good cook, but I've been so on edge about everything that I really haven't been able to eat. I hope this doctor I'm scheduled to see will do something to settle my stomach," said Margie as she put her fork and napkin into the empty plate.

When they were back in the car Alex said, "Well, how did you girls like that meal?"

Jennifer grinned. "It was good, but I certainly wouldn't go there alone even if the food is good."

Margie shook her head. "Neither would I. They acted like they'd never seen a woman before."

Alex grinned apologetically. "I'm sorry girls. I knew the clientele in these places was usually truckers except for the occasional 'lady of the night' who stops by, but there's not another restaurant of any kind for about twenty miles and Margie really needed to eat."

Jennifer and Margie looked at each other and then Jennifer said, "Well, please don't take us to a place like that again. I . . . I guess we did gain some valuable information though just in case we ever travel this road alone." She looked back at Margie. "Didn't we, Little Sis?"

"I thought you already knew it all, Jenns, but I sure don't know much about the world," said Margie.

"No, I sure don't know it all, by half, but I do know more than you, Little Sis. You're like a baby trying to learn to walk. Isn't she Alex?" asked Jennifer.

Alex glanced over his shoulder at Margie and chuckled. "She's pretty green, but Lieutenant Steve Hammer would certainly love to educate her."

"Do you still hear from him, Alex?" asked Jennifer and although Margie didn't say anything she was eager to hear his answer.

"I've heard once since the veteran's dinner, but it was all about that beautiful girl he met who got sick at the sight of him," said Alex.

Nobody said anything until Margie blurted out. "I didn't know him and I don't want to know him or any other man. I'm going to concentrate on getting my secretarial degree and getting a good job. I don't need some man cluttering up my life."

"Whoa! You sure are down on men" said Alex. "Men don't clutter up lives any more than women do. Or, at least, I don't think they do."

Margie leaned up toward the front seat. "I'm sorry, Alex. I didn't mean you and I really didn't mean that the way it sounded. I only meant that there is something much more important to me, than any man." Margie was about to cry and Alex heard it in her voice.

"I was kidding, Margie. Don't get upset. Of course, I do think men are pretty important, but then I am a man and of course I'm going to feel that way," said Alex.

Jennifer looked back at Margie. "You're tired, Little Sis. Just relax and dose off if you want to. Alex likes to say things to get a discussion started, but he doesn't mean any harm."

Jennifer turned on the radio and they rode the rest of the way listening to the mellow voices of Nat King Cole, Bing Crosby, and Perry Como.

When they pulled into the parking space at the Jacobs farm, Jennifer looked back and saw that Margie was sound asleep. Alex cut off the engine and also looked back. "She looks like a little lost girl, doesn't she?" he asked as he opened the door to exit.

Jennifer smiled. "Yes, she does. I think she really is lost in a way, but she is very determined. I hope that one day she will allow me to tell her story, but right now it's too raw."

She reached into the back and gently patted Margie's arm. "Little Sis." Margie jerked back with a wild startled look in her eyes.

"It's okay, Margie. We're home and you've slept most of the way here." Margie sat up and looked around her before relaxing and opening her door.

CHAPTER 37

Before two weeks had passed, Margie was enrolled in Peninsula College and was the owner of a good looking, though used, blue Ford coupe. She bought it from the Ford dealership where Alex worked after she had passed her driver's test and got her license.

She was scared to death when she started her driving lessons, but both Alex and Jennifer worked with her. Every evening they had her doing various driving maneuvers over and over until they felt she had mastered them and then made her park in any little nook (or so it seemed to Margie) that could be found.

After passing her driving test and driving all over the area for over a month she felt she was ready to tackle college. She drove carefully along the road leading to the college, since she hadn't driven that way before now. She parked in a spot near the student union cafeteria to get some coffee and a doughnut. *I'm so nervous that I'm going to be sick if I don't eat a bite of something* she thought as she stood waiting her turn to order.

In front of her a girl with shoulder length blonde hair was also waiting and Margie could tell she was getting impatient. She shifted her weight from one foot to the other and looked around the man in front of her to see how long the line was. Finally, she groaned and turned back toward Margie, "They're going to make me late for class. I hate to be late on the very first day."

The girl was pretty and had the bluest eyes Margie had ever seen. Her quick smile lit up her face when Margie said, "I'll be later than you and I don't really know where to go. I've never been here before."

An interested look appeared in the girl's eyes as she looked at Margie. She seemed to know how nervous Margie was for she said, "Don't let that bother you. Where do you need to go, I mean, what class do you want? I'll take you to it as soon as we get our orders."

"Won't that make you later? I don't want to cause you a problem," said Margie.

The girl smiled. "You don't know me, girl. Trouble and problems follow me around, but I'm not afraid of them. I'm Sue Davis and I have Mrs. King for accounting. She knows me and I'll get fussed at, but I just ignore it and go right on. What's your name?"

"I'm Margie Meadows. I just moved to Sequim. I transferred from the university in Seattle and I also have accounting with Mrs. King in first period. Is Mrs. King a good teacher?"

"Some people say she's good. I had her in high school and I can't say she's bad, but high school is a lot different than college."

She chuckled. "Well, my attitude was different in high school. Mom made me go to school back then, but now I need it for my job," said Sue with a knowing smile.

Finally, they reached the counter and ordered their food and Sue turned to Margie. "Can you walk and eat at the same time? Our classroom is upstairs and across the quad."

Margie nodded and followed Sue from the cafeteria. The doughnut seemed to lodge like a heavy load in her stomach and Margie began to feeling queasy as they neared the building. She threw out the remainder of her coffee and started up the steps to the Science building, but was stopped by Sue.

"Hey, are you sick? If you get much whiter you'll blend with the walls. Here let me have those books before you fall over," said Sue, reaching for the books Margie was clutching to her chest.

Margie released the books and took a deep breath. "I'm scared and I often get nauseous, but I think I'll be all right."

"Scared! Why? You take a class, you study, and you either pass or fail your tests, but either way life goes on, so 'don't sweat the small stuff.'"

"It isn't 'small stuff' to me. I need to have good grades to get a good job," said Margie.

Sue grinned. "I did tell you that I needed this class for my job, didn't I?"

Margie's eyes widened. "Oops! I'm sorry. That sounded very rude. I think I'm too used to being alone."

Sue laughed and tapped her shoulder. "It's okay, but we'd better get a move on or we'll really be in trouble."

This incident led to a mutual friendship for the entire semester. Sue revealed that her young and very handsome husband had been drowned when she was pregnant with their second child. Her mother was helping with the children so Sue could work.

Although Margie liked and trusted Sue she still did not mention her background except to say her parents were both dead. She often listened to Sue's philosophy on life and soon realized that she was the most 'life accepting person' she'd ever met. Soon she found herself trying to adopt Sue's attitude about life. *Sue is a girl with two young children to bring up alone. She has just lost the husband she loved, and has picked up the pieces of her life and is making the best of it. That's what I need to do*, Margie thought as she drove to and from the college each day.

Peninsula College was a really good school and Margie had no trouble getting work as a student helper to defray expenses. She had some money left after purchasing her car, but she feared dipping into her 'nest egg' any further and was glad she now had a job. Since she had worked in administration at the university in Seattle she was now working as acting secretary to the Dean of Students, a kind, gentleman named William Elton. Margie didn't know it at the time, but this job would lead her to a very well-paid position after she finished college.

A Fatal Beginning

Before the semester had ended Margie got to meet Sue's mother and her two little girls. This only increased her longing to hold her own baby as Sue snuggled her youngest close in her arms. Both little girls had dark hair and eyes, which Sue said was inherited from their daddy. The oldest girl, Leann, had a bright, chirping voice and a sweet smile that made Margie think of Rick, her first and only love. Margie felt tears well up in her eyes and quickly coughed and looked away to cough several more times before she turned back. "I don't know what I got strangled on. I'm sorry."

Sue shrugged. "It's probably sinus drainage since this is the middle of allergy season."

At the end of the semester, the two friends parted with promises on both sides that they would keep in touch, but as things usually happen, they lost touch and it was nearly forty years before their paths met again.

Margie did so well in her classes and was so efficient on her job that the dean advised her to submit some resumes to various employment agencies. She sent in materials to ten different agencies, but had little hope of receiving any replies.

Even though her goal was a well-paid job in order to help her son, her focus had not been as much on getting a job as it had been in finding out everything she could about her baby. She had asked Jennifer to find anything she could about him and she drove by the house on a monthly basis in the hope of seeing him. Once a man came out of the house carrying a bundle, which she knew was her baby, but she couldn't see him.

Jennifer had learned that the name given him by the Larkins, his adoptive parents, was William Richard Larkin. *I wonder if they call him Rick,* thought Margie since she knew that boys named Richard were often called Rick. His biological father was really Richard Allen Mullet, but everyone called him Rick. Margie thought the likelihood of him being given a name that closely like his real father's name was amazing. *God, is this your way of keeping me, the baby, and Rick linked together?* This was her first thought when Jennifer told her his name.

Later Margie often wondered how she was able to keep up her grades, work, and keep track of the movements of the Larkins. She realized that Dr. Auriel Moses, the psychiatrist Jennifer had gotten her to see, had helped her accept that bad things often happen to good people and that her mother would not want her to let it ruin her life.

Dr. Moses's advice had been, "Margie, keep in mind that your mother was willing to give up her life so that you could live and have a good life. Don't you feel you'll be letting your mother down if you stop trying when the going gets rough?"

Margie felt she was trying to live her life in a normal way, but she still had problems sleeping, and her stomach still hurt. *All I want to do now is to help my baby and to honor the memory of my mother. My sweet mother was the nearest thing to an angel that I've ever known,* thought Margie when she recalled all the abuse her mother had suffered.

A Fatal Beginning

CHAPTER 38

Jennifer and Alex tried to introduce Margie to various men they knew, but soon found that Margie had no interest. "Little Sis, are you telling Dr. Moses about your avoidance of men?" Jennifer queried.

"I've told her my whole life, but I don't talk about men, . . . well, not now, but I had to tell her my whole life when I first started seeing her. That was the hardest thing I've ever done. In fact, I walked out the first time I went to see her, but when I thought about helping my baby I went back. Now, she knows that I am concentrating on getting my degree and getting a good job. I told her that I didn't want to deal with any relationships and wanted to put that side of my life on a 'back burner' until I got all these other things straightened out," said Margie.

During the next two years Margie's existence was comprised of helping around the house, cooking on the weekends, going to school, studying, and driving up and down the street past the Larkin home. One week she dared to drive past the house for an entire week, but at different times of the day. After not seeing anyone the whole week she became very discouraged.

"Jenns, I believe there is something wrong with my baby. He's old enough to be outside and I drove past there at different times every day for an entire week and not once saw any child," complained Margie in a worried voice.

The sadness displayed on Margie's face moved Jennifer to tears. "Little Sis, don't worry I'll see if I can find out something for you, but I know he hasn't been brought in to the hospital. I look at admittances at least twice each week."

Margie's eyes lit up. "Is there a pediatric unit in your hospital? Or, If you know any of the nurses or doctors who work with children, can you ask them?"

A Fatal Beginning

Jennifer assured her that she would and the very next evening she came in with a big smile on her face. She found Margie in the kitchen alone and said, "You won't believe what I found out. It is just like some unexpected information just dropped right into my lap."

Margie grabbed her arm. "Jenns, is it about my baby?"

Jennifer grinned. "A woman was in the waiting room when Jerry Slater came in to see Dr. Culpepper and I heard her say Larkin. Of course, that caught my attention and so I acted like I was straightening the magazines and checking on empty coffee cups so I could hear what she said. She said she left her little girl with Mary Larkin since her little girl is 'in love' with Billy Larkin. She went on to say, that they had a very safe place to play since the entire backyard was fenced-in."

Tears slid down Margie's cheeks. "A girl in love with my baby, but he's not a baby anymore. He's growing up, Jenns. He's four years old or will be next month and I've never seen him, and sometimes I don't think I can stand it any longer."

Margie stopped to wipe her eyes and swallow the lump in her throat. "Jenns, I think that if I could just see him 'face to face' just one time I wouldn't be so distraught. The way it is, I just ache inside at the thought that I have a little boy and will never get to know him."

Jennifer dropped her head. "I thought that bringing you that news would help and make you happy, but it's made it worse for you. I'm sorry, Little Sis."

Margie quickly turned to Jennifer. "No, Jenns, you didn't make it worse. I was beginning to worry since I thought I should have seen him outside, but you brought me relief on that score. You telling me that a little girl loves my baby is so cute and so sweet, but it hurts to hear about some stranger knowing more about my baby than I do. At least, though, I know he is all right and just playing in a back yard, so I do thank you, Jenns. I thank you so very much."

Jennifer shook her head. "You'd better thank God. The chances of me even being in that waiting room are very slim and then for that woman to be talking about your baby struck me as being one of those 'miracles' Mom always talks about."

Margie dropped to a chair and covered her face as she sobbed brokenly. "I'm ashamed, Jenns. It was a miracle and I never once thought about God working it out. I hope He will forgive me."

Jennifer dropped to her knees in front of Margie. "Don't you dare start weighing yourself down with guilt. God is just proving to you that He loves you and is watching over you and little Billy."

Margie raised her head and said, "Thanks Jenns. I don't know why you are so good to me, but I really appreciate it. I've realized from the first that God had a hand on my life when I was allowed to live and then to meet you and your family. I would be all alone without you, Uncle James and Aunt Amy."

Jennifer rose to her feet. "Maybe you should keep a journal of the miracles being performed in your life, Little Sis. I think you'll see the path of a 'purposed God."

Margie didn't get a chance to question her belief in a 'purposed God' because they heard the Jacob's truck pull into the parking space beside the house. She knew they would be expecting food to be on the table and she had been talking to Jennifer. Margie darted to the cabinet and gathered the plates, glasses, and silverware to set the table.

James Jacobs stepped through the door, stopped and sniffed loudly. "I can smell something good, Amy, but it is not on the table as you predicted."

Jennifer turned to go up to her room, but stopped." It's my fault. I came in telling Margie about my day and kept her from setting the table. I'll be back to help as soon as I take my things to my room.

Amy laughed. "Now, you girls know how your dad makes a big deal out of nothing. He wanted to bet me that Margie would have supper ready before we left the store, so I told him I wasn't betting. He just didn't want me to linger in the store in case something caught my eye and I'd buy it."

James grinned and put his arm around Amy. "You're getting smarter all the time. It won't be long before you're smarter than I am."

"James Jacobs I've been smarter than you from the time I met you. I got a man who wouldn't even look at a girl to marry me, didn't I?" Amy giggled at the pretended look of chagrin on his face.

James shrugged. "I'm good for a laugh anyway even if I'm not too smart."

Margie finished putting the last dish on the table as she said, "I think you're smart enough to keep, don't you, Aunt Amy?"

Amy put her arm around James and said, "Come on, you pitiful man. Let me lead you to the table since I know you are starved nearly to death. It's been nearly four hours since you've had a bite to eat."

Jennifer had returned to the room and they all settled around the table and Margie thought how blessed she was to have been taken in and treated like family by these wonderful people. "Uncle James, I know you like western movies so how would you like it if I took us all to see Shane, with Alan Ladd? It is showing at the theater in Port Angeles. We could go to the four o'clock showing and get home before dark."

James looked around the table. "Well, don't just sit there, looking dumb. Do you two ladies want to go? I know I'd like to, since Alan Ladd is my favorite actor."

"When? I mean what day, Margie? I don't want to be gone in case Alex if free," said Jennifer.

"Well, let him come too, but he'd have to pay his own way," said James with a dead serious look.

"Alex has brought food out here on three or four evenings, Dad, so don't start acting like he's a sponger," said Jennifer in a bristling tone.

"I don't really care who else is going, but I want to go and I really don't care what day. You get the tickets, Margie, and I'll be ready," said Amy.

"What about this coming Friday, if I can get the tickets?" Margie looked around for approval and seeing every head nodding she smiled and rose to her feet. "That's settled then, and Jenns, if Alex is free and wants to go I'll buy his ticket too."

This turned into a monthly outing to a movie, a festival, a western rodeo, or some form of entertainment for the whole family. Margie explained to all of them that Dr. Moses had encouraged her to start doing things that were different from what she usually did. "So, really I dragged my family into helping me have so-called entertainment. To be honest though, it is the best I've felt in a long time and I thank all of you for going along with me."

"Thank you! Why Margie, I think the rest of us need this just as much as you do. Just look at Amy and Jennifer's faces. They look a heap happier than they did the night we went to see Shane," said James.

A Fatal Beginning

CHAPTER 39

Since Margie had attended winter and summer classes she was able to graduate with degrees in secretarial work and office management in August of that year. She was very happy to leave school even though she knew she had learned many things other than her office skills and this contributed to her happiness. She now had more confidence and was more adapted to living life among strangers and in crowds. She was also more trusting, but still didn't allow many people into her confidences.

She put in job applications, but had narrowed her search to Sequim, Port Angeles, Shelton, Seattle, and Forks before she left college, but hoped she didn't get a job in Forks. That town had too many bad memories and she didn't know if she could really work there or not, but if a super job was offered she knew she'd at least try it.

Jennifer cautioned her to be careful and not take the first job offer she received. "You're more qualified than half the people out looking for work, Margie, so you can afford to be selective."

Margie grimaced. "I know I can do the office work, but I don't have any social skills, or at least they are very limited."

Jennifer grinned. "For a girl who was never more than twenty miles from home in her life, I think you do well, Little Sis. You can't see the 'you' that others see. You'll do fine except for the fact that some man may try to play the flirtation game, especially since you are so pretty."

"I'd just walk out if that happened to me," said Margie.

"No, don't be hasty. My advice is to give him a cool look and walk away the first time, but if his actions still persist then threaten to file a grievance unless you don't like the job anyway," advised Jennifer.

A Fatal Beginning

One of Margie's applications and resumes had been mailed to Nippon Paper Industries, but it was the last one to respond with an offer of an interview. Since this company was big and also located in Port Angeles, it was very appealing to Margie. While attending college she had become acquainted with the town and felt comfortable driving in it. She eagerly replied to that offer, which had given all the pertinent information about the date, time, and place for the interview.

Margie had received seven previous invitations to be interviewed and had responded to each. Three of them had explained that a girl had been hired the day before or at least that week. Two of the interviews made Margie want to walk out before they were finished. Those two were scheduled for the same day and Margie felt very defeated. She had decided she didn't want to apply to the other two companies, but she had hoped she would hear from the Nippon Paper Industries. Now she feared they were no longer interested.

That evening she talked to Jennifer. "I'm about to give up, Jenns. That Mr. Walters, with the television station, was so eager to pat my shoulder or hold my hand that I felt disgusted and couldn't wait to leave, but he wasn't as outright offensive as Mr. Altizer, the man at that tractor supply company. That man only looked at my face when I first entered his office. After that he was smiling or making suggestive remarks. He even had the audacity to say, 'Would you require extra pay if asked to do personal errands or things like that?'

Jennifer gasped. "What did you say to that?"

"I said, 'What sort of errands are you speaking of, sir?' and he smiled and said, 'Well, you're an adult and must know that men will find you attractive, and . . .' I didn't let him finish. I jumped to my feet and said, 'Good day, Mr. Altizer. I don't feel I would fit your requirements" and I walked out.

Jennifer laughed. "Geez, I wish I could have seen that. I'm so proud of you, Little Sis. Don't give up though, you still have one more that hasn't replied, don't you?"

"Yes, but I don't feel like they're going to reply since it's been nearly two weeks," said Margie.

"Tomorrow is another day, Little Sis, and we'll just have to pray harder tonight.

When Jennifer arrived home the next evening, Margie had the letter in her pocket and pulled it out as Jennifer stepped into the kitchen. "Look at this! I sent my request for an interview two weeks ago. I must have been their last resort. Is that a bad omen or not, Jenns?"

Jennifer scanned over the letter. "I don't know, Margie. It may be that your resume looked so exactly like the person they wanted to hire that they were wary. I can't think of why a company this size would have any other reason. They haven't seen you. They could have talked to someone at the college, but that would only make them more interested. You're going, aren't you?"

Margie took the letter back and put it in her pocket. "You bet I'm going. I know Port Angeles and I wouldn't feel like I'm in an alien world. I applied for a position as a secretary, but I could do anything as to the office work. I hope it is a personal secretary. When you work for just one person, you don't have to adjust to so many different personalities."

"You'll do fine and I'll bet you get the job. Where are Mom and Dad," asked Jennifer since she could tell that Margie had cooked their dinner.

Margie smiled. "Jerry Slater called and wanted them to go to an auction with him. It seems that he trusts Uncle James's 'know-how' about bidding on farm equipment at auctions."

Jennifer laughed. "Yes, and that tickles Dad. He loves to think he knows more than Jerry Slater. They are really good friends, but unless you really know them you'd think they had a feud going."

During dinner, the discussion was all about the job interview and everybody had an opinion or advice. The women had done most of the talking, which was unusual, since James Jacobs was a talker and loved to approach things in a logical manner, or so he often proclaimed. When Margie pushed back her chair from the table, James spoke up.

"Wait just a minute, Margie. I've been thinking this over while you women have been babbling. Did you ask about the salary offered? If you didn't there's a few things to think about. You have to decide how much your trip to and from the place will cost. Gas, oil, tires, and insurance ain't cheap, and also figure in housing. You'd have to pay rent if you didn't stay here, and we want you to stay here at home, but they don't have to know that. Another thing is vacation and whether it is paid or not." James hesitated as he looked around the table. "You women just talk about clothes, and stuff like that, but I don't want you to go in to that interview without some costs in mind."

James had their attention and Margie sat down again. "I hadn't thought about those things, Uncle James, but I don't know what kind of salary I should expect." She looked at Jennifer. "What should I ask, Jenns? I guess I need to do some research before I do anything else."

Jennifer had a thoughtful look on her face. "Gosh, Little Sis, I have no idea what you should ask. I know what nurses get paid, but what a 'high-powered secretary should receive, I haven't a clue."

Amy broke in. "Why not call that Jane Lewis that you worked for at the university. Wasn't she a secretary?"

Margie looked at the wall clock. "It's only seven, and she doesn't go to bed for hours yet. I'm going to call her right now." She jumped to her feet and turned to smile at Amy. "Thanks, Aunt Amy. I should have called her as soon as I graduated."

An hour later, the family once again gathered around the table and laid out the barebones of what Margie needed to find out in an interview. Jennifer pulled the notepad over to view it more closely. "You know, Little Sis, you need to make a copy of this and whether you get this job or not, it will be useful in any interview you have."

A Fatal Beginning

CHAPTER 40

Armed with all her interview information Margie drove slowly into Port Angeles on the scheduled morning and parked at the side of the building marked Parking for Nippon employees. She was dressed in a newly purchased brown business suit with a cream silk blouse underneath. Her shoes were dressy, but not spike-heeled as a more modern girl may have worn and her purse went well with the outfit. Margie looked very professional, or so Jennifer had told her as she went out to the car.

She opened the glass doors leading into a reception area and walked up to the desk. "My name is Margie Meadows and I'm here for an interview with Mr. Paul Seaton."

The girl looked up and smiled. "Wow! I think Mr. Seaton is going to be surprised. You did graduate from Peninsula College, didn't you?"

Margie's eyes widened. "Yes, I did. What did this Mr. Seaton expect? I mean, you act surprised. Am I not what this Mr. Seaton is looking for?"

The girl sobered. "I . . . Well, you are very pretty and from what the college told him, I think he assumed you were very bookish and prim."

"Doesn't he want someone who likes books?" Margie's voice showed alarm.

"No . . . no, I don't know. I've probably already said too much. I'll buzz his office." The girl put in the call. "Tell Mr. Seaton that a Miss Meadows is here for her interview. . . . Okay, I'll send her right up." Margie's stomach had begun churning as bile rose in her throat. *Stop this, you're here for a job and if it doesn't go well you won't be any worse than you were before,* she scolded herself silently as the elevator swished to a stop on the second floor.

A Fatal Beginning

She exited the elevator and turned right as per directions and saw a door with President Paul Seaton etched on the glass panel. She stopped in front of the door and took a deep breath before she knocked.

Margie's knock was answered by a short, well-dressed woman in her late fifties, whose eyes had a startled look as she tried to smile, before asking, "You are Margie Meadows, aren't you?"

Margie smiled warily since the girl downstairs had told them she was coming up, but she replied. "Yes, I am."

The woman pulled herself into a more correct posture as she looked down on a paper in her hand and said, "Yes, we have you on our schedule. Come in please."

She stepped aside and Margie walked past her into a nicely appointed room furnished with a large desk in front of a wide window, showing a panoramic view of the city. Margie stopped and stood hesitantly waiting for the man behind the desk to speak.

When he just sat staring as if puzzled, the woman who ushered her in said, "Mr. Seaton, this is Margie Meadows. She is here for her appointed interview for my replacement."

Mr. Seaton was a man of middle-age, not handsome, but certainly not ugly, in Margie's estimation, and also, for some reason, he wasn't pleased to see her.

Well, I won't be hired here and it is my last interview, Margie thought, as what confidence she had built up started oozing away.

The man suddenly came from behind his desk and put out his hand. Margie, who felt tremors of fear run through her, put out her hand to find it clasped in a warm, firm handshake.

"I'm pleased to meet you, Miss Meadows. You are the Margie Meadows who just graduated from Peninsula College aren't you?"

"Yes Sir. I graduated three weeks ago," replied Margie.

Mr. Seaton pointed to a chair in front of his desk and said, "Please take a seat."

When Margie was seated, Mr. Seaton turned toward the woman who had taken a seat beside Margie, and said, "This is my secretary, Hilda Rasher, who finds it necessary to leave us."

Margie turned toward the woman and again saw the puzzled look on her face, but still smiled and said, "I'm glad you're here. I'm a little nervous."

Both Mr. Seaton and Miss Rasher seemed surprised by this, but Miss Rasher said, "Is this your first job interview?"

Margie answered no and hoped they didn't question her about all of the others, but felt certain they would. She didn't plan to reveal anything about her former life or her birth name. She hoped she had put that behind her forever.

The interview began and, just as she thought, she was asked about the other interviews. She told what happened without naming any names. She was asked about her family and had to tell that both her parents were dead. She explained that the Jacobs family had welcomed her into their own family, so she wasn't alone.

When this part was finished she was asked to take a letter, which Mr. Seaton would dictate, Margie felt a little easier since she knew she was very good with shorthand. She took the letter, typed it, and placed it on Mr. Seaton's desk for approval. She also took part in a make-belief telephone conversation with another business, with Mr. Seaton and Miss Rasher listening in. This made her uneasy and by the end of the call she was again feeling nauseous. *Oh Lord, please keep me from vomiting until after this is over*, she thought.

With firm control, she kept her nausea from growing worse. When she put down the receiver, her two listeners sat back and looked at each other, while Margie sat quaking inside.

Finally, Mr. Seaton said, "Miss Meadows, you have proven that you know all about the job of secretary, and that you have knowledge of the intricacies of business. You have also proven that you know how to react to other businesses, but to be honest, you are not what we, I, expected. You are much younger than we had thought and also much more attractive than we were led to believe."

Margie had been so nervous, fearing she would mess up on her secretarial tasks, and now she wanted to scream or strike out. She felt it very unfair to be turned down because of her youth or her looks. With a white face and tightly pressed lips, she slowly rose to her feet and stood looking at Mr. Seaton. In short crisp words, she said, "I don't know who you spoke to at the college, but to be told that I know what a job entails, yet be turned down because of my youth which is twenty-three, or my looks, which shouldn't have any bearing on my competence for the job, is very upsetting. Thanks for allowing me to interview."

Margie turned toward the door when Mr. Seaton said, "Wait! I didn't say you would not be hired. The college described you as rather introverted, intelligent, but very studious and straight-laced, which in our minds does not describe you at all."

Margie stopped when she heard 'wait', but now she turned back to Mr. Seaton. Clamping her lips together for a moment, she drew in a breath in an effort to keep control and said, "How old or how unattractive does one have to be to be hired?"

Mr. Seaton saw that she was upset, but he was in a quandary himself. Having been very pleased with Margie in the interview, and not wanting her to be hurt, Miss Rasher spoke up. "Miss Meadows, please don't be offended. Mr. Seaton has hired hundreds of people and he looks at all aspects and eventualities of each of his personnel and of course has his reasons to hire whomever he feels is the best fit for the position."

Margie turned even paler as she realized that her words were, 'way out of line.' She dropped her head to fight the threatening tears for a moment and then looked up.

"I'm so sorry. Both you and Mr. Seaton are right, but I had such hopes of finding a job in Port Angeles. I have no excuse, except that I am very nervous. I'll know better on my next interview. I thank you both and again, I'm sorry."

Margie turned to leave and Mr. Seaton said, "Miss Meadows, I normally would not do this, but I feel you need some answers. This interview that you just completed was for my personal secretary. If hired, in that position, you would be required to attend conferences and meetings in various places. Most of the people I meet with are men, and I have found that attractive ladies, such as you, can become a distraction."

All the talks she and Jennifer had about flirtatious bosses flashed through her mind. She turned and tried to smile. "I see. Thanks for telling me, but I don't feel there would be a problem with me. I'm told that I can be very, uh 'off-putting' around men, whatever that means. However, you don't know me and can't hire on my word only. I did so hope to get a job here in Port Angeles. Thanks again."

Margie walked quickly from the room, closing the door gently behind her and with tears streaming down her cheeks she dashed to the elevator. On the way down, she scrubbed her face and tried to look poised as she stepped back into the reception lobby.

The receptionist met her as she started toward the front entrance. "Miss Meadows, you've been asked to please return to Mr. Seaton's office."

Margie gave a surprised gasp. "What?"

A Fatal Beginning

"Hilda Rasher just called and told me to stop you and ask that you return to Mr. Seaton's office," said the receptionist.

Seeing Margie hesitate she said, "I'd go if I were you. She sounded as if it was very urgent that I catch you before you left the building."

Margie smiled. "Thanks. I guess you're right. Wish me luck."

This was the beginning of Margie's twenty-year position with Nippon Paper Industries, and her lasting friendship with Paul Seaton, his wife, and their family.

During her twenty-year tenure, Margie was a part of most of their family holidays and vacations. Alice Seaton, his wife and Sarah and Shelley, his two ten-year-old twin daughters came in to meet her on the second day on the job.

So, after three weeks of anxiety, bad dreams, and wrought nerves Margie became the private secretary of Mr. Paul Seaton, President of Nippon Paper Industries in Port Angeles, Washington at a splendid salary, plus healthcare and paid vacations.

She stayed on with the Jacobs family for the first month and once or twice each week she drove by the Larkin home hoping to see her baby. In the first week of the second month, Mr. Seaton told her that it would be a good idea if she lived in town since he often had to go to unexpected meetings.

"There are some nice apartments in a gated complex at the end of my street and I believe you could afford the rent. I'll get Alice to check on it for you if you like," said Mr. Seaton.

Margie agreed and the following week, Alice picked her up at the office and took her to look at a two-bedroom apartment. Margie loved it and with the help of Alice Seaton and the Jacobs family she soon moved into her own place.

Amy and Jennifer Jacobs knew how to shop for bargains and during the next month they helped her scour Goodwill stores, bargain sales, estate sales, and every place they could think of to get furniture as cheaply as possible.

At first, Margie adamantly refused to go into debt. "I'll just get a bed and a sofa now and buy the rest as I find it," she explained, but Jennifer refused to allow that.

"Little Sis, this apartment is too nice to start like that." Jennifer had helped Margie with her banking and finances and knew what she had so she felt safe in saying, "Margie, you have quite a bit left from the sale of the farm, so use some of it. It is like an investment." Jennifer laughed at Margie's expression as she pulled her out the door to try another estate sale.

With patience and persistence from Jennifer, it wasn't long until Margie found her apartment completely furnished with some really nice pieces of furniture.

The evening the living room furniture was delivered, she and Jennifer placed every piece then stood back at the door to survey their handiwork.

"Jenns, this looks really nice. It is much nicer than anything Mom ever had even if it has been used. That sofa and chair looks as if it has never been used at all, doesn't it," said Margie with pride in her voice.

A Fatal Beginning

CHAPTER 41

During the two months of hectic activity and the stress of adjustment to a entirely new and totally independent lifestyle, Margie had no spare time to drive by the Larkin home. However, she had dreamed about her baby several times and planned to start again as quickly as possible.

Now that her little boy was four years old, she felt she would have a better chance of seeing him, so she planned each week to have some time to drive by the house. "I'll have to go in the evenings and I will be less likely to see him," she grumbled since she worked until five o'clock each day except Saturdays.

Margie and Jennifer talked most evenings and they decided that if Jennifer wasn't expecting Alex she would agree to ride with Margie past the Larkin home one evening each week.

"Margie, Mr. Larkin is probably home on Saturdays, wouldn't that be the best day?" asked Jennifer. Margie agreed and Saturdays became her days to drive that way, but each time she wore sunglasses or sometimes a hat and sometimes a ball cap. After a full month of not seeing even the man or the woman, Margie was getting very discouraged until Jennifer called her to say that she'd heard that the Larkins had been away on vacation.

A week later, Jennifer called Margie at work. "Little Sis, I think you'll want to hear this, but I'm not sure I should tell you. I've prayed about it though and I think you should know, so I'll make it quick. Little Billy Larkin is to go to a Christian Preschool. He'll start next month. I know you're always worried that he may be sick or something. You have to know that him starting school means he is well and healthy and that's why I felt I should tell you."

"Find out where it is, Jennifer. I can go by there without being noticed," said Margie in an excited voice.

"No. Margie, I'm not going to tempt you by finding out where it is. I just know you won't be able to stay away and you're getting more and more desperate. You'd get caught and I'd lose my job," said Jennifer.

Margie knew she was excited, but tried to regain her usual calm voice before replying. "Jenns, I promised and I won't break my promise. I'll just keep driving by ". . . but she suddenly blurted out. "Jenns, he'll be coming out to the playground. Oh Jenns, I might get to see him."

Margie, swallowed repeatedly as tears clogged her throat and she knew Jennifer would know it if she spoke, so she waited for calm, but Jennifer cut in. "Little Sis, you've never seen him. There will be lots of little boys on that playground."

Margie groaned and heaved a labored sigh. "You're right, Jenns. There has to be a way, though. I think I could die happy if I could just see him full in the face."

"I know, I'm going to get myself in trouble, but I'll see if I can find out more about it for you. You have to promise me, though, that you will never go into that school or try to contact him. Little Sis, you know I would lose my job and never be allowed to work as a nurse again . . . or maybe be fined or sent to jail," warned Jennifer.

"I promise, Jenns, that I will never make any contact or speak about him to anyone else as long as he is a child. When he is an adult, however, I will try to be a part of his life," said Margie.

Jennifer hesitated since she knew that Margie's stomach problems and her frequent nightmares had become a part of her past, but desire to see her baby seemed to grow stronger as she aged.

Finally, she said, "Margie, like I said, I'll try to find out, but promise me that you won't go near that school unless I'm with you."

Jennifer heard Margie's sigh before she said, "Thanks, Jenn. I promise I'll pick a time when you can go with me before I go by the school."

Jennifer started to say bye, but was stopped. "Jenns, try to get a picture of the school or his class or something. We may not be able to pick him out if we don't know what he looks like, but even though you'll think I'm crazy for saying this, I think I'll know him," said Margie.

"You're weird, Little Sis. How could you know him if you've never seen him?" asked Jennifer.

"I knew you'd say that, but I still think I'll know him. You have to remember that I carried him close to my heart for several months," replied Margie in a satisfied voice.

"Every mother carries their babies, but they have no idea what they will look like until they're born and can look at them. You didn't get to look at your baby so how are you going to recognize him?" asked Jennifer.

Tears were now streaming from Margie's eyes as she whispered, "Because I saw him in my dreams, Jenns. I've seen him in dreams several times, but I've never been able to see the color of his hair . . . his face is the thing that stands out in my dreams. I don't know why I've never noticed the color of his hair."

"I've gotta run, Little Sis. I'm on the clock and Nurse Grimsby will chew me out good if I don't finish the BP rounds," said Jennifer and hung up the phone.

Just as Margie replaced the receiver, Alice Seaton came through the door. "That must have been a really important call. I've been trying to get you for the past half-hour," she said as a wide smile lit up her entire face.

Margie grinned. "It was an important call. Every call coming into this office is important even when the boss's wife calls. Why were you calling me?"

"Have you had lunch? There's a new restaurant two blocks down that I want to try out and I don't want to eat alone," said Alice Seaton.

Margie smiled. "I haven't eaten, but let me see if Mr. Seaton has anything he will need me to do for an hour. This has been a rather busy week and he is planning that conference back east next month."

"Well, don't tell him that his wife is interfering with business or he won't let me go to the conference. He knows I want to visit the Statue of Liberty and Ellis Island," said Alice.

"Ellis Island! Most everybody wants to visit the Statue of Liberty, but I wouldn't have thought many people would want to visit Ellis Island. I think I would though. What's the attraction for you?" asked Margie.

"I want to see what Dad's real name was before they shortened it at Ellis Island?" replied Alice.

"Shortened it? How do you know that? I know some people had names that were difficult to spell and so their names were often spelled incorrectly and from then on it was pronounced incorrectly, but I didn't know they were shortened." Margie sounded puzzled.

Alice shook her head. "You see, Dad was hit by a crane on a construction job when I was small and I couldn't ask him. Mom said he told her some strange name that she couldn't pronounce and so she only knew him as James Daniel Hornick."

CHAPTER 42

Margie didn't hear from Jennifer for another week, but when she did hear, it was good news. On Tuesday evening, she had just walked into her apartment when the phone rang. She picked it up to hear Jennifer's excited voice.

"Get a pen, Little Sis, I have a name and address of the school little Billy Larkin will be attending," said Jennifer.

Margie ran to an end table, used as a phone and information center, and grabbed a pen. Sliding a notepad into position she said, "Fire away, Jenns. I'm ready."

When Jennifer hesitated, Margie said, "No, Jenns, I won't go there unless you are with me, so give me the address."

Jennifer again hesitated a moment before saying, "That neighbor of the Larkins who uses our clinic for her family's primary care brought her little girl in for a check-up. I heard her talking about her little girl being happy to attend this school since Billy Larkin would be going there as well. I couldn't ask her about the school and wondered how I could find out, but I heard her say the school needed proof that each child had a physical before they could be enrolled and she gave the address of where the information needed to be sent. So, being the nosy-parker that I am, I looked on the file after the nurse took her into the doctor's office. The address is Olympic Christian Preschool, 118 Ahlvers Road, Port Angeles, Washington 98362."

Margie wrote the address down and breathed a relieved sigh. "Jenns, this is wonderful and I believe that I pass that road when I go out to that Farmer's Market where I got those peaches for Uncle James."

"Alex is coming over this evening about six o'clock. It will be two hours before it gets dark so we could get him to drive us around and find it. Would you like that?" asked Jennifer

Margie got a puzzled frown on her face and said, "Have you told Alex about my baby"

"Lord, no, Little Sis. Do you think I'm crazy? I'll never tell anyone until you tell me too. I plan to tell Alex we want to drive around and try find a nice, new restaurant," explained Jennifer.

Margie laughed. "Good idea and you can tell Alex that I'll buy our dinners."

Jennifer giggled. "I told him you thought he was a Scrooge with his money, so he'll believe you really do think that."

Margie laughed. "I just noticed him checking his billfold before he went into stores or restaurants."

When Alex and Jennifer walked into her apartment at six o'clock, Margie met them at the door. "Hello, Jenns, I see you've brought Scrooge with you."

Jennifer gurgled with laughter and so did Margie, seeing the shocked look on Alex's face.

"Scrooge! What's Jennifer been saying about me?" asked Alex, giving Jennifer a puzzled look.

Jennifer put her hands up as if to ward off a blow. "Don't blame me. I'm not the one who worries about money all the time. I didn't tell Margie anything. She noticed it herself. You know; things like looking in your billfold before you go into a restaurant or in stores."

"So I guess you told her I was a miser, didn't you, Jennifer?" asked Alex who was looking upset.

Margie grinned. "Alex, I was only joking, but I did notice you doing that and I asked Jenns if you were frugal with your money. Jenns immediately said that you were not, but when you were at home your brothers were constantly taking money from your billfold and you just had a habit of checking."

Alex relaxed. "That's true and I've tried to break myself from doing that. I took a girl out once and she liked expensive food, which was all right, but when I went to pay, there was only a twenty-dollar bill in my billfold. Luckily, I had my checkbook with me or I would still be washing dishes."

Margie patted his shoulder. "I don't think you're a scrooge. I guess I'm just comfortable enough with you to joke about things. I must be learning social skills since my counselor says I'm doing better."

Jennifer, who had gone to the bathroom, came back into the room. "Well, we've established that you aren't stingy so let's go find a really classy restaurant."

"Not too classy, though, Jenns. Remember, I told you I was buying if we found a good restaurant," said Margie.

They pulled out of the gated complex where Margie lived and turned right since Jennifer had said she wanted to see what was on the outskirts of the city. "Today we'll drive west and see what's there and another time we'll go in the opposite direction," said Jennifer, looking right to the left as they drove.

They drove several blocks when Margie saw the street sign with the name Ahlvers and exclaimed. "What a strange name for a street. Let's go that way and see what's on that road."

Alex pulled up to the light and stopped. "I'll bet this will be a totally residential street."

"Why do you say that?" asked Jennifer.

"The trees! Busy industrial streets are not lined with trees. Anyone want to take my bet of five dollars that there are no restaurants on this street?" asked Alex.

Margie giggled. "You can't check your billfold, so are you sure?"

Alex laughed. "Trying to be cute aren't you, Little Sis. Are you going to take my bet?"

"Yes, I will. In fact, I'll double it. If we find a good restaurant on this street you will owe me ten dollars," replied Margie.

Suddenly there was a school zone sign and a pedestrian crossing on the street and located on the left was a long, low, brick building with Olympic Christian Preschool prominently displayed on the top of a cross, which stood at one side of the entrance. From the back seat, Margie reached up and squeezed Jennifer's shoulder as they drove slowly in front of the building.

As they passed, Margie saw that an area on the right side of the building was fenced in with wire and held swings, slides, seesaws, and what she thought was a sandbox. At the end of this area was a row of trees and then a red light with a four-way stop.

I could hide in those trees and watch him on the playground, thought Margie as she smiled with inward excitement.

CHAPTER 43

Before the light turned Alex asked, "Do we go straight or make a turn?"

Margie started to say, make a turn, but Jennifer piped up with, "Go straight, since you and Little Sis are betting on finding a restaurant on this street."

"Oh yes, you're right, but if my opponent wants to make a turn and forfeit her bet, it's all right with me," quipped Alex, looking back at Margie with a wide grin.

"Don't you dare make a turn off this street, the ten dollars I'm going to win will help to pay for our meal," said Margie.

They approached a wide curve and just on the other side a large neon sign flashed the words Port Angeles' Elegant Dining. Margie yelled, "Stop! Stop! I want my ten dollars."

Alex pulled into the parking lot, but couldn't find a parking spot. "This must be more than a restaurant. I'll bet it's one of those 'anything goes' night spots that's always raided by the police," he said as he turned to circle the lot again.

Ahead of them a party of diners had just exited the door and Jennifer exclaimed, "That woman in front is at least ninety and her friends aren't much younger, so I think you're wrong, Alex."

Margie gurgled with laughter. "He's thinking of how much money he has in his billfold." She reached up and patted Alex's shoulder. "I'll take a check, Alex, so don't get so upset."

He looked back at her with a dour look on his face. "You're getting in a lot of practice in being cute, aren't you?"

Margie laughed again. "Yes, I am and it really feels good. Thanks for giving me all this encouragement."

Jennifer grinned. "Alex, does this little cutesy girl sound anything like the Margie who vomited when Lieutenant Hammer wanted to meet her?"

Alex chuckled. "No, she doesn't. Are you sure that's Margie Meadows we're hauling around?"

Just then a car backed out of a parking spot and Alex sped into it before the car, waiting behind him, tried to edge its way into it. Their former bantering stopped as they exited the car and walked toward the restaurant.

When they stepped through the door, Margie thought, *I'm glad there's only three in our party. I'll bet this place is very expensive,* but she smiled at Alex and rubbed her thumb against the tips of her two front fingers to indicate money. Alex raised his eyebrows and grinned.

Before the waitress came to seat them, Jennifer stepped close to Margie and whispered, "Can you afford this, Little Sis?"

Margie couldn't answer since the waitress was leading them to a table. Once seated, they looked around and immediately realized that they were in a place far more luxurious than their usual haunts. That was confirmed when a wine waiter appeared to take their order. Margie looked at Jennifer who looked as lost as Margie felt, but Alex seemed completely composed as he placed their orders.

When the waiter went away, Alex said, "I hope you ladies don't mind, but I ordered a light dinner wine for you and one a little more hearty for myself."

"I don't want you to drink and drive, Alex," whispered Jennifer as she placed her hand on his arm.

"I'm not having it on an empty stomach, Jennifer, and besides one small glass will not make me drunk."

Margie saw that Jennifer was, like herself, far from knowing anything about wines, but she also knew that lots of people had wine with their dinners without any unwanted side effects, so she said, "Thanks, Alex. I'm pretty ignorant about wines or any kind of alcohol, but I'm told that I need to learn before I go to New York with Alice and Paul Seaton."

When the waiter came back with their drinks and to take their meal orders, Alex asked about the house specialty. Learning that it was Chicken Kiev in Wine sauce, he ordered the same for each of them. The waiter smiled and said he'd made a good choice since it was very good. He poured their wine and then left.

On their way home, Margie noticed that they were all a bit more jolly than they had been on the way there, but thought it was because she and Jennifer had located the school that her little boy would be attending.

Jennifer looked back at Margie with a wide grin. "How much did that cost you, Little Sis? Don't forget that Alex owes you ten dollars."

Margie leaned up and poked Alex in the shoulder. "Yes, Mr. Scrooge, you owe me."

"I thought that once a man was, as my brother says, 'going steady' with a girl that her allegiance should be to you, but here's Jennifer teaming up against me."

With this kind of laughing banter they finished the trip and when they deposited Margie at her door she waved and said, "I'll call you tomorrow, Jenns, and thanks again, Alex", then suddenly said, "Wait just a minute. Get out that billfold and give me my ten dollars."

Alex stepped out of the car and pulled his billfold from his pocket and opened it. He fumbled around for a second and then walked over closer to the street light.

"Don't try to pull that trick on me, Mr. Scrooge. Hand over my money or I'll call the cops," said Margie, walking toward him.

Alex looked up with alarm on his face. "Shh, don't talk so loud . . . I really don't have any money, Little Sis."

By this time Jennifer had gotten out of the car and came to where they were.

A Fatal Beginning

"What do you mean, you don't have any money? You just got paid yesterday, so you have to have money. Quit fooling around, Alex. It's late and we all have to work tomorrow," scolded Jennifer.

"That's just it, Jennifer, I don't have any money. See for yourself," he said as he pushed the billfold into her hands.

Jennifer went through the billfold and looked up at him and then at Margie. "It's gone. I know you said you always kept back at least two hundred each week for emergency expenses, but you don't have even one dollar."

"I did, Jennifer. I had two hundred and ninety dollars when I left the office this afternoon. I stopped at a supermarket to buy a few things and pulled out a ten-dollar bill and paid for it, but I put my billfold back in my pocket .... Jennifer, somebody in that line of customers behind me had to swipe my billfold," said Alex.

"No, they didn't, Alex, there's your billfold," said Margie, pointing to Jennifer's hand.

Jennifer looked stunned. "You're making all this up, Alex."

Alex put his hand down in his pocket and pulled out a roll of bills. "I wish you could see your faces. I had you both convinced, didn't I?"

Margie heaved a sigh of relief. "I don't know about, Jenns, but I was ready to offer you a loan."

Alex grinned and handed her a ten-dollar bill. "Thanks, Margie. You have a kind heart."

Jennifer hadn't said a word and Alex looked at her. "It was a joke, Jennifer. What's wrong?"

"I don't know. I'm stunned, I think. Are you sure you didn't drink too much of that wine?"

CHAPTER 44

That night Margie lay fantasizing about seeing her little boy. Oh *God, I don't know if I could keep from grabbing him and running away*, she thought as tears streamed down her cheeks. Before she finally went to sleep, she planned the first trip by the school that she and Jennifer would make.

She hurried to work on Monday morning, wanting to review her schedule in order to make plans with Jennifer. When the intercom came on, it startled her since Mr. Seaton was planning to come in an hour later that morning. Shaking her head in annoyance, Margie answered the intercom and with pad and pencils hurried to Mr. Seaton's office.

Before she was seated, Mr. Seaton said, "I hope you haven't made any major plans for several weeks or maybe a month, and you'll have to clear my schedule as well."

Margie knew her face fell, but she tried to not let it show when she said, "Why? Has something happened?"

"That meeting I had scheduled in New York has been moved up to this week. In fact, we'll have to fly out tomorrow evening and Alice may not be able to go. She can't unless their grandmother can take the twins for several weeks," said Mr. Seaton.

"Several weeks!" Margie swallowed her disappointment and said, "I thought it was to be a one-week deal."

"That's the way it was planned, but now several other businesses want to meet with us to see if they can become a part of the venture. Carl Paxton, the man I have been conversing with, called me this morning and it seems we have no other alternative since the main office wants to expand," explained Paul Seaton. He got up and pushed his hand through his hair as was his habit when perturbed.

"Does this cause a problem for you, Margie?" asked Mr. Seaton and Margie crimped her lips together and said a hesitant no. Her mind was in turmoil though since that would mean another month or more before she could have a chance to see her little boy.

She sat as if in a daze until Mr. Seaton turned and without looking at her, said, "Well, you see what you can do with our schedule. Give any of the in-house issues to Patrick Randall. I know you don't like him, but he'll do anything to move up the ladder and he knows that I'm aware of it. He'll do a good job.

Margie returned to her desk and began the thousand and one things that would be necessary before Mr. Seaton could be away for a month. *I'll deal with that awful Patrick Randall first,* she thought as she picked up the phone and called his secretary.

Patrick Randall was one of those lecherous men who undressed every woman he met with his eyes. He was such a creep that Margie was always on edge around him, and felt that with the least bit of encouragement he would do much worse. She always remained behind a desk if possible when she was in his presence.

His secretary said he would be free at 10 o'clock and Margie noted it on her desk calendar before proceeding to the next task. It was 9:30 when her phone rang. Mr. Randall's secretary said that her boss could see her now if she was free to come up to his office. Margie said she was on her way, and picking up the plans for what he needed to oversee while Mr. Seaton was away, she left a message for Mr. Seaton and went out the door.

Mr. Randall must have been waiting at the door since it opened before she knocked. "There you are, Miss Meadows, looking as beautiful as ever. I don't know how you do it. You're as fresh and sweet-smelling as newly purchased roses."

Margie edged passed him saying, "Good Morning, Mr. Randall. I have a list of things that Mr. Seaton would like for you to take care of while he is away. Would you like me to explain them to you?"

Hearing Mr. Seaton's name put a glow on Mr. Randall's face. "Come right on in, Miss Meadows. I'm so happy Mr. Seaton thought of me to help him out. Did he personally ask for me?"

"Yes, he did. He said you would do a good job." Margie could almost feel him swelling with pride right behind her. She went to the other side of his desk and took a seat.

"That desk is so broad, Miss Meadows . . . does everyone here call you, Miss Meadows?" he asked with a beaming smile.

"Yes, they do, sir," said Margie bluntly. "Now this first one is basically a routine that I believe you have taken care of before, haven't you?" She pushed the papers toward him and he glanced at them.

"Yes, that's the personnel grievance procedure so I already know all about what to do. In fact, I pretty well know about as much about Mr. Seaton's end of the business as he does, but I want to know how he wants it done," said Mr. Randall, starting to come around the desk.

Margie stood up. "Please call your secretary in, Mr. Randall. She'll have to do the spreadsheets anyway, so there's no point in both of us explaining it to her."

Mr. Randall grinned as he put his hand on her arm. Margie jerked her arm away and gave him a baleful glare. He chuckled as he said, "Touchy aren't you. I meant no harm."

With a stony expression, Margie repeated, "Mr. Randall, call your secretary, please."

Mr. Randall shrugged. "Oh well, if you insist."

"I do insist, Mr. Randall. I need to get all this taken care of since Mr. Seaton will need me in another twenty minutes," said Margie as she began laying the different projects into separate piles.

Mr. Randall flipped the intercom and requested his secretary and soon Margie felt much more relaxed and hurriedly went through each project with both Mr. Randall and his secretary listening and asking questions.

Margie didn't really relax until she was outside Mr. Randall's office and she thought, *Thank God I don't have to see him very often. If I did, I believe I would look for another job.*

CHAPTER 45

Margie didn't have time to do anything about seeing her little boy except to tell Jennifer to learn all she could and keep her posted. She also asked Jennifer to come by her place and get the gate pass and the house key so she could check on her apartment while she was away.

Alice Seaton did get to go with her husband and Margie, which made Margie extremely happy. She wasn't uneasy around Paul Seaton, but a boss didn't go shopping, sightseeing, and rarely met his employees for lunch. As it, she and Alice spent happy hours in Central Park, visited the Statue of Liberty, made the tour of Ellis Island, and shopped more than Margie felt she could really afford.

Mr. Seaton always went with them to the theater or special dinners at night and twice he took them to spots where they could dance. When Margie was told about those events she worried about with whom she would dance. That worry was solved when she was introduced to James Harrison, president of a foundation that did entrepreneurial projects to improve communities. He was based in Huntington, West Virginia at that time.

Mr. Harrison came to see Mr. Seaton after an all-day meeting during the second week they were there. He was introduced to Margie who was very impressed and felt very comfortable around him. He was a big man, and nice looking, but he was also a gentleman in his manner and Margie was happy to have him as a date and dance partner.

Before the month was up she and Mr. Harrison were together quite a bit and Margie knew she liked him better than any man she'd met since Rick Mullet, the father of her baby.

On the last week, as they were dancing, James, as Margie now called him, asked if she was satisfied with her job."

"Yes, I am. Mr. Seaton and his wife have been wonderful to me and Mr. Seaton is great to work for. Why do you ask?" Margie didn't know what to expect.

"You are so efficient, and easy to talk to, that I thought about offering you a position with the foundation I'm managing, but if you are well satisfied I guess that's out," said Mr. Harrison.

Margie looked up at him with a smile. "That's the nicest compliment I've ever had, James, and I thank you, but I need to stay where I am for the present."

He smiled also from his kind blue eyes. "I thought so, but the job will be open if you ever change your mind. Actually, we have just begun delving into projects for business enhancement in various communities. We are trying some pilot projects, but on a small scale, right now."

"I'll bet that was your idea, wasn't it? I mean, I've heard you mention that business, if approached in certain ways, would be a great enhancement to the development of better communities," said Margie.

James smiled. "So, you've been really listening. I'm impressed, Margie. I think you care about people as well."

"I am interested, James. I think people need encouragement to realize how much potential they have. Most of us walk the path laid for us by our friends, our parents, fate or whatever without once thinking that there may be another way that would be better. Mostly, I think, we're held back by fear, or at least that's what held me in bondage for a long time," said Margie.

The music stopped and James stood still looking down at her. "What kind of fear held you back, Margie?" he asked with an intent look.

Margie's eyes shone with tears, but she blinked and put her hand over her mouth. In a shocked voice she whispered, "I'm sorry. I'm talking too much. Please forget that I said that, will you?"

James patted her arm. "I'll not mention it, Margie, but if you ever need someone to talk to, I will certainly be willing to listen."

Margie turned and James took her arm and walked beside her back to the table where she was seated. She looked up as he pushed in her chair and whispered, "Thanks, James. I may take you up on that someday."

He pulled out a business card and said, "Here, put this in some place where you won't forget it. You may someday find that a friend is what you need most and when you do you'll have a way to contact me."

Margie thought she would succumb to weeping, but closed her eyes for a moment and kept herself in check before saying, "James, I've never had a man offer to be a friend to me and I can't tell you how much I appreciate it."

The next morning Mr. Seaton and Alice came to her room and told her to pack. "The other company that we planned to meet with has changed their minds so we decided to see if we can get a flight back home today. Is that all right with you?" asked Mr. Seaton.

Margie's first thought was, *Great! I'll go this next week to see if I can see my little boy*, but she smiled happily at the Seatons, as she said, "Nothing would please me more. I'm getting a little homesick."

So, at nine o'clock that night Margie was back in her own apartment and on the phone with Jennifer. "Jenns, have you been out to that school? Is he really a student there?"

Jennifer chuckled. "I thought you'd say you were glad to hear my voice or something like that. I have driven by the school and I've seen lots of little boys, but I don't know if I've seen Billy or not. I do know that he is enrolled there and that each student wears a name tag while there, so I've parked across the street and watched kids come out, but I haven't seen one with a tag having his name on it."

Margie sighed and said, "Well, at least we know to look for a name tag if we ever get close enough."

Jennifer added, "I heard that the school was going to bring a beginner class to the clinic next week to help them learn to not fear doctors and nurses. It may be his class and if I find what day they are coming I'll try to have some errands to run for our doctors that will take me to the clinic."

"Great! You may even get to see him and I won't have to guess which one he is, but I still think that I'll know him if I ever see him," said Margie.

They spent the next hour on the phone talking about Margie's stay in New York with her describing all she had seen and done.

"I wish I'd get to travel. You are learning and doing so many things that I always dreamed of doing, but I probably will just dream all of my life," said Jennifer.

Margie hurriedly said, "Oh no, Jenns. When you and Alex marry I think you will travel many places together. You just wait and see."

CHAPTER 46

Margie spent the weekend with the Jacobs family since she hadn't seen Amy and James in several months. It was like going home and in a way it was, since she had been so lovingly accepted as a family member.

On Monday, Margie knew that she would have to meet with Patrick Randall again and therefore dreaded it. *I wish Mr. Seaton would call him in and take care of that. I can barely stand to be in the same room with that awful man,* thought Margie as she pulled into her space behind the office building.

She opened her office door and immediately began work on the numerous things that had to be done to take over the reins again. Soon the intercom interrupted her activity. Mr. Seaton wanted to dictate some letters and armed with pad and pencils she quickly left her office.

After taking down ten letters she sat back and dropped her pencil on the desk. "It piles up, doesn't it? I'm glad we didn't have to be away any longer."

Margie rose to her feet and turned to go as she said, "I think I'll go take care of the projects you put Mr. Randall in charge of while you were away. I hope he did a good job, but I dread even talking to him."

Paul Seaton was instantly alert. "Margie, has that man accosted you or made suggestive comments. If he has, he won't be working here much longer. I know he has six children that need his income, but I won't have someone working for me who doesn't respect women."

Thinking of the six children Margie answered, "No, Mr. Seaton, he hasn't actually done anything overtly except with his eyes. He just gives me the creeps and I don't like to be alone with him."

Mr. Seaton nodded. "Well, you won't have to see him about this because I called him down this morning and I'll have to say he did a good job."

A Fatal Beginning

Margie sighed with relief. "Thanks, Mr. Seaton. Now I can relax."

The rest of the day was spent in doing her normal secretarial chores, which were many after being gone most of the month. By the end of the day, however, she felt she was back on an even keel even though she had worked two hours longer than usual."

Margie's phone was ringing as she stepped through her front door. She dashed to the phone, leaving her door open. It was Jennifer.

"Little Sis, I've been calling since five o'clock. Where have you been?" Jennifer's voice sounded worried.

"I worked over Jenns. There was a backlog of work that I needed to catch up on and I don't like to leave things undone," said Margie.

She heard Jennifer sigh before saying, "That's all right then. I was worried that some lecherous man had carried you off somewhere."

Margie laughed. "Well, I didn't have to deal with the only lecherous man that I know anything about. Mr. Seaton tackled that before I got in this morning and I could have hugged his neck, but one doesn't hug their bosses."

Jennifer chuckled. "So, Mr. Randall didn't get to feast his eyes today. That's good news since Alex and I think that with a little more counseling you might black both of his eyes."

"Mr. Seaton says he has six children and for that reason I wouldn't describe how awful he is around me. I feel sure that Mr. Seaton would let him go in a heartbeat if I told him how the creep acts around me," replied Margie.

"That's great to know, but I still worry that he will try to get you alone and then it would be his word against yours. Maybe you should tell Mr. Seaton how awful he really is," urged Jennifer.

Margie shivered before saying, "Talking about him gives me the creeps. Let's talk about something else. Have you heard anything else about my little boy?"

"Okay, Little Sis, we won't talk about him anymore, but make sure you are not in any place alone with him. I think he's getting pretty bold and I know you don't encourage him," said Jennifer.

"You're right, I certainly don't, but I swear he almost acts like that my avoiding and dismissing him is encouragement. Does that make sense?" asked Margie.

"It does with a weirdo like him. So, please be careful, Little Sis," cautioned Jennifer, then heard Margie say, "What are you doing here and how did you get through the gate?"

"Who is that, Little Sis?" Jennifer had almost screamed.

Margie laughed. "It's Alice Seaton, Jenns. Can I call you back?" She could hear Jennifer's 'thank God' before she hung up.

"What are you doing, leaving your door standing open, Margie? I know this is a gated complex, but what if somebody besides a friend got in? Don't you leave that door open again, not even if the President calls," scolded Alice.

Margie nodded and said, "You're right, Alice. I had my arms full and the phone was ringing, so I admit I was careless. I'll be more careful from now on, I promise."

Alice put down the bundle she had in her arms. "I found the curtains we were looking for that would match the rug and bedspread in your guest room and since I was passing by I thought I'd just stop and leave them. My mother used to live in this complex and I have her gate pass, but don't tell anybody."

The curtains were the exact match they had both been looking for, but had never found. "I found those at a 'going out of business' sale at the J C Penney's store in the downtown mall that is closing," she bragged.

Anyway, the curtains were hung and the two friends parted in the best of spirits. A car turned into the complex just as Alice exited it and she recognized Patrick Randall and wondered what he was doing there as she drove away.

Margie called Jennifer back. "Jenns, you started to tell me something about Billy when Alice came in. What was it?"

"Oh, yes, I think you may have a chance to see him tomorrow, but not unless I am with you," said Jennifer.

"How?" questioned Margie, her voice filled with excitement.

"Well, the kids are going to be playing ball in that fenced in area at the side the school building and I thought that you and I could wait in the trees and with binoculars we may be able to see him," explained Jennifer.

"What time will that be?" asked Margie.

"I heard that it would be around three-thirty, which will make it difficult for us to get away, but if we have to we can both be sick and ask to leave early," said Jennifer.

"I'll ask Mr. Seaton in the morning and I'll be home by two-thirty. Will you come to my place and pick me up? I could come to your place, but for some unknown reason I'd rather you came for me," said Margie.

"That's what I planned to do anyway, otherwise you'd have to leave your car in some unprotected parking lot," said Jennifer.

After they hung up, Margie wondered why she was so sure that Jennifer needed to come for her since she had a good car and was also a very good driver.

Oh well, I guess everybody gets feelings about things. I'll ask Dr. Moses about that next week, she thought as she made a salad for her dinner.

Preparing for bed that night, she dropped to her knees beside her bed and begged the Lord to allow her to see her baby. "Oh Lord, you know my heart and know that I so long to see my baby. Yet Lord, you also know that I want the best for my little boy, so Lord, if it isn't good in thy sight then don't let me see him. I think my heart would break, but Lord, you know me better than I know myself, and what I want may not be what's best for me or him. Lord, please just let us both live to help each other. Amen" she murmured before climbing into bed.

Puzzled, she lay there thinking, *why did I ask that my baby and I be allowed to help each other. There's no way a little boy could help me.* Finally, she gave up puzzling and drifted off to sleep.

A Fatal Beginning

CHAPTER 47

The next morning, she was up, dressed, and was eating breakfast when the phone rang. *I wonder who is calling me at this hour*, she thought as she picked up the phone.

"Good morning, my beautiful Miss Meadows," said a familiar voice and chills ran down Margie's arms. She quietly replaced the phone and stood wondering how he had gotten her personal phone number. Suddenly, she realized that he must have gone through anything he could find in Mr. Seaton's office while they were away.

Margie stood shivering as she tried to decide what she should do and couldn't decide. Finally, she called Jennifer. "Jenns, that creep got my phone number somehow and he just called me. I'm getting scared."

'You march right into Mr. Seaton's office and tell him what's been going on and let him take it from there. That man needs to be locked up. Thank God, your office is only separated from Mr. Seaton's by that glass partition. You'll be safe while there at the office, but don't get on the elevator if he is anywhere near," cautioned Jennifer.

When Margie got to the office she looked all around and finding the elevator empty she went safely up to the second floor and into her office. She looked at Mr. Seaton's office and saw that he had a couple of men with him. Margie went to work on her usual duties until the intercom blared, requesting her for dictation.

Once inside and seated, Margie sat waiting for Mr. Seaton to turn from the window and begin. When he did he looked troubled. "When Alice came to your place yesterday she said she passed Randall's car going toward the gate. Does he have someone living in that complex?"

Margie's eyes became large and her mouth fell open in surprise. "God, I sure hope not. I'd have to move."

A Fatal Beginning

"You've not told me everything that has been transpiring between you and Randall, have you, Margie?" ask Mr. Seaton.

Before Margie could respond the phone shrilled and Mr. Seaton picked it up. A big smile crossed his face. "James Harrison! Good to hear from you. Are you in town? Good, and yes, I'm available. The hotel dining room is fine. I'll be there in ten minutes." Mr. Seaton hung up and looked at Margie while rubbing his hands together in satisfaction.

"Miss Margie Meadows, I think James Harrison has rekindled that deal that fell apart in New York. He's here in town. Hold down the fort. I don't know if I'll be back in the office today or not," he said as he smiled at her.

Fearing he would leave before she got in her request she interrupted whatever he was going to say. "Mr. Seaton, may I leave at two-thirty today? There is something very important that I need to see about."

Mr. Seaton smiled. "Yes Ma'am, you may leave at two if you want to. Actually, you can take the rest of the day off if you need to."

Margie rose from her seat. "I only need to leave at that time. Thank you and please tell Mr. Harrison I said hello, and I do hope your meeting is successful."

Margie didn't leave her office even for lunch. She was now afraid to be alone anywhere in the building. Three more offices were next to hers and each had plate glass fronts so she felt that should anything happen she would have help from all three sources.

When it neared two o'clock, she called Jerry Henson's office and asked if he was going to his usual meeting that evening. When he said yes, Margie said, "Let me know when you're leaving and I'll go down with you. I'm not feeling well and I'm going to leave early myself." Jerry agreed and Margie was all ready when he stopped at her door at two-fifteen.

Luckily, Jerry's car was only two cars away from her own, but still he walked to her car with her and saw her inside before returning to his own car. Margie breathed a sigh of relief and quickly pulled out of the parking lot and drove home.

When she reached home she called Jennifer and found that she had left for the day. She only had time to hang up the phone and change into slacks, tee shirt, and a jacket with a hood before her doorbell rang. Cautiously, Margie opened the peephole in the door and saw Jennifer.

Margie told Jennifer about Alice seeing Patrick Randall driving up to the gates of the complex. "Jennifer, I have the strangest feeling. I think that man is trying to get to me, for some reason."

"That pervert. If he shows up here, keep your door locked and call the police. I feel like calling the police myself," said Jennifer.

They both went through the apartment checking every window, and every door before taking their handbags and going out the door, which they locked behind them. As Jennifer drove out of the complex and was passing the last house, she suddenly said, "There's a car exactly like yours. Who does it belong to?"

"I think it's a new couple. I haven't seen them, but they just moved in last week. That's the place Alice Seaton's mother lived in before she moved next door to Alice," said Margie.

Jennifer drove through the gate and onto the highway with both girls looking both ways. Jennifer shook her head. "We've got to stop this. Randall was probably only looking the place over when Alice saw him. He would have to have a pass to get through the gate."

Margie sighed with relief. "That's right. Let's forget about him and go see my baby."

Soon they were on the Ahlvers Road and drove passed the Olympic Christian Preschool before they turned left down the street where the play area was located. They parked down the street about three hundred feet below the school, but on the same street. Jennifer stopped and turned to Margie.

"Now, what do we do? Those trees are pretty thick, but if anyone saw us sneaking around through those trees I'm sure they would call the police."

"Let's wait a while and then go walking up the street. If a ball game is going on, we'll stop in the first open place and stand watching the game. Nobody would think that is suspicious, would they?" asked Margie.

Jennifer agreed and the two girls sat trying to relax and get as calm as possible before they decided to start. Margie looked at her watch. "It's three-forty-five, Jenns, let's go."

They strolled along and found that others, both men and women, were doing the same thing. They smiled and spoke to the nearest two women who were also walking. One of the women said, "Oh look! Those little boys are playing ball. Aren't they cute? Let's stop and watch them play."

Jennifer said, "My nephew is supposed to be playing, but I don't know for sure, so since we're down this way I thought we could watch the game for a while and then leave if we didn't see him."

The other woman said, "This is just our evening walk, but those little fellers are so cute it would be a shame not to watch for a bit."

The four women walked up close to the fence, but with several feet of space between them and stood watching.

Jennifer laughed and said, "Look they have shirts with their names on them. If one of you happens to see a shirt with Billy on it, let us know. That will be my nephew." The women agreed and silence reigned except for a few chuckles when the little players did cute things.

Margie hadn't said a word, but stood with her eyes riveted on the little boys. She was getting tired and was beginning to think he wasn't in the group when the game seemed to be coming nearer the fence and someone hit a ball that came over the fence. Margie grabbed it up intending to toss it back when a little boy, with hair the rich auburn color of Margie's, came running toward the fence.

Jennifer looked at his hair and then looked at Margie's and, as he got closer she saw the name Billy emblazoned on his shirt. When he got to the fence, Margie reached over and handed him the ball. The little boy looked up and smiled then said, "Thank you, lady," before turning back to the game and yelling, "I got it."

Everybody stood perfectly still until one of the women said, "Oh, how sweet . . .," she didn't continue since they all gasped in shock as Margie sank slowly to the earth.

A Fatal Beginning

CHAPTER 48

Jennifer's eyes were enormous as she looked down at Margie's ashen face and realized that Margie must have recognized her son. She sank to her knees beside Margie her and started calling her name.

Two men came over and asked how they could help. "She wasn't feeling well. I think she's fainted. If you all will stay with her, I'll run down and get my car and perhaps you can help me put her in it. I'll take her home or to the ER if she doesn't revive soon."

Several people nodded, and Jennifer sprinted back to her car and soon pulled to the curb beside the group. Margie was still comatose, but her pulse and heart rate seemed to be normal. After Margie was put into the back seat of the car and the door was closed, one of the men said, "I'd take her to the ER if I were you. That seems to be more than a faint."

The man was right. Margie Meadows was once again in a coma. When she hadn't responded by the time Jennifer was back on a through street, she turned north toward the hospital. She pulled into the Emergency Room bay and started to get out when an ambulance attendant opened the door and stepped outside.

Jennifer stepped out of the car and said, "Please come and help me. My friend has fainted, I think, and I can't get her to respond."

Soon Margie was on a gurney and being wheeled into the hospital. They were met by a nurse, who took one look at Margie and motioned for a doctor.

After thoroughly examining Margie and asking Jennifer what had occurred and noting all the details, the doctor put in a call to a specialist that happened to be in the hospital.

The specialist examined Margie also and pronounced her in a coma. "We'll put her in a ward and tomorrow do further testing. Are you her next of kin?"

"I'm her, well, I call myself her sister, but my family sort of adopted her when she first came to our area. As far as I know she has no relatives. I know that both her parents are dead," said Jennifer.

The doctor motioned for an orderly to take Margie to a room on the second floor and Jennifer rode the elevator with her and followed her into the assigned room. A nurse came in and began the intake requirements while Jennifer looked out the window upon hearing numerous sirens blaring.

"I wonder what that's all about. It looks like the ER is going to be very busy for a while," said Jennifer and the nurse stepped to the window to look.

"It looks like the police escorted the ambulance. That must be an attempted murder or at least I hope it was only an attempt," said the nurse and Jennifer agreed.

Soon Margie was settled and Jennifer sat down and picked up her hand. Once again, Jennifer began to talk to Margie and was still talking when the specialist came through the door. Jennifer recognized him. "You're the doctor who treated Margie when she was known as Elaine Archer, aren't you?"

The doctor stopped and swung his gaze at Jennifer. "Nurse Jacobs . . . You must be an angel in disguise. I always said that your intervention helped to bring her around. As I recall Archer was not her correct name, but I've forgotten what her true name was."

Jennifer smiled. "She had it legally changed after she recovered." Jennifer would have said more, but the doctor's pager came on asking for his assistance and he walked hurriedly from the room.

The next nurse that came into the room knew Jennifer. "Jacobs, what are you doing here? You were leaving as I came on duty this evening."

"I know, Sarah. I promised this sister of mine that I would go somewhere with her and it's a good thing I did. We hadn't been there a half-hour when she fainted, but she hasn't just fainted, she's in a coma," said Jennifer.

"What caused that? Did she fall, get scared or something?" asked the nurse.

Jennifer hadn't thought about an explanation until now, so she shrugged her shoulders. "I'm not sure. The specialist didn't get to examine or do any testing when that clang of sirens arrived. I guess we'll have to wait until he can return."

"Are you going to stay with her? The doctor hasn't given us any directions as to treatment yet," replied Sarah.

Jennifer stood looking down at Margie and whispered. "Yes, I'll be staying with her, at least tonight." When the nurse, Sarah, went away Jennifer called her mother and Alex."

Amy Jacobs was concerned about Margie. "Jennifer, what happened to cause this again? She didn't see somebody who reminded her of her father, did she?"

"No, Mom. I don't really know what caused it and the doctor hasn't had time to examine her yet. He came to the room, but an ambulance came with a police escort and he was called away," explained Jennifer.

When she called Alex, his first words instead of 'hello' were, "Jennifer, have you heard the news? I guess you haven't since you're not at home, are you?"

"Alex, I'm at the hospital. Margie is here. She fainted, or I thought she'd fainted. The doctor says she's in a coma. What news are you talking about?"

Jennifer stood listening in shocked amazement as Alex said, "Thank God, you're not at Margie's place. Some pervert sneaked into that community and almost killed a woman. If her husband hadn't arrived home early he would have finished her off. The news is saying that all three of them are in the hospital."

Jennifer was shaking so badly by now that she could barely talk. She whispered, "Alex, can you come over here. Margie is in Room 226. This is awful."

Alex's voice came back laced with fear. "Jennifer, are you hurt? Why is Margie in the hospital?"

Jennifer pulled up a chair and sat down. Her legs were trembling so much she couldn't stand. "No, Alex, I'm not hurt, but come on over here. I need you," she said through a sob-choked throat.

"Hold on, Sweetheart. I'll be there in fifteen minutes," said Alex and the line went dead. Jennifer sat huddled in her chair beside the bed, still holding Margie's hand, which she'd held from the moment she'd entered the room.

Her thoughts were chaotic as she thought about somebody in a gated community being attacked. Suddenly she remembered the car that was exactly like Margie's and she convulsively gripped Margie's hand. She was so distraught that the slight quiver in the held hand went unnoticed.

Fear and dread skittered along her spine as she thought about Margie's fear of that awful Patrick Randall. *He's weird*, she thought, but still found it hard to even think that someone who worked for an influential national company would actually try to physically harm anyone.

When Alex walked through the door, Jennifer dropped Margie's hand and rushed to him, to be clasped in a warm embrace. "You're trembling like a leaf, Jenns. I guess that means you've already listened to the news."

"No, I haven't. When you said it happened in Margie's gated complex it threw me into a tizzy. Alex, Mrs. Seaton told her husband that Patrick Randall was pulled up to the gate of the complex as she left it yesterday.

That made me leery of him. Margie has been telling me how creepy he acts around her. Could he be involved in this awful event?" asked Jennifer, swallowing back the threatening tears.

Alex picked up the TV control hanging on the side of Margie's bed and clicked it on. The police chief was being interviewed. "It seems that Mrs. Cheevers had rushed home to get ready to attend a concert and had failed to lock her door. She didn't take time to switch on the lights, but hurried to get a shower and dress."

A deputy came and mumbled something before the chief continued. "She had taken her clothes off and started to enter the shower when a man's voice said, 'Oh, my beautiful Miss Meadows' and grabbed at her from behind. Startled, she side-stepped and he only grasped her arm as he lunged against the shower door. As he fell he jerked her forward and they both fell into the shower stall. She was on top of him and when he saw her face he became very angry and started cursing and hitting her with his other hand. She screamed and began to struggle with her attacker. Mr. Cheever came home and saw a strange car there and rushed into the house through the open door and heard her scream." Again, the chief was interrupted. He stood waiting until the deputy was through before continuing.

"Mr. Cheever probably saved his wife's life, but he pounded her attacker into a pulp. If the gate-keeper hadn't heard the commotion and called the police that man would not be alive right now. He is in critical condition as it is."

A reporter shouted. "Do you have the man's name?"

The Chief said, "No. He is unable to talk, but we will soon have his identifying information. I've told you all I have at present."

"How did he get through the security guard at the gate?" Another reporter shouted as the Chief ended the interview.

Margie stirred and since Alex was standing closer to the bed, he noticed it first. "Jennifer, she's moving."

Jennifer pulled out of Alex's arms and leaned over Margie. "Little Sis, are you awake?" she whispered and picked up the hand lying on the blanket. Margie didn't open her eyes, but her eyelids twitched.

"She's coming out of it, Alex. Go out to the desk and tell one of the nurses," said Jennifer and Alex left.

Jennifer felt a twitch in Margie's hand as she held it. She leaned down close to Margie and heard a whispered, "He spoke to me," then Margie slipped away again.

Jennifer laid Margie's hand on the top of her blanket and then again leaning close she whispered. "Yes, he did, Little Sis, and I thank God he did. You told me you asked God to let you and your baby help each other and your prayer was answered today. In going to see your baby you escaped the work of an evil man."

When Alex came back with the nurse Margie was sound asleep, but she had a smile on her face.

Adda Leah Davis

Made in the USA
Columbia, SC
28 September 2024